The Monk's Prophecy

Andrew Ritchie

Frontispiece artwork by Alister Ritchie

About The Author

Andrew Ritchie was born on the 3rd October 1933 in his parents house, Cove Manor, in Kirkpatrick Fleming Dumfriesshire. He attended primary school there, before going to Lockerbie Academy. He inherited Cove Estate and King Robert the Bruce's cave in 1958 before spending two years mining Rio Tinto Zinc in Elliot Lakes, Ontario Canada. Returning home to Scotland he married Alice Winder in June, 1960 and they celebrated 50 golden years together in 2010.

When his eldest son Alexander died his second eldest son Alister returned home from the Army and set up Lightning Protection Services working with his father all over the United Kingdom, whilst Alice managed a caravan site in the grounds of Cove Estate.

Prior to the Motorway bypass being built, Alice showed large numbers of visitors the famous cave that once sheltered a King.

Andrew is now retired and lives with his wife Alice a mere six miles from the town of Lockerbie which became the site of the most infamous of all terrorist attacks which brought down a Jumbo Jet Aircraft flying to America.

Each year Andrew and his extended family carry out a re-enactment of one of his boyhood games. They all assemble on the old bridge over the river Kirtle and armed with air rifles they hold a competition to see who can destroy the most balloons and tiny home made walnut shell Galleons complete with masts and sails which have been lovingly constructed by Andrew before being set adrift on the river further upstream by his son Alister.

This book is Dedicated to my Wife Alice and our children namely.

   Alexander, Alister, Anne and April

My son Alexander was killed in a motorcycle accident at 29 years of age.

' The speed limit is three score years plus ten
The Bible says man, will live 'till then
So never Hurry
And never Worry
A contented Mind
Is a blessing Kind
Better by far, than a purse well Lined'

Foreword to the series

The Tales of Green Snow'

In the Scottish Borders, between Gretna and Lockerbie, in a small rural village called Kirkpatrick Fleming, hidden in the grounds of a beautiful estate called Cove, you will find a cave. The cave nestles high above the Kirtle Water and is believed to hold the key to the success of one of Scotland's greatest Kings, Robert the Bruce.

You could be forgiven, dear reader, for thinking this is the story of a King and a Spider but no, indeed it is not. More recently and yet commencing at a time before the explosion of technology, when little boys fired real ammunition, not hand held controllers of an X BOX or a PLAY STATION and at a time when respect was born from pride, independence and helping ones neighbour. A young boy grew up and used his photographic memory to recall events from a period now consigned to history.

A time, post war, when common sense prevailed.

From his early school days, filled with laughter, sadness and later, terrifying exploits through life's journey, to find the love of a childhood sweetheart, fact and fiction become impossible to separate. Sex, the most powerful emotion to drive man, is explored with great sensitivity and hilarious wit. Were there really ladies of the night able to entice the young naive traveller into a Tibetan Brothel? Did a beautiful woman, loved and cherished by her husband, really fall deeply in love with one of her own fair sex? An eye for an eye, a tooth for a tooth.

From a spontaneous clip around the ear from the village Bobby to the horror of being lifted clean off the ground by big Tom Braithwaite's massive farming hands, all accepted as justifiable punishment. A time so different from the politically correct, red-taped, twenty-first century. The author captures moments we can only dream of and as his story unfolds he earns the same level of respect as the King who sheltered in his humble cave, on his own land, and patiently watched a little spider spin and re-spin his broken web until success was eventually his reward.

Sheila Richardson

The Monk's Prophecy

Andrew Ritchie

Contents

'The Monk's Prophecy' was first published in the United Kingdom
In 2012 by King Robert the Bruce Publishing. This is the first book
In the series 'The Tales of Green Snow.'

Contact email: **KingRoberttheBrucepublishing**@mail.com

Address: King Robert the Bruce Cave
                                   Cove Estate,
                                   Kirkpatrick Fleming
                                   DG11 3AT

Paperback 978-0-9573780-1-8
Hardback 978-0-957-3780-2-5

Printed and bound by CPI Group (UK) Ltd, Croydon, CR0 4YY

1.

The English Teacher

The sun streamed in through the picture window of the large Victorian bedroom as John gazed at the tiny perfect features of his soul mate Cheng Eng. Peacefully asleep, her long black eye lashes framed the perfect oriental, almond shaped eyes as she rested her head gently on John's shoulder. The King size bed with its pure white sheets and large soft feather pillows brought back memories of the days and nights they had spent in their tiny one-man tent high in the Tibetan Mountains.

John's mind began to relive those dark days on top of the cold white snow of the upper reaches of that mountainous region and a comfortable feeling of warmth and well being began to steal over his whole body as he watched the sleeping girl. Life had been an adventure then, a hard cruel existence with no known end in sight and yet as the Tibetan monk had predicted all those years ago, in the tiny Scottish village of Eskdalemuir. John and Cheng Eng were destined to endure many hardships before their life together would begin to turn towards the true meaning of peace and harmony. Watching the sleeping girl, John's mind slipped backwards through the years to the first time he had set eyes on her. He remembered every little detail of that first meeting.

As John duly finished his cup of coffee he knew instantly that it was now midday break, which would be an ideal and opportune time to make enquiries about the young schoolteacher from England, who was teaching on a temporary basis. As the last of the stragglers emerged from the school doors, he went into the school grounds, getting some strange looks from the pupils who were milling around in small groups all over the playground. On entering the school building he saw a very long corridor with doors at regular intervals. He stopped and put his ear to each door, on hearing no noise, he kept on repeating this routine until he came to a door where he could hear voices in conversation.

There was wording on each door but as it was in Tibetan, he couldn't decipher any of the words and his phrase book wouldn't be of any help what-so-ever. He gave a sharp loud knock on the door, but because nothing happened he was in a bit of a dilemma, he didn't know whether to open the door and walk in, or knock again. He was just about to knock again when a small bespectacled Tibetan man, who was obviously a teacher, confronted him. John looked beyond him at the many male and female teachers, drinking cups of tea, and as he did, they all turned their heads to stare at him, standing in the now open doorway.

The Tibetan teacher garbled something, which John didn't understand. Replying in English he intimated that he was looking for an English teacher whom he had been reliably informed was teaching at this school. He had the sense to speak loud and clear, so that it could be heard by all, most were now engaged in conversation with each other in several small groups, clearly this was the teachers staff room.

He was just starting to think that he had been misinformed or misled, as he couldn't see any school staff who looked English, they all looked oriental, however, his mind was soon put to rest when a small Chinese girl stood up from one of the tables and made her way to the door where he was standing, and said something in the Tibetan language which instantly made the bespectacled Tibetan teacher return to the table he had vacated a minute or so before. The young Chinese girl then said in perfect English. "Excuse me for asking, but why did you follow me to my place of work. you are staying at the same hotel as I am. I saw you last night in the hotel dining room and again at breakfast this morning, and I could hardly be mistaken by the mountaineering boots you have on your feet."

This accusation took him by surprise and he began to explain all about his mission and quest for a map showing the exact height of the mountains. He had certainly not followed her to work and was only following the information given to him by the hotel receptionist, who would be able to verify his statements. The Chinese girl seemed to relax as she spoke.

"Okay I will believe you, but I can't help you right now, it will have to be after school hours so I shall bring you a map with the information you require from the school library. We shall meet in the hotel dining room tonight, but please go away now."

She closed the door abruptly, hardly giving him time to say thank you. Turning on his heels he started to walk back along the corridor and out of the double doors into the playground, where again the pupils there subjected him to strange and weird glances, in the end he was glad to get out of their sight.

John realised he hadn't quite got over the shock of finding out that the English teacher was a young Chinese girl, he had fully expected she would be English, however at the same time it didn't really matter as long as he got the information he required. One thing was imprinted on his mind, there was just no way would he allow a similar situation to develop as had happened with Gillian. By now he had left the school and was slowly retracing his steps through the town. He decided that when he reached the café, where he had stopped earlier for a coffee, he would pass some time with a snack and another cup of coffee.

Being approximately half way back to the hotel it was a logical stopping point, and when sitting at a table he could leisurely think of what he could do to put some time in before returning to the hotel. It would be boring, having to return to the hotel room and just sit around waiting until it was time for the evening meal. Passing a shop, which was the equivalent of a newsagent back home, which also doubled up as a post office, he had an instant great idea; he would buy two airmail letters and write back home to both

Ruby and his parents.

So forthwith he ventured into the shop and by pointing to what he wanted, made his intentions known to the very elderly shopkeeper who spoke no English. Nevertheless he was able to obtain the two airmail letters and a pen. After paying, he left the shop, not knowing how much the items had cost. All he could do was hold the money from his pocket in the palm of his hand and allow the shopkeeper to take what he wanted from the collection of coins.

He had noticed that the old shopkeeper bowed most respectfully and clasped his hands in front of him as John was about to leave the premises. An old customary 'Thank you,' he thought, which must have been handed down from times way back in the mists of antiquity. He arrived at the café with the outside tables and chairs and had barely taken a seat when the same waiter, who had served him previously, came with a menu. Since the menu card was not in English he just had to take potluck and point to one of the listed sections, hoping that he would like it, when it was served up.

As soon as the waiter went away with his order John started to write one of the letters, however before he could start he had to get the new pen to work, it wouldn't write at all at first, he had to find something to scribble on to get it to function, and it was no use trying it on the airmail paper, for it was too thin, and besides it would totally spoil it with scribbles on it. He thought about it for a few seconds and decided the only thing, which would do the job, would be to scribble on the outside of his mountain boots. After a few efforts he succeeded in getting the new pen to work.

The waiter reappeared with the ordered meal and placed it in front of him. He fervently hoped that the waiter wouldn't notice the expression of disgust etched all over his face as he looked down at the meal. His stomach was doing somersaults and churning at the sight. He was surveying, incredible as it may seem, an animal's whole eye in the middle of the plate surrounded by a grungy mixture of goodness only knows what. The eye appeared to be looking straight up into his own eyes.

Just as soon as the waiter was out of sight, and making sure no one at the tables around were watching, he discreetly and quickly picked up the eye and popped it into the airmail letter, wrapped it up and slid it into his trouser pocket. Then he went through the motions of pretending to eat while all the time he was slipping down onto the other airmail letter situated on his knees, portions of the grungy mess which he couldn't even attempt to taste, not even if he was paid to.

Eventually the entire grungy mess ended up in the airmail envelope rather than his stomach. As luck would have it, his new wallet was inside his jacket pocket so he didn't require negotiating his hand past the now wrapped up meal to get money out to pay. He couldn't pay fast enough and get out of there and back to the hotel.

All the way walking back along the street he felt the urge to vomit and couldn't wait to find an opportune moment to find a place to dump the two envelopes and their contents from his pockets. The opportunity didn't come until he reached the hotel, where there were two large tubs of flowers flanking either side of the hotel entrance, so bending down and pretending to smell the fragrance of the flowers. He swiftly took out the contents of his pocket and dropped them amongst the flowers, still wrapped in the airmail envelopes.

Only then did he make his entrance into the hotel and tried to put on a brave face as he walked past the receptionist, who caught his attention and asked him if he had been successful in finding the school teacher.

"Yes! No problem" he said, and thanking her for her help went straight along the corridor to his room and took a drink of water from the bedroom wash hand basin, as he still felt sickly.

He lay down on top of the bed, and must have dosed off to sleep, and quite a long sleep it was, because he awoke to find it was now dark. If he rushed he would just be in time for the evening meal! Losing no time in going along to the hotel dining room he noticed right away as he entered the room, that the young Chinese girl was sitting at the table where he usually sat by himself, so she obviously, unknowingly to him, had been keeping a close observation on him. Pulling out a chair he sat down opposite her apologising for being late, the young English teacher just smiled and explained that she herself had only just arrived and she asked him how he had spent the day after visiting the school. He explained that he had bought a pen and two airmail envelopes intending to write back home to his wife and parents and how it had gone so drastically wrong. This had the young Chinese girl in fits of laughter as she could see the funny side of it all, whereas on his part it was serious, being such an unexpected shock to him.

It interested him why she had chosen such an isolated place to teach English so he asked her why. She told him that her parents lived in Hong Kong and being financially secure they had sent her to England for a university education and she had qualified as an English teacher. She also had relatives living on Mainland China, whom she had never seen, and this was the better of two worlds, as it was the golden opportunity to visit these relatives in china and her parents in Hong Kong after her two-year contract expired.

"I see." He said, as the waiter arrived to take their orders.

As soon as the waiter left the table with the orders she asked about his mission.

Reluctantly he went on to explain that he had first started mountaineering back in the English Lake District but decided he wanted to try the highest mountain ranges of the world, so that's why he was here. He couldn't for the life of him divulge information about the true significance of his mission, for fear that foreign governments could be alerted and begin taking an active interest in his activities. He went on to explain that he required the height of the mountains from her, as the map he had, gave no reference to the height of each individual mountain and this was so essential to his mission. If he were to see two mountains of similar height with a smaller mountain between them, then that's where he would head. That was the vision, which had been so graphically displayed in his dreams.

After a long chat over the evening meal, the Chinese girl opened a briefcase, which she had removed from under the table, and on opening the briefcase, she produced from it a folded up map which she handed to him saying
"Please return it at breakfast tomorrow morning" He thanked her very much and said he would go right away and transfer all the readings onto his own map. The young girl, much to his astonishment said,
"The night is young so why rush; let's go into the lounge and talk."

He wanted desperately to find an excuse to leave as he was beset with thoughts of the events with Gillian crowding back into his head but he couldn't force himself to, after all, she had gone to the trouble of obtaining the map for his sole benefit. So, much against his better judgement, he gave way to her offer. Settling down in the hotel lounge, he bought drinks for them both, making sure he was on soft drinks as he blamed the excess alcohol for the experience with Gillian. Lets face it, it had all started off in similar circumstances.

As the night wore on he explained about his wife who had herself been a teacher, but now she had set up her own farming engineering business, and was doing well, and his mother watched their twins daily, freeing her to work.
Eventually he got back to the subject of his mission and

explained that he was starting to walk in the direction of the mountains first thing in the morning after breakfast, rather than have to wait five days for a bus. The Chinese girl warned him to be careful, as there were bandits in the foothills who would think nothing of attacking and robbing an innocent lone traveller. He assured her that he would be alert and on his guard at all times, especially as he carried no weapons except for an army style Swiss penknife.

Of the many precautions he had taken, one was keeping his money notes under the heel of both stockings so if he was robbed of his mountain boots he still had money, as it would be highly unlikely that bandits would stoop so low as to take his stockings. Eventually it dawned on John that he had not formally introduced himself and he corrected this situation immediately. The young teacher replied,

"I am known as Cheng Eng Yew."

He thought her name had a very nice ring to it and said, "Let me guess! Cheng Eng Yew is twenty two" to which the young girl clapped her hands and said.

"Good for you"! And told him he must have a gifted intuition and should make a fortune on the horse racing if he could put such a gift into gambling. Laughing, he said, "I am afraid I'm not into that, it's not my scene."

Then he got a surprise, which to say the least he certainly wasn't expecting, when she gave him a kiss on the cheek and whispered into his ear that she would be very sad when he left in the morning as it was so much nicer to sit at a table with someone rather than be alone. Continuing to explain that was why she had first noticed John in the dining room, where he had sat at a table on his own, just as she had, adding "I noticed that you had a book which you were engrossed in."

John explained that it was his Tibetan phrase book, and he had been silently rehearsing for different scenarios but so far he had not had the confidence to put any phrases into practice, nor for that matter, the opportunity, as most people he had come into contact with spoke English. She said,

"You will be exceptionally lucky if you can find anyone who can speak English when you reach the area you are going to, that's for sure, and also I cannot over stress you must be vigilant at all times".

"Don't worry," he said, "I will be."

Asking him to say a phrase from his book, she explained that the Chinese and Tibetan languages were very similar but with different dialects and in some words there was a small but almost indistinguishable difference. After searching the phrase book for a moment John came out with a phrase, to which she responded.

"Very good, very very good."

She repeated the same phrase, word for word, which in English meant, I am delighted to have met you. After a few more phrases were exchanged it was getting late, the bar had closed down and they were the only ones left in the lounge. Taking the initiative he reluctantly said,

"It's late and I have most thoroughly enjoyed your

company and can barely wait until morning to see you again, but I really must go now, as I still have to copy from your map all the altitudes of the mountain peaks and transfer them to my map, and I'd prefer to do that now rather than leave it until morning" and with that he rose from his seat and taking her hand in his he gentlemanly assisted her up.. Lo' and behold she wouldn't let go of his hand, so they walked hand in hand out of the lounge and along the corridor to their rooms. They came to his room first where he stopped to unlock his door, and was just about to say goodnight, see you in the morning, when she threw both her arms around his neck and started to kiss him. John's willpower wasn't very powerful and he felt he couldn't refuse her affection so he put both his arms around her waist and cuddled her in return. Although he intended to break away, he found it was now impossible as he was drawn to her like steel to a magnet and was so carried away that he dropped the map which he was holding and made no effort to retrieve it.

How long they continued cuddling and kissing in the doorway was anyone's guess, but his arms were aching. Eventually he slowly removed his arms from her waist; she likewise removed her arms from around his neck, as her arms must also have been aching from the lack of circulation. He gave her one last kiss and said "All good things must come to an end, now we must go our separate ways." He had no sooner said this than she put her arms around his neck again and gave him a long lasting passionate kiss, then turning around swiftly said ,

"See you in the morning." and proceeded down the corridor. As he entered his room he bent down to retrieve the fallen map, and then switched on the light before getting his own map out of his rucksack and recording all the altitudes of each individual mountain peak, never realising how many there were. It took him much more time than he had anticipated but eventually the job was completed.

He was in for a disappointment because he couldn't see what he had hoped to see, two mountains side by side by side at almost the same height with a smaller one in the middle. This was a bitter disappointment to him, as he had felt so confident it would be there, just as it had appeared in his dreams. Getting undressed and into bed after switching off the light, he couldn't settle to sleep as now he had lost confidence in his mission, and was having second thoughts that it would end up in failure because he had not found on the map what he had so confidently been expecting to find.

It had a serious repercussion on his previous enthusiasm and high spirits, his mind was so plagued by actively thinking about defeat, there was no chance of him getting any sleep. He was tossing and turning from one side to another.

There was a gentle knock on the door and a voice could be clearly heard in the stillness of the night saying, "It's me, Cheng Eng." Still fully awake he quickly got out of bed, switched the light on and unlocked the door. There she stood with just a towel wrapped around her. As for him,

13

he only had a small pair of underpants on.

"I just can't get to sleep for worrying about your safety when you leave here in the morning," she said,

"So forgive me for troubling you but I just had to see you again, I couldn't possibly wait until morning."

"No trouble at all," he replied,

"on the contrary I greet you with open arms, so he put both his arms around her just to prove the point, and as he ushered her into the room and locked the door he admitted that he had also been unable to sleep because, after recording all the altitudes of all the individual mountains, he couldn't find the two peaks of almost identical height with a smaller mountain in the middle, which was so important to his mission. Both of the maps were laid out on the bedroom floor, going over to inspect them she said,

"OK, let me see now, let me have a look for you." She got down on her knees and first of all looking at the map in its horizontal position, slowly scrutinising the peaks from top to bottom, then she turned the map to a diagonal position he hadn't thought of, and there plain as a pikestaff could be seen, lined up right on the Chinese Tibetan border, were the three peaks, exactly lined up, now that the map was in a diagonal position.

"I can't thank you enough, you have made my day, you really have. I can't believe how stupid I was, not to think of turning the map in different directions until they lined up. I can never thank you enough" He again cuddled and kissed her to show his appreciation. Drawing a straight line on the map from where he was now, to where he wanted to be on the plateau in front of the middle peak, he estimated it would take the best part of three months to get to the eventual destination, as some of the mountainous terrain would be the hardest in the whole world to negotiate on foot. The nastiest part of the journey would be from the hotel to the foothills, which he hoped to do in only five days. Again putting both of her arms round his neck and kissing him, she reiterated,

"I am terribly worried for your safety, and my mind will not be at ease until you are safely back from your mission, so will you promise me you will come back to this hotel when you return."

"I promise," he said. She then whispered in his ear,

"Every minute in your company is precious to me, so can I stay here with you tonight"?

"Your wish is my command, since I feel the same way you do, mind you it's only a single bed, but where there's a will there's a way." As they got up from their knees on the floor she dropped the towel from around her waist and he took off his pants.

They were now both naked, and while they put their arms around one another he remembered to switch the light off, as he could reach it from where he was standing. They both got into the single bed where they kissed and caressed each other for hours, culminating in full sexual intercourse. She lay underneath his plunging male member and felt a steadily increasing sexual excitement, which was turned into a full climax by the extra stimulus of a sudden fear of the ferocity of his manhood within her small body.

2

The Native Hunter

In the morning they were awakened by the sound of people walking along the corridor and the sound of room doors closing as people were leaving to go down to breakfast. This posed a problem for her as she had only a towel to drape round her, so how could she scurry along the corridor back to her room? His solution was to put his anorak around her shoulders after she draped the towel round her waist, and then unlock the door and when it was all clear; she made a successful quick dash along the corridor into her own room. He then had a wash and a shave, taking his time and almost enjoyed the experience, as this would be the last shave he would have for months.

When John and Cheng Eng were reunited at the breakfast table, he observed that she had been crying. As she handed him back his anorak he asked her why she had been crying. It was such a sensitive issue she burst into tears, sobbing that she couldn't come to terms with him having to part on such a dangerous mission and that she wanted to accompany him. She just couldn't cope with the worry of not ever seeing him again. Taking a hanky from his pocket and gently drying her tears, while holding her hand he said, "Don't worry I shall return I promise you and I shall be thinking of you all the time, rest assured."

Because the waiter was standing beside the table he had to take his hand away from hers to allow him to put down the two breakfasts.

After breakfast, although they left the dining room together, he had to go to his room to collect his rucksack and she to hers to collect her briefcase. They waited for each other, and then they both made their way to the hotel reception where he paid his account and handed in his room key. She had to wait in the reception area for the taxi, which came every morning to run her to the school, before bringing her back in the evening after the school closed. She thanked him for the return of the borrowed map and put it in her briefcase to return it to the school library. He replaced his own map back into his rucksack. At that moment the taxi arrived and after he escorted her to it, he gave her a final kiss and cuddle and noticed she was crying again. Although he tried not to show it he too was emotional at their having to part. The taxi moved off and he waved until it was out of sight.

Lifting his rucksack onto his back he started making his way out of town in the opposite direction from the school. Within half an hour he was well out of sight of the built up area and started to enter the rural countryside where as before he kept off the road and started to walk across country, only using the road when he had to cross a ravine, or a river. That meant that the road was never far away. By midday John was ready for a break, he sat down at the base of a large tree and reckoned that he must have covered approximately five miles since leaving the hotel.

His break wasn't too long, only enough time to eat a handful of dried cereal, and drink water from a nearby stream, then he was on his way again. While he slowly trudged along with his heavy rucksack on his back, he kept thinking of Cheng Eng. He realised he was fretting for her company and felt that a special bond had formed between them, in spite of the fact they had only known each other for such a short time. The events of the night before had been so different to his experience with Gillian.

John also thought about how Cheng Eng had come to his rescue by finding and locating what was needed on his map, he had found that most extraordinary. It lifted him out of his dejected depression, although he still felt bad about not accepting her offer to accompany him on the venture.

She would have jumped at the chance, given just a little encouragement and it was now causing turbulence in his mind. The more he trudged on, the more he thought about it, it kept nagging at the back of his mind. Sometimes it was so bad he had to fight against an impulsive urge to go back to her.

After four hours of walking he felt he couldn't go any further, he found a secluded part in the Dense forest with a small stream running though it, and decided this was the best place to spend the night. There was a ready supply of water, which was crystal clear, and was obviously sound and fit for drinking. Taking the rucksack off his back he gave a welcome sigh of relief, as it was so heavy, the more he walked the heavier it seemed to get, so true to say the last mile seemed the longest. He sat on his rucksack resting for a good ten minutes before contemplating doing anything; he then started to unpack his Bibby tent, and to erect it.

This took very little time, he had practised many times before leaving home, to familiarise himself with the procedure and also to see how long it would take him in all weather conditions. In inhospitable and sub-zero temperatures with gale force winds and driving snow blizzards, it could be a matter of life or death. That was the importance of being able to get it erected with the utmost speed. Your tent was your shelter from the elements, and seconds could be a lifeline in those circumstances.

He had just finished this task when he thought he heard a faint sound in the distance. At first he thought he must have imagined it, everything went into a deadly silence. A few seconds later, he could have sworn he heard it again but the sound was from a good distance away. Was it a cry for help, or perhaps an animal of sorts? For that matter he couldn't even be sure from which direction it came from.

One thing for sure, he was perturbed by it, but being cautious he decided not to do anything about it at this time. Sitting down by the stream he took off his mountain boots and stockings and with great relief put his bare, sweating, burning hot feet into the cool water of the stream. Ah! Heaven indeed!

This reminded him of the biblical story where Christ Jesus

after a long hot walk in the desert, arrived at a household where a member bathed and anointed his feet, to soothe them after the gruelling punishment they had been subjected to. Not only were John's feet being soothed but also the comforting sound of the water trickling over the stones into the pool had a most calming affect on his mind. He thought, if people in busy towns and cities who were so stressed up with the pressures of this day and age, could come to a place like this, it couldn't help but be most beneficial to both mind and body.

He was almost day-dreaming in the natural tranquillity of the surroundings, when he was suddenly brought back to reality when he again heard a distinctive high-pitched sound. This time certainly much nearer, and it sounded like a human noise, not that of any animal he could think of. Having said that, he was now in a foreign country with many animals and wildlife, all of which he was unfamiliar with. It could quite possibly come from an animal, which frequented this part of the world.

One way or another he wouldn't be at ease until he found out for sure. There was little chance of him sleeping in a tent with the thought of a predatory creature in the vicinity. Hastily he removed his feet from the pool, shaking off the drips, and not bothering to dry them, with a struggle he put his wet feet into the stockings, then getting to his feet he pulled on his mountain boots. Taking his binoculars from his rucksack he cautiously proceeded to search in the direction of the sound he had heard. His progress was painstakingly slow as he avoided even treading on a dry stick on the forest floor in case the noise of its snapping betrayed his presence.

He was now in a state of full alert, and he reproached himself for having been so stupid to come to a place like this, without firstly finding out all about the local wildlife. As he tip- toed intrepidly forward he again heard a call, this time much closer than before. It seemed to be travelling directly towards him, he froze in his tracks, almost afraid to breathe, his mind played for caution, what was he to do? If it were a dangerous animal he had only an army penknife for protection, and that was back at camp.

Looking up at the surrounding trees, and seeing one that looked like easy access, he lost no time in scaling up from branch to branch until he was nearly at the very top. This was an ideal surveillance and observation post, an ideal place to survey the forest below, nothing could move below without being spotted or heard. His heart was definitely doing overtime after the supreme effort he had put into climbing up the tree. It was a good few minutes before his heartbeat returned to normal.

He was listening intently all the time, there were birds calling from the trees, all of whom he couldn't relate to, as they were completely different to the ones back home. Just then his ears picked up what he thought was the sound of twigs snapping underfoot, this sounded very near. Swinging his binoculars in a wide slow sweep, he couldn't see anything untoward and was just removing his binoculars from his eyes, when he definitely heard the same noise again, this time it was unmistakeably the same something on the move, and so much nearer than before.

Still in a state of high suspense, he once again put the binoculars to his eyes and slowly swept around the surrounding area, suddenly he heard a yelp which sent his heart racing, it was so near and yet he still couldn't see anything through his binoculars, then as he was about to take the binoculars from his eyes he noticed a movement of something passing a tree and then stopping.

He couldn't believe what he was looking at through the binoculars; it was a young dark haired girl bending down doing what looked liked tying a shoelace. Since he had expected to see a wild animal, he was wondering if his eyes were playing tricks on him, but this was nothing to the shock he was about to get. A second later a shout loud and clear came to his ears. "John!" He almost dropped his binoculars when he saw it was Cheng Eng.

"Cheng Eng, over here"! He shouted in return.
Looking through his binoculars again he saw her get back up from stooping down, he also noticed she was limping badly as she slowly made her way in his direction, guided by his call. He once again shouted,
"I am over here Cheng Eng!"
He then started to make his way down the tree, branch by branch, stopping at intervals to shout out that he was high up in a tree, but was making his way down.
By the time he got down from the tree, she was only a few yards away.

He ran to her with arms outstretched to greet and

22

console her, because she was crying, with tears running down her cheeks. While kissing and cuddling her he asked her "Why are you crying?"

"My foot is terribly painful," she replied. He immediately bent down and to his horror saw a broken stick protruding out of her trainer-like shoe.

"You can't walk on that," he said with compassion, and immediately put her over his shoulder and bending over, started to make his way back to his tent beside the stream. He tried to go as fast as he could while at the same time consoling her and putting her mind at ease, but the journey was painstakingly slow.

"You will be all right now," he told her, "I have a First Aid kit in my rucksack back at camp, and we should not take long to get there."

By the time they got back to the tent, and he had laid her gently down by the stream where he had been soaking his feet so recently, he was completely exhausted, but exhausted or not he wasn't going to waste valuable time in getting his breath back. He treated her injuries as an accidental emergency, he could see she was in pain and had a fever already and was in shock.

He grabbed his rucksack throwing everything out, scattering items all over the place until he reached his first aid kit. Giving Cheng Eng two tranquillisers for her pain, he advised her to chew them before swallowing, this allowed the medicine to get into the digestive system quicker. Until now his binoculars had been round his neck and only now noticing this, he took them off. Looking around at the scattered contents of his rucksack he collected his tin mug, and half filling it with the crystal clear water from the stream he gently put one arm around Cheng Eng's shoulders and with his other hand gently offered her the drink by putting the mug to her lips and coaxing her to drink, which she did slowly until the mug was empty. He explained to her that she would have to be brave and swallow her pain as he was now going to extract the splinter of wood from her foot.

He was quite unable to remove the shoe to dress her wound without first removing the splinter. On closer inspection he noticed that this was not a natural twig of wood from the forest floor but was a piece of wood fashioned by man. Realising only just in time that it was in fact the broken shaft of a small arrow, and had he tried to pull it out, it would have caused irreparable damage to her foot, not to mention the excruciating pain that she would have had to bear.

He now realised only too well, why he had heard the sudden yelp while he was up the tree, what he didn't understand was how the shaft of the arrow had broken. Although she was still shaking, trembling and sobbing he had to ask her how the arrow had broken and exactly what had happened. Through her sobs she was able to explain, that whilst running through the trees in the forest she felt a sudden, burning pain in her foot and at this same instant she heard a snapping sound of wood breaking when she tripped and fell on her hands and knees. Pulling her close he embraced her and said,

"I also heard that same snap while I was up in the tree. I can now understand what happened" he added,
"as you were running, the small arrow penetrated through your shoe into the side of your foot, the arrow shaft must have broken when it got caught on a tree as you ran between them, causing you to fall down. I shall have to cut your shoe very carefully to get it off without any movement to the remaining piece of arrow shaft. You will have to be very brave while I cut your shoe off."
Still sobbing she indicated that the pain was now easing but that there was still a burning sensation in her foot.

Time was now critical as it would be dark in an hour so John wasted no time in getting his knife out and very slowly, after first removing the lace, started to cut the fabric off the trainer shoe in a straight line right up to the arrow shaft, it was comparatively easy then to remove the remainder of the shoe. To his amazement there was not a speck of blood to be seen, he had expected the shoe to be soaked with blood from the nasty wound, but the flesh of the foot was so tightly adhered to the arrowhead that it had prevented blood loss; he gave a sigh of relief that it hadn't severed an artery.

Now the big decision had to be made, how to extract the arrowhead, he was no surgeon and it looked like surgery would be required. Time was important, and he had little of it to think things over. He remembered two things, the half bottle of brandy and the chocolate covered Kendal Mint cake that Reg had given him at the airport send off. John took off his heavy mountaineering jacket which was thermal-lined, and put it on Cheng Eng to keep her warm as she was getting cold in the chill of the night air.

Taking the Kendal mint cake from his rucksack side pocket he broke a bit off offering it to her to try. She took it thankfully, although she didn't know what it was, so he explained to the best of his abilities what it was and that it was manufactured near the village next to where he lived. At first she just nibbled at it, but seemed to acquire a taste and said she liked it, so he broke off and gave her a much larger piece, by the time she had finished it she had calmed down considerably. Obviously the tranquillisers were now having an effect, he thought.

Taking the brandy bottle he opened it and told her to have some but to keep taking small sips. As time went on he noticed that she was getting drowsier and drowsier, until she fell into a sound sleep with the brandy bottle still clasped in her hand, but with only a quarter of the brandy now left in the bottle, just what John hoped would happen, because now she was warm and in a deep sleep.

He could now carry on the task of removing the arrowhead from her foot, after firstly removing the brandy bottle from her hand, he screwed the top back on, and put it down beside what was left of the Kendal mint cake.

The next thing that he did was to get his penknife and open the blade ready to act as a scalpel to make the necessary incisions either side of the broken arrow shaft allowing the withdrawal of the barbed arrow head. Nerves got the better of him and he was trembling. He knew that at that moment he was in no fit state to start.

Without thinking and working more by intuition and impulse he opened the brandy bottle and gulped down most of what was left, leaving just sufficient to use as a steriliser, he drained the last few drops on the surrounding area where the incisions where to be made, and on both sides of the blade. He couldn't resist the temptation to finish off the last of the Kendal mint cake while he was at it.

Then with the expression of his heart in his mouth, he forced himself to make an incision, he felt like closing his eyes as he forced himself to do it, but knew only too well they had to be kept open. After the first insertion he felt more capable, maybe the brandy was giving him a helping hand as he seemed to gain confidence. To his great relief the barbs of the arrowhead were just under the surface of the skin so the incisions he had to make were not too deep.

Parting the flesh with the knife, with his other hand he gently waggled the broken shaft from side to side, almost the same as one does to a slack tooth to enable it to be pulled out by the roots, practising the same technique to extract the arrow head, it slowly but surely came away in his hand, it had been painstakingly slow at first but then all of a sudden it came out.

Next he had to act quickly pressing the now open wound together, and bandaging it tightly with the one and only suitable dressing from the first aid box. His timing could not have been any better as it was now almost dark. Darkness seemed to come on you all of a sudden in this

27

part of the world, not like back at home where you had the gradual twilight before darkness. What didn't help was that they were in the shade from tree foliage, this certainly accelerated the darkness. After he had finished bandaging her foot, with a bit of a struggle he carefully lifted her into his tent. As she was still in a deep sleep, it was his turn to try and get to sleep in a very cramped tent, which after all was designed for one person and it was a real squeeze for two people.

Unable to settle he was restless, and was beginning to think that he would never get to sleep. It was on his mind all the time, just how had that arrow been fired into her foot? He came to the conclusion that it had come from a poachers trap, set off by a trip wire, which had been set up to kill a wild animal. He was confident that there was no one around in the vicinity where she had been.

He was also worried about her wounded foot, should she be taken to a hospital, or at least see a doctor regarding the wound he had bandaged, she may well require stitches. With all this going through his mind, it was little wonder that it took a long time for him to get to sleep, but eventually he made it.

Early the next morning he awakened to the noise of a morning chorus of birds. Listening intently to it he thought how wonderful it was, a truly beautiful experience, he wished Cheng Eng could share it with him, but she was still in a very sound sleep. He could have easily spent all morning listing to the birds but he was very hungry as he hadn't eaten anything for almost twenty hours, apart from the piece of Kendal mint cake, so even though he was reluctant to get up he found the pangs of hunger took control.

As soon as he had wriggled out of the tent, and wriggling was the only way it could be done, as the tent was only one metre high. It had been built and designed to withstand a hurricane force gale, and that's why it was so low to the ground, to offer minimum resistance to the wind. Going straight to the pool he splashed cool water all over his face to freshen up, then he gathered some of his dried cereal, mixed it with water from the stream and ate it heartily. Looking round he surveyed the scene where the contents of his rucksack were scattered, he picked them up and replaced them, then he went back to check on Cheng Eng who was still sleeping. He knew that the longer she slept the better; because when one slept the body's natural Healing process was working at its maximum efficiency.

Now that he had tidied up and had his the breakfast he was ready to move on, but didn't want to leave her here sleeping. However he had an irresistible urge to go back into the forest to where she had been struck with the arrow. Throwing caution to the wind he returned to the forest, after firstly writing a small note explaining his absence to Cheng Eng, and left it at the entrance to the tent with a stone on it to keep it in place.

He proceeded with extreme caution and kept a wary eye on the ground looking for trip wires, he did not want to be struck with an arrow like Cheng Eng. Eventually he reached the bottom of the same tree, which he had climbed up, and used yesterday as an observation post, so it would be plain sailing now to locate the exact spot where she had yelped in pain and fallen down.

Within a few minutes he had found the spot were she had been shot, and just a few paces to the rear, he found just what he had expected, the broken arrow shaft, which incidentally was a flightless arrow held on a line of cat gut, which he followed back to a pile of leaves, the line just disappeared into the pile. He bent down and very slowly pulled at the line, but it wouldn't give, it was obviously anchored to something under the leaves.

This made sense because when the arrow had been fired and struck a moving object it could only go so far before coming to the end of the tether. Although this seemed common sense to him, what he couldn't understand was the lack of a trip wire to set the trap off. In an effort to solve this puzzle he got down on his knees and started to move the leaves from where the line disappeared into the pile. Clearing the last of the leaves away he uncovered a very large flat stone, what intrigued him was not only it's shape, but the fact that it had a hole in its centre used for tying on the cat gut.

The hole was indeed large enough to accommodate the arrow shaft, the broken shaft fitted into the perfectly round hole and confirmed his findings, and because it had no flight, the arrow shaft was able to move through the hole with ease. After closely studying it for a while he worked out that there must be some mechanism under the stone to set it off.

Spreading his arms out he got to grips with the circumference of the stone and just as he had predicted the top of the circular stone moved and lifted off, exposing a beautifully made cross bow which had been secured by several brackets to the base of the stone. It was almost like removing the circular lid of a giant sized biscuit box and to find inside a miniature cross bow.

The stone lid was a work of art and fitted perfectly. On closer examination he saw a piece of broken gossamer fine catgut round the trigger of the cross bow with a miniature pulley wheel just behind the trigger. Now he understood! What was left of the trip wire operated the trigger mechanism. The fine cat-gut, as fine as could possibly be, was tied to the trigger of the cross bow, then round the small pulley wheel and out through the hole and ended up anchored to a tree trunk opposite, it had obviously been broken as it had activated the trigger and then dragged down to anchor height by Cheng Eng as she fell over.

He now knew that the whole idea of the set up was to catch a rabbit or similar animal. It could be any small animal as he was not fully aware of the variety of wildlife which existed in this country. Anyway he had now seen all he wanted to see, so he carefully replaced the stone lid and covered it all with bracken to leave it undisturbed and just as he had found it. He felt tempted to look for the trip wire but decided it was more urgent to get back to Cheng Eng in the tent. Still on his hands and knees he swung round to pick up the arrow shaft, and got one of the biggest frights of his entire life when he saw a pair of light brown bare legs and feet, so close that being squatted down he couldn't see above knee height. He froze with fear; he felt his throat dry up as he broke out in a cold sweat, his body literally trembling with fear. His mind flashed to schooldays when he had read, that in faraway lands there were naked head hunters who were still cannibals.

These thoughts wouldn't get out of his mind and he was petrified, unable to even look up. Knowing that the few phrases of the local language he had learned were of no material use here, and besides, he was too frightened so he couldn't speak. The stranger remained motionless, and he too was completely silent. John felt sure his heart could be heard pounding away. It was a good job he was young, because the state he was in now, an older person in the same circumstances would have suffered a heart attack without a doubt.

Inner instincts told him that he was in great danger. Should he look up now? He could almost imagine that the person standing over him was holding a huge machete knife just ready to chop off his bent head. It was only then that he came up with the one and only instinctive thing to do, which was to put his hands together and with head bowed down, not much more than it was already, and to say a prayer in silence to God for help. No sooner had he made his Silent prayer than the fear left him and he gained his normal self-confidence, it was indeed a miracle.
Slowly arising to his feet he saw for the first time the

stranger confronting him, he was naked except for a green loincloth held in position by a large leather black belt. John's eyes where almost riveted to the two large hunting knifes on the belt. He wore one on either side of him. Over one shoulder he carried a large bow and on the other he had a container full of arrows.

He looked about twenty years old or thereabouts, with black hair, brown eyes and standing about five and a half feet tall. Since his prayer John was still without fear, so he bent down slowly and picked up the shaft of the broken arrow, in sign language he pointed at the arrow and then to the side of his foot and making a crying sound of pain, he straightened up and gestured for the native to follow him.
Walking away he noticed that the native without as much as a murmur was following him in complete silence.

Soon they arrived at John's tent, where he calmly picked up the broken arrow head and then showed the native hunter where it had been in the side of Cheng Eng's foot, although still asleep her foot with the blood stained bandage could be quite easily seen at the doorway of the tent. The native seemed to understand because without any words being spoken, he bent down and picked up some grass.

Holding the grass in one hand he pointed to the sun with his index finger, and slowly moved from the sun to a different position in the sky, looking at his finger he started running on the spot while at the same time dropping his other hand to the piece of grass at his feet, then turning on his heels he ran off into the forest, John was left totally bewildered by this, but did not have time to dwell on it as Cheng Eng was now awake and calling for him.

Making his way to the tent he greeted her and asked her how she felt.

"I am very tired," she said.

"That's to be expected" he sighed,

"you just stay where you are and I shall prepare you some breakfast"

When John returned, she gave a short cry, stating that she had no feeling in her left leg; it was her left foot, which had been damaged by the arrow. He explained the situation in full to her and let her know that the arrow been removed.

He retrieved the arrowhead and eased her mind by showing it to her, on seeing the arrowhead her eyes opened wide in astonishment.

"Was that in my foot?" she asked.

Lifting the cover from her legs he helped her to sit up and have a look. When she saw the heavily bandaged foot she asked if he had contacted a Doctor yet. He explained that he had been unable to do so as his first priority had been to remove the arrowhead and that he had done this while she slept.

"Let me get you some breakfast and I will tell you all about it" he said, remarking that he had already had his breakfast some time ago.

Later while she was eating the cereal that he had prepared for her, he related the whole story to her and all that had happened while she had been sleeping. He missed out no detail and finished off with the peculiar antics of the native before he ran off into the forest.

She seemed to understand what the native was trying to tell them, and explained that when the native pointed at the sun, then moving his finger over the sky, he was indicating the passing of time, running on the spot meant he was going to run somewhere, and it would seem he intended to return later on. She never failed to amaze him with her abilities; she had been quick to understand the messages from the native while he on the other hand had little idea what they meant, it all seemed so logical after she had explained it.

When she had finished her breakfast she asked him to help her out of the tent and on to her feet because she needed the toilet. He had to fully support her because she could not bear to put her injured foot on the ground. What was more worrying was the fact that she was paralysed all down her leg. With quite a struggle he managed to get her a few yards into the undergrowth and later back into the tent.

After that he took the opportunity to ask her why she had followed him into the forest. She explained that on arriving at the school on the morning he had left, she just couldn't settle and felt she had to accompany him on his expedition as it would be much more exciting and adventurous than being in a classroom all day teaching young students. By mid day she had handed in her resignation to the head teacher, who wasn't amused to say the very least.

She had lied to him saying that her parents had been involved in a serious road accident in Hong Kong. John could understand why she didn't give the real reason.

Returning to the hotel by taxi she informed the hotel manager of her plight, she settled her account, and not even taking time to change into more suitable clothing, arranged for her belongings to be put into storage to await her return. Getting back into the taxi, she had instructed the driver to wait and she got him to drive her along the road running parallel to John's cross country route until she came to a spot which she thought was right. She paid the taxi driver telling him that a friend was going to pick her up here in half an hour.

Looking at the vast jungle and placing all her faith in God to help her find him, she set off in pursuit. Her previous experience of orienteering was used to her practical advantage, however when she did find him it was more by providence than her skills. She had alternated between running a few hundred yards then walking, and shouting to him at regular intervals. When she had finished with her explanation she laughed and asked him why on earth he had been up a tree.

He thought, how pleasing it was to hear her laugh, anything to keep her mind off her injuries, laughter is one of the great healers. However he was more worried than he wanted to show her, now that she was paralysed and needed help to get around, how could he possibly manage to carry her to a place where she could receive proper medical attention? It was almost mid day by now, and he offered to fetch them both a drink of cool water from the pool

On returning to the camp with the water, John saw the young native hunter come running out of the forest up to the tent with something clasped in his hand, and without a word he squatted down at the entrance to the tent opened his clasped hands and showed them a selection of leaves which he put on the ground.

Turning his attention to Cheng Eng and without a murmur, he commenced very gently to unwind the bloodstained bandage on her foot; he looked at the wound very carefully and then placed a yellow coloured leaf over it followed by a green leaf, he repeated this until all the leaves were used up. After washing out the bandage in the stream he returned and commenced to wrap it around her foot. Then after tying it securely he stood up, and pointed up to the sun, and very slowly with his index finger he went round in a very large circle while at the same time walking with an imitation limp until two full circles had been made, then he picked up the grass, which he had thrown down on his previous visit, pushed it against the side of the foot he had been limping with. Throwing the grass away he started to shake his leg in all directions. Then, in a flash he turned and quickly ran back into the forest and was gone from their sight.

Cheng Eng had observed all this from her position in the tent, she also noticed that the visitor had not uttered a sound in all the time he had been there. Crouched down at the entrance to the tent John asked,

"What do you make of all that then?" She smiled and said, "I know exactly what it means, in two days from now I shall not be limping and that's when the bandage has to be removed." He could sense the newfound confidence which was now brimming over in her, she had only managed to laugh once in his presence so far, but was now laughing and smiling at the thought of making a full recovery in two days.

He felt relaxed and at ease now that she had brightened up. She said that she couldn't get over how the native hunter, while looking so menacing and ferocious was actually so kind and gentle, and wondered if he was dumb because he had not uttered a sound in their presence.

"I am full of gratitude for all he has done for me, and I suspect we shall never set eyes on him again, but one thing's for sure, I shall never forget him"

"I can honestly say that I won't forget him either, but for a different reason, for as long as I live he will be my guardian angel but I will also remember him for giving me the biggest fright of my life", John answered,

"I reckon I could go through ten lifetimes without ever getting such a fright again, how on earth he ever managed to creep up on me so silently I'll never know. I did not hear even so much as a leaf being stepped on."

"Yes," she replied,

"the lord above works in mysterious ways his wonders to perform."

Looking into her eyes he smiled and said,

"Never a truer word have you spoken."

38

Then giving her a quick cuddle and kiss he asked if she had any washing to be done as he had to attend to his stockings which were in a poor state after the first days walk.

"Well John," she said,

"to be honest with you I prefer to change my underwear each day, but in my rush to get here I left it all at the hotel, I only have with me what I'm wearing."

He indicated that, this was not a problem for him and because she was unable to fend for herself he helped remove her under garments for washing.

Down at the stream a bird caught his eye, it was a bird that was completely different from anything he had seen back home. Being a keen bird watcher he was unable to resist being interested in it, it had a lovely and interesting chirp, one that he recognised from the early morning chorus that had awakened him. He got so carried away with things and not paying attention to what he was doing, to his horror he suddenly realised that in the bundle of washing he was doing was all his money, he had completely forgotten to remove it from his stockings where he had placed it for safe keeping.

Now he had to part the notes as they were all stuck to each other being soaking wet, he separated each one and put them on the bank of the stream held with a stone to prevent them from blowing away as there was now a breeze. He rushed to get back to the tent to explain to Cheng Eng why he had taken so long. Once again Cheng Eng placed her tiny hand over her mouth as she couldn't stop laughing, she saw the funny side of the situation, which eradicated John's anxiety. Anyway, time consuming as it was, the notes all dried out except for where the stone was pinning each note down which of course he had to move on each note to enable that last wet patch to dry. Her underwear dried out very quickly being made of very flimsy material, but as for his stockings, his mother had hand knitted them in the thickest ply wool she could obtain; they took ages to dry out. In the meantime he had no choice but to walk about in his mountain boots without any stockings   Cheng Eng had to be eased out of the tent, head first then helped onto her feet so he could assist her into the trees for the toilet, this was an essential service which had to be provided several times each day It was a much harder task getting her back into the tent than it was to get her out, but like everything else, by repetition it was easier as one got into the knack of it. Just like the staple diet of dried mixed cereal and water, after a while you just took it in your stride although it was a tremendous change to the hotel meals especially when it came to the evening meal. When you had a portion of dried cereal and water, all you could think of was the last delicious evening meal back at the hotel.

Later that same evening John got the map out just before it got dark and they plotted together over it to find out where exactly they were now, and the best course of action to take when she was able to walk unaided. After much deliberation she came up with two choices, first choice was to get to the road where the once weekly service bus would hopefully stop and pick them up as fare paying passengers, and go on to the small village in the foothills. Secondly to just keep walking cross-country until they achieved their objective under their own steam.

After an exhausting and very long discussion it was unanimously agreed that rather that waste time going miles off course to the road, in the uncertain hope of catching the bus, it was preferential to keep going on walking as long as her shoes would stand up to the journey, there was a whole side of one of the shoes missing where it had been necessary to cut it to free the arrow head. They had another long discussion about the supplies that would have to be purchased when they got to a trading post, as she literally had nothing with her, apart from a flimsy dress and a damaged pair of soft shoes, totally unsuitable for climbing, so he said that if and when they reached their destination which was four full days walk away, she would have to decide whether to carry on the expedition with him or wait for a week until the bus would take her back.

She told him in no uncertain terms that she had fallen in love with him and would sooner die than go back, saying that not only did she love him but loved his spirit of adventure and that her mind would never be at ease if she parted from him. She would be devoted and dedicated to him, and although she knew he had a wife and twins back home, that was of no consequence as she would always take the background role as his lifelong devoted mistress. To say the very least he was left speechless, but he was not prepared to reject the loving offer made to him.

When all that had been said he took her in his arms cuddled her and whispered asking God to forgive him but he, as a married man, had fallen in love with her. He couldn't resist the temptation of making love with her there and then, time and time again until they both finally exhausted themselves and fell asleep.

Neither awoke until well into the next morning, and far too late to hear the wonderful chorus of the birds which he had heard the previous morning. This morning breakfast was a treat, not only did they have the usual cereal but for an extra treat they shared a bar of chocolate covered Kendal cake, which he got from his rucksack.

Later he helped her down to the pool where she washed in the crystal clear water. After she was settled in the tent again he said that he was going bird watching, but he would be within shouting distance away and if she needed him then she should just call out for him. With that said he made his way to the edge of the forest where he was in his element because he had never seen such brilliant coloured birds before, nor for that matter heard the lovely calls that they were making.

After a while he felt a bit guilty about having left Cheng Eng by herself in the tent with nothing to do. In an instant he had an inspiration, he saw some long flat tapering leaves so he cut off half a dozen or so with his knife and then returned to his rucksack outside the tent, took out his Biro pen, returning to the stream he picked up a flat stone and made his way back to the tent where he started cutting the long straight stiff leaves into equal length segments. She could see him working away, so she asked him why he was cutting the long leaves so carefully into such precise measurements. He laughed and said, "Wait and see." After John had cut the exact amount he required then, with the point of his pen, he made dots in patterns and then with the point of his knife he cut out the dots. Chen Eng was still left guessing, and she looked on until one by one he eventually got through the entire pile.

Slowly but surely he finished the last one, then with his pen he drew a straight line through the exact middle off each and stacked them all up into a neat pile and handed them to her, saying,

"Now we can pass the time away."

She smiled and clapping her hands together squealed with joy.

"How clever, ingenious and enterprising" and she turned each one over and examined it.

She told him that she hadn't played a game of dominoes for years, and never thought she would play with a domino set made from leaves.

"Let's start after lunch," he suggested,

"we shall have lunch first, it has taken so long to make the domino set it is now well past midday. We will have the rest of the day to play with the dominoes".

She said that she had not wanted to disturb him while he was busy but had wanted to go to the toilet.

"Right, first things first," he said, and helped her out of the tent, and because she was still limping he supported her to the edge of the forest, then back into the tent afterwards.

Only then did he mix up some of the dried cereal with water from the stream and after they had finished their cereal he again went to his rucksack and put his biro pen and his knife away. He broke a portion off a Kendal mint bar and gave it to her as an after lunch treat, which she really appreciated. Then the rest of the day was spent playing dominoes in the tent, those home made improvised dominoes were a Godsend as the time just flew by, game after game was played until it got too dark to play anymore.

It was time to settle down for the night but John wasn't able to get off to sleep straight away because he kept thinking about the sign language of the native hunter telling him that Cheng Eng would be able to walk in a couple of days. He did worry in case the native hunter's sign language prediction didn't work out, if it didn't, what was he to do as they couldn't stay here indefinitely. It was obviously a worrying position to have to contemplate, so while she was fast asleep he was wide-awake with worry. Eventually after what seemed like an eternity he did get off to sleep. It was Cheng Eng who had to wake him in the morning; she was excitably shaking him and saying that the feeling had now come back to her foot and leg. Half asleep he gave her a cuddle and said

"God moves in mysterious ways, his wonders to perform," and bleary eyed crawled out of the tent, the restless night and lack of sleep was telling on him now. Looking up at the sun he saw that it was now in the position where the native hunter had pointed before he threw the grass on the ground then shook his leg before running off into the forest.

After what Cheng Eng had just told him, John had some faith in the native's predictions, so he started to unwrap the bandage from her foot, then he parted the layers of leaves, and couldn't believe his eyes as the last leaf was peeled off, there wasn't even a mark where the wound had been. It was as good as witnessing a miracle; there was no way one could pinpoint where the lacerations had been. To say he was gob smacked would be an understatement, and he excitedly told her to have a look for herself.

Sitting up and having a look, she was equally amazed at how well her foot had healed, she stared at it in amazement and commented on how remarkable it was to think that the native hunter, who would have been unlikely to ever have had inoculations, vaccinations, antibiotics or any of the other modern medicines, was probably more healthy than the majority of the world's populace who relied on present day man made medicines. She also marvelled at the inside knowledge of natural cures he was aware of.

John laughed and said,
"I totally agree with you, that native is quite unable to walk down the street to a chemist. Another problem with modern drugs is the occasional serious side effects, and here you are, fit again without as much as a headache."
"I suppose" he added,
"you could liken it to keeping a wild animal caged up in a

zoo for years and then releasing it into its natural environment, it just would not survive. People nowadays are a bit like that, they rely so much on drugs and antibiotics that their bodies have lost their own natural resistance and immunity to most ailments."

"There is a lot of logic in what you say," she said in reply, and started to move forward and pull herself from the tent "Look" she added,

"I feel quite independent now" and with that she stood up, rather shakily at first, and made him laugh as she tried to move her foot about just as the native had done, then to his astonishment she ran to the forest to answer the call of nature. He stood and shook his head in amazement, to think that just a few days before she was quite unable to walk, and now she was running, she surely had shown great faith in her healer.

Later she came running, almost bouncing back to the tent explaining that she had never felt better and more fit in her whole life than she did right now. He was so pleased and relieved to see her happy, only now was he able to confess to her about how worried he had been. She threw her arms around his neck drawing him to her, she kissed him and said,

"From now on I will be a great help to you and not a hindrance." He cuddled her with affection and whispered,

"I can tell you now that I missed you the moment I left the hotel, I'm so glad you're with me now, on my own I would have been solitary and lonely, and this would surely have got me down".

She reminded him that the feeling was mutual and that was why she had followed him on his expedition.

Collecting the leaves and dressing that had been on her foot she said that she wanted to keep them as a lifelong reminder of the native, his kindness and the whole escapade, she asked if he would keep them for her, so he packed them in a side pocket of his rucksack along with the unique dominoes, which he had so proudly made. It would soon be time for them to be on their way to the trading post for clothing and provisions, in the meantime they sat together down by the pool eating their dinner come lunch, consisting of the usual cereal which he had mixed to his own recipe. Suddenly she nudged his arm and whispered, "Look a fish" and pointed to where it was.

Seeing the fish he exclaimed

"Well I never, to think that I have been down to this stream so many times and had yet to see a fish, and you spot one first time down here."

"You should remember," she replied,

"that when you were here you were looking at the birds, had you spent the same amount of time looking in the pool I'm sure you would have spotted a fish."

Then she told him to look a few feet behind the fish and nearer the banking and he would see another, just a bit smaller. It took him several seconds to see it; if its tail hadn't been slowly moving he would not have spotted it, as its natural camouflage was so good. She suggested that it would be exciting if they could try and catch a fish, if he were to go upstream and she downstream, then wade towards each other, they would trap the fish between them. He disagreed saying it was not a good idea, having no cooking facilities, he did not want to eat raw fish so he suggested they forget about it.

"Ok" she said, smiling,

"my motto from now on will be live and let live."

He answered, "Walk and let's walk," this made her chuckle at his quick humour.

While she was washing the dishes in the stream, he took down the tent and folded it up ready for packing in his rucksack, and taking the newly washed pans from her, he placed them beside the now neatly folded sleeping bag, and was about to pack the items away when she stopped him.

"Now that I'm fit" she said,

"I can see no reason why I cannot help carry the load, in fact I insist upon it, not only will it help you but it will be excellent exercise for me, not to mention the good experience."

"I can understand your point," he replied,

"But it's just not practical to carry loads under your arms".

"No! No! John, I shall carry them both on my back just in the same way as you carry your rucksack, she said.

"How can you" He exclaimed,

"when you have no shoulder straps to hold the load"

"Ah, but I soon will have straps in a few minutes, you just wait and see" she replied. He was disturbed to say the least, when she asked him for a loan of his knife, and had reservations as to what she intended to do with it. Accepting the knife from him she asked him to show her where he had cut the long narrow leaves which he had used to make the dominoes. She followed him a few paces behind until they arrived at the place where the leaves grew.

"Ah, just what I need" she said, and proceeded to cut down the longest ones in the bunch. By the time she had cut down what she required there were very few leaves left in the group. Giving him back the knife, she gathered together an armful of the long green leaves and he followed her back to the camp.

3

A Long Hard Trek

Sitting cross legged he made himself comfortable and sat watching as she collected three long leaves and skilfully started to pleat them together, leaving a few inches undone at either end. Then she asked him to try and make one following her example.

"I have never done this before," he said,

"nor have I seen it done before." Nevertheless he was keen to try so he willingly set to work. It amused her that he had never seen pleating done before. "Don't you have a sister then?" She asked. "No" he answered, "I was an only child, the nearest I got to having a sister was when my mother accepted Ruby as being her daughter."

"That explains it," she said. "Explains what?" he asked,

"Well" she replied, "If you had a sister you would probably have seen your mother pleat her hair in the mornings prior to her going to school." Eventually when he had completed it to her satisfaction he noticed that she had done another two, her speed and experience were showing him up no end. When they had completed ten, the ends were spliced together to make two full circles, each of five. Each circle was then twisted into a figure of eight.

Then she placed the rolled up tent and the sleeping bag in one end of each strap she had made, then put her arms through the other ends of the loops, and hey presto she was now able to carry part of the load on her back with comfort. John was full of admiration at her skill and ingenuity, and was impressed beyond belief. Now with their back backs fully loaded and fitting comfortably they set off on their journey together.

Within the first hour they had emerged from the forest and onto open ground. They were about a hundred yards onto this open ground when John suggested they have a break as it was also time to take a compass bearing and map reference to make sure they were on a true course to their destination.

Removing his rucksack and getting out his map and compass, he was setting this up when she said
"Hey! Look!" and pointed to the edge of the forest where they had just come from, and there in the shadow of the trees could be seen the native hunter who had contacted them before. They both waved to him, but he simply turned on his heels and ran back into the Forest.
"I wonder how long he has been following us" she said, "just think, if we had not stopped here, we would never have known of his presence."
"I am also wondering why he was following us," he said.
"maybe he was making sure that we did not set off one of his traps again,"
"Although unseen he was scouting our progress and would have probably come to our rescue if we had been in a direct line of one of his traps again," she answered.
"Sounds logical, but then on the other hand, maybe he was

keeping a watch on you, to see if your wound had healed properly," he answered.

"To think," she said,

"he must have been watching us all the time since before we broke camp this morning".

"Let's put this away" said John,

"we will never know," and laughing he continued,

"you will not catch me going back into the forest to engage in sign language to find out, no chance!"

"That goes for me too," Cheng Eng replied.

John took a compass reading from the map, he found that they were only a few degrees off course, it was better to rectify it at this stage rather than later.

They were soon under way again, and were able to make much quicker progress, not having to fight their way through the forest now that they were on open land. It was bright and sunny with a slight breeze blowing, making it an ideal day for walking; in the distance scores of cattle could be seen grazing which meant that this plain at the bottom of the foothills to the mountains was obviously cattle country. It amazed him that there were no fences; the cattle here had the freedom to roam as they pleased.

Four hours had passed since they emerged from the forest, and by now the sun was well down on the horizon. They were both very tired and hungry. John threw off his rucksack with a sigh of relief, and they both sat on it together, it was wide enough to accommodate them both, and with room to spare. Its width had caused him problems in the past, he remembered on one occasion just being able to get through the hotel room entrance door, with it on his back, but he had to take it off to get through the much narrower bedroom door. Mind you, it was the largest one now available and it had been designed to carry as much camping gear as possible, not necessarily suitable for going through doorways, he thought.

Pointing to a line on the map he told her it was either a stream or a river, and as it was necessary for them to have water they would continue to it after they had a little rest. Hunger got the better of them and as they sat together they shared a bar of the chocolate cake, they both enjoyed not only the cake but also the rest; he could quite easily have put his feet up there and then. She could see that he was weary so she said,

"You're like me John, very tired but I think we should be going now if we are to give ourselves a chance of finding the stream before it gets dark, I do hope this stream is not too far away."

Reluctantly he got to his feet, and gave thanks to God that Cheng Eng was fit again and able to share both the load and decisions with him, for he doubted that he would have made it thus far without her help. His feet were burning and sore with walking and his mountain boots felt as if they weighed a stone each. He almost envied her with the lighter footwear and vowed that when he reached civilisation, he would purchase a similar pair for himself as they were much more suitable for walking on flat land. They had estimated it would take them about three days to reach civilisation if they kept to the current schedule. He was looking forward to getting his feet up for a well-earned couple of days rest in a hotel, if there were any there.

They chatted together as they walked, she confessed that she was looking forward to the break back to civilisation, but on the other hand she would be quite happy to resume their adventure, which would take them into the wilderness for a couple of months.
"One thing is for sure we won't be doing this walk again, I don't care how long we have to wait for the once a week bus, next time we will be on it," he said painfully.
"I second the motion," she said laughing.

It was now late and becoming very dark as the clouds were crowding out the stars and moon, and they were not in sight of the river.
"I can see no sense in carrying on," he said dejectedly. We are quite liable to lose our sense of direction and we could be in danger."

They were both so exhausted that they spent very little time over their late meal of cereal, which neither of them enjoyed because they had no water to mix with it. They wasted no time in putting the tent up and getting bedded down for the night. He said he would just have to dream about putting his bare feet in the cool stream and having a drink of water. "Me too." she replied, and that was the last words spoken, before they both went into a sound sleep.
Seeing that John was still sleeping when she wakened in the morning, she was careful not to disturb him and very slowly and quietly shuffled out of the tent and put her

footwear on. She was dying for a drink, so decided to see if she could see any sign of the river.

The grass was soaking wet, either there had been rain through the night or there must have been heavy overnight dew. She had only walked about half a mile when the flat ground suddenly sloped away and there before her was a wide river. She was so excited she couldn't help but run down the slope to the rivers edge where she got down on her hands and knees and started to drink the water. By now dehydration was starting, even her throat was dry, so one can imagine what a relief it was to quench such a thirst.

As soon as she had taken in a sufficient supply of water, she got up from her hands and knees and started running all the way back to the tent to inform John that she had found the river and how close it was. She got back to the tent out of breath and full of excitement, she just couldn't let him sleep any longer, she must waken him to give him the good news, so she shouted "John!" and shook him again shouting "John!" and giving him an extra good shake which woke him up. Immediately she blurted out, "John, guess what?"

Struggling to come to grips with such a sudden and surprising awakening he said "What"?
"I've found the river, and it's so near, less than half a mile away, get up quickly and come and see!" she exclaimed. Taking a long and deliberate yawn he said, "Good work my dear, I am desperate for a drink, to be truthful I'm longing for a cup of tea or coffee, but water will sustain my thirst,

even my throat is dry."

"Mine was too." She said,

"What a relief it was to find the river and get a drink from it."

Just as soon as he was up and out of the tent, John said "Lets take the dry cereal with us, we can mix it with the water and eat our cereal breakfast on the riverbank, which will be quicker than bringing water back to the tent".

"Can I make a suggestion?" She asked.

"Surely" he answered, as he fastened up the laces on his mountaineering boots.

"Well, rather than leave the tent and go to the river, then having to return for it, why not pack up now and go to the river, we are going in that direction anyway?

"Spot on and good thinking Cheng Eng, ten out of ten, for that is exactly what we shall do," he replied, and started to take down the tent. When it was down, he left her to roll it up and fold the sleeping bag inside, and then using her home made pleated shoulder straps she got it on her back.

He loaded his rucksack on his back and with her leading the way they set off together. When they reached the river, he felt like kicking himself for stopping last night so relatively near to the water. However on the first sight of the river he wasted no time getting to it, as he was absolutely desperate for a drink. He dropped his rucksack on the ground and ran down to the edge of the water. There he couldn't stop drinking and it took ages to quench his thirst. There were cattle also drinking at the edge of the river and looking on with great curiosity, but after a while they slowly wandered off back to their grazing. In the meantime Cheng Eng was busy mixing up water with the dry cereal for their breakfast. When they sat down to eat their water mixed dry cereal, he said to her,

"It must be at least two hundred metres to cross the river, and I note it is shallow at the edges but I am worried that midstream it could be too deep to cross."

In reply she said,

"As a general rule, slow flowing wide rivers are shallow, by comparison narrow fast flowing rivers are usually deep, as the strength of the current keeps scouring out the bed of the river and prevents sedimentation, so if that is a good yard stick to go by, this part of the river should be no more than knee deep in the midstream."

His reply was,

"I only hope you are right, because if not, it will mean a big detour to the bridge which is about a days walk away from here."

She had been quiet for a while, and he wondered what was on her mind.

"Are you OK?" He asked her.

"Well John to be frank" she said,

"would you mind if I ask a rather personal question? It is bothering me considerably, and I'd like to get it out in the open then my mind will be at ease".

Noting his nod of consent. She continued,

"Well John, when I went into your rucksack to get the cereal to prepare for breakfast I was dismayed to find a pair of ladies knickers."

He laughed and said,

"Well I can put your mind at ease, I am not a transvestite and they're not my wife's nor did I bring them to fulfil some personal fantasies during my expected six months absence from a woman. It's a long story how I come to have them, but alcohol had a hand in it. It could take me an hour to explain fully, tell you what, tonight at bed time I shall reveal all, that's a promise."

Smiling she said, "I can't wait for tonight."

"Right" he said, "our priorities are to get across this river so let's tie our footwear round our neck and see if we can wade across."

He was first to wade in and exclaimed that last night he had been crying out to be able to place his feet in this cool water, now it was more of a bind than a benefit. Slowly but surely they made their way across the wide river, and just as she had said, it was no more than knee deep in the middle. However it was still a relief when they were both safely on the other side. It was time now to put their footwear back on, check the map, and then prepare for the twenty mile hike that lay ahead of them. "You know," he said, "it is quite possible we could have wandered off course in the darkness last night." She checked the map again and he took another compass bearing. There did not seem to be another stream or a river marked on the map for at least two days walk, and it was only a few miles from the village they were heading towards.

Although it was pleasing to see that they were so close to habitation, the thought of two days without water was not so pleasant, so they decided to drink as much water as they could while they were here. Down at the river edge they cupped their hands and drank their fill, until they both felt bloated. Groaning he said,

"I can never understand how some people can go down to a public bar and within an hour or so can down pint after pint of ale."

"John," she replied,

"you can spot them a mile away, men with their stomachs protruding way out in front, I think it looks disgusting."

He had to laugh at her apt description, but went on to say that being so bloated he had better rest for half an hour to give his stomach time to settle.

Later while they both sat at the riverbank he asked her if she was any good at stone skimming.

"Stone skimming," she exclaimed,

"what is that?"

Picking up a round flat stone, he said,

"Watch this." He held the stone between his forefinger and thumb and threw it along the surface of the water and it bobbed on top of the water until it reached mid stream where it lost its momentum and sank to the river bed.

Her eyes were wide open in amazement; it was obvious that she had not seen this done before. Deciding to have a shot herself she selected a stone, which he could see was quite unsuitable but he said nothing, she threw it, only to see it sink to the bottom. Suppressing the urge to laugh, as he felt that was more diplomatic, considering the disappointed expression on her face.

He gave her a kiss and a cuddle and agreed that it was much more difficult than it appeared. He told her there was a knack to it and one that could only come with experience.

"Firstly you must find a suitable stone," he said,

"Ideally it should be round, flat, with a smooth surface all over, about half an inch thick and between three to four inches wide. Depending on whether you are left or right handed you throw it with your best hand, holding it loosely between your thumb and forefinger. When you throw it, make sure that your hand is in a horizontal position and level with the surface of the water,"

He went to great lengths to position a stone in her right hand and let her throw it. The result was a dismal failure, but it did not deter her determination and she kept trying and trying.

Eventually he decided it was time to go, trouble was he could feel the water in his stomach swilling around with each throw, and it was not pleasant. Because she had not mastered the art of skimming he showed her once more how it was done, and it was a beauty, it skimmed four or five times on the surface of the water.

"That's marvellous!" she said as she watched in sheer astonishment, and continued,

"I wish I could do that."

"Don't worry" he said,

"you will master it, all it takes is practice, when we come to the next river you will get plenty of time to practise then, but right now it's time to be moving on again."

They hadn't gone very far when she stopped and said, "I've just had an idea."

"Oh, what's that then?" he asked.

She continued, "Your first aid kit is in a fairly large plastic bag, if you emptied the first aid items into your rucksack I could use the plastic bag as a water container."

"Good idea," he replied and emptied out the contents of the bag, she took it and said,

"I won't be long, I'll just run back and fill it, why don't you put your feet up for a few minutes."

He made himself comfortable by sitting on his rucksack and watched her run back towards the river with the bag.

After a while he began to worry about the delay of her returning, she seemed to be taking ages, maybe she had burst the bag. He had visions of her trying to repair the broken bag with a shoe lace or something similar, or perhaps worse, maybe she had fallen in and was in some other trouble. Deciding to investigate he made his way back to the river, as he approached he could see her throwing stones across the water in an attempt to skim them.

He sat in silence and watched her, appreciating her dedication in trying to master stone skimming, he was sure she would make it one day with plenty more practice, right now it was comical to see her pitiful attempts. After a while she started to rub her arms and was finding out just how painful it can be if you continue to throw stones making use of muscles that have not been used for a while. She was quite oblivious to the fact that he was a spectator, but when she eventually did see him she gave a start of surprise and shouted,

"Right I'm coming now."

Returning with the now full water carrier, she handed it to him, and shook her head and explained how she had got carried away with herself.

"I could have stayed at the river throwing stones for hours, if my arm hadn't been so sore."

He chuckled and remembered all too well what it was like. After getting kitted up again they agreed they would both take turns in carrying the water. They also agreed to purchase a more suitable carrier along with their other supplies later on. They continued their journey step after step, mile after mile, chatting as they progressed.

John told tales about his childhood just after the Second World War. Children then had no videos or television, and no computer games to keep them occupied. Most of the children in his village used to meet up at the back swimming pool to spend literally hours and hours after school, in summer and spring and on school holidays, stone skimming or catching little fish in nets and putting them in little jam jars. It was almost as competitive as stone skimming. Who could throw the farthest or who caught the most fish in the jam jar.

Whoever caught the most fish was no problem to resolve, but with stone skimming it always ended up in arguments as to which stone skimmed the farthest, and on many occasions it came to a fight.

"I came up with an idea to put two fence posts on the bank

at the far away side of the pool and another two posts in the middle of the pool, he said, then a fine gauze net was stretched from the two far away posts to the two posts midstream, the net was only just under the water level, and it worked a treat. Everyone had their own stones and had scratched their Initials on them.

At the end of the stone skimming session there was no bickering about who threw the winning stone, everyone could wade in and retrieve them and use their stones again and again, and that way when you had the ideal stone you didn't use it under the old system as it would be lost for ever after the first throw"

She said,

"That was a really good and practical idea." she then asked if girls played stone skimming.

"Some did and were very good at it," he replied,

"however most girls preferred just to sit on the grass banking making daisy chains, perhaps gathering bunches of primroses or wild hyacinths or just sitting on the banking as spectators. That's what we used to do, make our own entertainment, and believe me people didn't have much money then, my father was a labourer for the water board but he is now a supervising foreman for the same company, he left school at fourteen and has worked all his life for the same employer, and is due to retire at the end of this year with fifty-one years service."

"That's quite an achievement." She replied.

"It sure is." John said,

"I take my hat off to him."

"Has he made any plans for his retirement?" She asked.

"Oh! He has plans believe me; he will be in his element spending time in his vegetable garden, which is his pride and joy, he spends every minute of his spare time in it or else with his bee hives, he has just taken up bee keeping," he then added. "Dad likes nothing better now than sitting in his fireside armchair nursing his twin grandchildren."

"Like my mother they both adore their grandchildren, and being twins my mother can nurse one while my father nurses the other, there is never a dull moment in our house."

"Do you think when you look back to your childhood days, your generation were more contented than the children of today?" She asked.

"because today's children appear to take their technological equipment for granted."

He thought for a moment or so and said,

"I suppose it's the old saying what you never had, you never miss, and I know one thing for sure, you didn't hear of drug abuse, mugging, joy riders, and even mad cow disease, it would be a better society today if we got rid of all these things don't you think?"

"I most certainly do," She agreed.

By now it was midday and it was really hot, with thousands of insects and flies of all kinds around, as the air was calm today, not even a hint of a gentle breeze, and the heat was getting to him, especially his feet, they were pounding and sweating so much that it would have been heaven to see a large tree where they could rest in the shade, but there wasn't a tree in sight so there was no choice but to rest where they were.

Removing their rucksacks he said that he must take off his boots and give his feet some fresh air.

"Wouldn't it be great," he added,

"to be granted a wish, I would wish to be over there in those snow capped mountains where I would be able to really cool off."

"That's fine" said Cheng Eng,

"but if you were suddenly transported there, you would soon be wishing you were back down here in the warmth again, remember, you have to get accustomed gradually to drastic changes in temperature,"

"You are quite right," he replied,

"what I have just said on the spur of the moment was quite irresponsible, but was meant more as a bit of fun, more than anything else."

She then opened the water carrier and made up two portions of dry cereal. John was very grateful for her idea of the plastic water carrier, in today's heat it was truly worth its weight in gold. He noticed that there was still sufficient water left for their needs tonight and tomorrow morning. He suggested that they rest up for one hour; this being the hottest time of the day, no matter what direction you looked in you could see the shimmering heat waves.

They both sat with their back against his rucksack and the heat seemed to sap the strength from them and made them both very drowsy. Taking the water carrier, which was now lukewarm, he placed it over his face as he lay back. She had been chatting to him, but after getting no response to a question, she noticed that he had fallen asleep. Looking at him she almost laughed at the comical sight before her, he looked so funny with the water carrier on his face, his mountain boots and socks at his side and with his bare feet sticking up in the air. Soon the intense heat got to her and she also became tired and fell into a deep asleep.

Two hours later she was the first to waken and was startled to see only a few yards away, a ring of cattle all standing perfectly still and curiously looking at the two of them. Her first reaction was to abruptly waken him up and he wakened with a long yawn and then removed the water bag from his face and rubbed both his eyes just to make sure they were not deceiving him.

"I see we have an uninvited audience" he said.

"Look around," she said in alarm,

"they have completely encircled us."

In annoyance, she swatted at some flies buzzing round her face.

"I notice they brought a swarm of their friends with them" he said, as he also attempted to swat the flies away from his face.

Although only a couple of hours had passed and the sun had gone down nearer the horizon, it was still very, very hot. As he put his stockings and mountain boots back on, she remarked on how there had been no cattle in sight before lunch. She found it incredible that they had arrived almost out of nowhere.

"I suppose," he mused,
"they must have been following us from a distance. They are very inquisitive animals and this may well be the first time they have seen backpackers. When I was a boy, a familiar sight was to see a herdsman, in the winter months, walking with a sack of oats on his back and with all the cattle following behind him until he reached their feeding troughs, where he emptied the oats out for them to eat. I suppose we would be the same, let's suppose that right now we saw in the distance a very unusual object, and it was slowly moving, had the body of an elephant and the long neck of a Giraffe, and with the head of a lion. We would be very much afraid, but we would probably risk everything to take a photograph to prove our point when we told the story to others later on."

"How are we going to get past them John, they are all around us?" She asked.

"No problem," he said, "as soon as we walk towards them they will scatter."

"I wish I had your confidence," she said, moving as far back from them as she could.

"Well now's the time to put it to the test," he said, returning his rucksack and water carrier to his back and moving off.

Very quickly lifting her pack she followed closely behind, in fact so close, she was almost hiding behind him. Just as he had predicted the cattle moved away as they got closer to them. She kept nervously looking over her shoulder and noticed that the cattle followed them again at a safe distance; she asked how far they would follow them.

"Oh just until it gets dark," he said

"Well I am glad to hear that, I don't think I would be able to sleep to-night if that lot was around the tent" she added.

"Don't worry," he said,

"cattle lie down to sleep at night so they won't bother us"

It reminded him of an incident some years ago, and he went on to tell her about the time he had broken his arm. Just before Christmas time, he had been working part time in a hotel, when he had an accident and Bob the hotel owner had driven him to the casualty department of the local hospital to have an x-ray, and how Bob had waited while John's arm was put in plaster. On the way back, they had come across a herd of black bullocks on the road. And on that pitch-black dark night how both he and Bob had herded them into a field nearby.

She was fascinated by his true story and listened intensely. Looking back she was pleased to see that the cattle were now a good way behind, it was getting dark now and they were so far behind they were just visible and no more. Seeing this he said,

"They won't follow us now until day breaks so I suggest we set up camp here for the night, if that are okay with you Cheng Eng."

"So long as you can assure me that the cattle will not annoy us any more tonight that's fine by me," she answered. They soon had the tent erected, and it was then time for their usual meal of dry cereal with water.

Later on while busily eating their meal she asked him to explain more about his accident and how he managed to break his arm when he was younger.

"Well it's quite a long story, basically the problem was that a ladder we had been using to put up Christmas decorations was well past it's use-by date, so much so that I mentioned it to the boss but he assured me that it was alright as the handy man had used it regularly, anyway I was putting up the last of the decorations when the ladder collapsed and I landed on the floor breaking my arm," he explained.

"What bothered me most was not the six weeks my arm was in plaster, but the fact I could not drive my own car and had to rely on others to run me around, the incident must have played on my boss's conscience because not only did he pay me my full wages, he also bought a new ladder, an aluminium one this time."

They were soon settling down to sleep and were just nodding off when she remembered that he had promised to explain to her about the ladies underwear she had found in his rucksack earlier.

"Okay," he groaned,

"a promise is a promise," and with that he explained the whole situation from the beginning. Because she found it quite hilarious she just couldn't stop laughing. But he could not laugh, as the whole experience had been a nightmare to him, which he could well have done without. It was as if he had been kidnapped and had to find his own way out of the situation. By this time he was so tired he fell asleep to the sound of her laughter.

Next morning they were up at the crack of dawn as they hoped this would be the last day before reaching civilisation, and where they would rest for a couple of days before tackling the uninhabited high mountains before them. As they ate their morning cereal mixed with the last of their water supply John remarked that goodness only knows how they would have managed without water, it really was worth its weight in gold. She airily replied. "There would be no life on this planet earth if there was no life sustaining water, look at the profusion of the wild flowers around us, they are most beautiful, they really are and we couldn't have picked a nicer location to pitch the tent."

"You couldn't have summed that up any better." John replied. It had been dark when they pitched the tent but the wild flowers proved a very pleasant morning surprise.

Then she asked, "Have you ever thought about municipal gardens, why they are laid out so precisely that you could almost measure between each flower with a ruler, the exact distance between them just like a carpet design, it's all wrong in my opinion as that was not the way nature intended. It looks unnatural as a man made pattern. Looking at all those beautiful wild flowers growing as nature intended is natural and beautiful."

He looked into her eyes, caressed her and giving her a kiss said "I couldn't agree more, I hadn't given the subject much thought until now, that you have brought it to my attention, but there is one aspect I have in mind which is on the same wavelength and that is, in the autumn I have many a time admired a carpet of autumn leaves with all their glorious tinted colours on the ground and how

70

wonderful they look naturally, then I think that if they were empty crisp packets and bits of newspapers, sweetie wrappers, food take-away packages or empty cans of soft drinks etc, how horrible it would look, a totally disgusting sight"

"You're right John, man has a lot to answer for, especially the pollution of the natural environment with radioactive radiation of the atmosphere, the rivers, lake's and seas of the world, are permanently polluted with man-made toxic chemicals."

"Not only in the rivers and seas but also on the land," he interrupted, "the world's natural rain forests are being cut down at an alarming rate, which will have long term disastrous side effects environmentally."

Their interesting discussion had to close, as it was now time to proceed before it got too hot, it was most important that they reach their destination before nightfall. So with that thought uppermost in their mind they got the tent down, packed up and got on their way.

The flat open plain was now far behind them, and their travelling was becoming more laboured as they were now climbing into the foothills of the mountains. These hills reminded John of his homeland in the Lake District. Travelling on, and as the miles slowly passed by, it was getting decidedly warmer. The sun rose high in the sky and it would be a safe bet it was going to be a sweltering hot afternoon, and as they had suspected it would be difficult travelling in this heat.

Today however there was the consolation of some

large shady trees dotted around on the landscape, there was no such cover on the open plain, which they had just left.

This must be sheep country; he noticed a few sheep around and reckoned that these animals were very different from those back home.

As they travelled on in the blazing sun they had a welcome and unexpected find when they came across a rock outcrop, which had a trickle of fresh crystal clear water oozing out from a fissure. Both got down on their hands and knees and eagerly drank their fill, they tried and tried again in vain to collect water in their home made carrier, and finally had to give up. Two hours later the sun was at its highest and just like yesterday it was uncomfortably hot, so they decided to have a well earned mid- day break and both thankfully slumped down under the nearest tree with it's shade from the sun's furnace like heat.

After they both had some dry cereal, and he had removed his heavy footwear allowing his very hot feet to cool off, being dog tired with the heat, they both fell into a deep sleep. After a couple of hours he awakened feeling fully refreshed and raring to go. Firstly however he had to awaken Cheng Eng. She awakened cheerfully also feeling the benefit of her mid -day siesta. In next to no time, he had his footwear back on, and both were loaded up with their backpacks and off they went.

Time seemed to pass so quickly and as nightfall approached they realised that it looked like another night in the tent for them, as it seemed likely they would not reach their objective to arrive in the village before nightfall.

They decided to continue in the darkness in an effort to reach the river, which was the last barrier between them and the village. This would allow them to cross the river in daylight and reach the town some two miles further away. Neither were aware whether they could wade this river or not, however when they finally did arrive it seemed most unlikely, although they could not see it, the noise it was making sounded so loud it was likely to be very fast flowing, whereas the last river on the plain was so placid it was silent.

"We shall check the map in the morning to see if we are Going upstream or downstream to get to the place where a road bridge crosses the river," she said.

After they eventually got the tent erected, which took them a considerable amount of time in the total darkness, she volunteered to go down to the river with the plastic bag and get some water while he got the dry cereal out of the rucksack, she then made her way to the river without hearing him advising her to be careful. Shortly thereafter he heard a scream, and straining his ears could hear nothing apart from the noise of the river.

His sudden response was to drop the bag of cereal and run stumbling towards the river, in the darkness he was directed by its sound and naturally, the nearer he got to it the louder it became. His heart was pounding with shock, he just stopped in time to see that the ground on which he was standing dropped away in a sheer vertical slope, and as he stood petrified in fear not knowing how far down it was to the river, he broke out in a cold sweat and shouted "Cheng Eng." He tried not to visualise what could have happened to her going over the edge, she could by now be washed downstream. Just then he heard her scream again, but was quite unable to tell what direction it came from.

He felt so hopeless and helpless because being pitch black he couldn't tell which direction was downstream, he knew he had to do something and was just about to jump down into the river below, even although he didn't know how far down it was, he just closed his eyes gritted his teeth and said silently to himself, into the valley of death I go but I fear no evil, and just took a large breath of air when he heard her shout,

"Over here John!"

The shout came from behind him, at first he thought his ears were deceiving him, so he shouted again

"Cheng Eng, where are you?"

Her reply was "Over here!" This time there was no mistake; she was definitely behind him, however when he turned round he still couldn't see anything, so he headed towards her as she kept shouting,

"Over here!"

Drawing closer he eventually saw her outline in the darkness, her arms and head were sticking out of the ground, and when he reached her she warned him,

"Be careful the ground is hollow under here."

Getting flat down on the ground he wriggled the last few yards towards her, telling her to grab his jacket with both hands and hold on as hard as she possibly could, his body would be slowly rolling away from her, and hoped this would get her out. With this said, his plan was put into operation, and slowly but surely as he made his body roll over, and with her hanging on with all her might this method of extracting her worked a treat. They both got back to the tent as soon as possible and cuddled and comforted each other for ages, having had such a traumatic experience they now had no stomach for eating so they just went to sleep.

They hadn't been sleeping for long when they were both awakened by a violent storm of thunder and lightning, the lightning flashes were so brilliant they lit up the interior of the tent, she was scared and clung on to him as if her life depended on it. Pulling her to him he held her in a tight embrace. "Don't worry," he whispered, "the chances of us being struck are very remote." Trying to comfort her further, he told her about the time Ruby and he were in old Sam's farmhouse during a very violent storm, when it took a direct strike and brought the gable end and the chimney stack down. That was the time when Ruby found an old box with gold coins in it.

By the time he had explained how the old farmhouse had been renovated, this time with a new lightning conductor system installed, the storm had passed over, and they went back to sleeping. When they both arose from the tent in the morning, the noise from the river was much more intense, the flow of water was much greater because of the night's rainfall. There was no need for water to mix with their breakfast today because the cereal had got soaked where he dropped it last night.

Realising that she had dropped the water carrier last night she questioned the wisdom of not trying to retrieve it, but he was adamant that neither of them should return to the place of her accident, and pointed out the extreme danger in doing so.

"The more you think of it," he said, "the more you see it was a blessing in disguise when you fell down that hole last night, a few more steps and you would have been over the edge and into the river, and it was also a miracle," he continued, "that you called out just when you did, because I was just about to jump into the river to search for you, and from what we can see now, that would have been certain death,"

She threw her arms around him and kissed him repeatedly, saying." Please forgive me for all the trouble I have caused you."

Returning her affections he said, "You are no trouble at all, believe me, I wouldn't be without you for all the tea in china, let's Pack up and have a look at the map for the bridge that crosses the river, and hopefully by mid-day we should reach our destination."

Further investigation showed that they had a trek of about two hours before reaching the bridge, however there was no rush as they had all day ahead of them.

As they were leaving they heard a loud thud, and felt a shock wave of vibration underfoot and witnessed a most spectacular sight, when a huge area of land suddenly disappeared before their very eyes, sliding down into the raging river. Spectacular as it was, it was also extremely frightening to see the results of the torrential rain and the power of the swollen river. Needless to say, they wasted no time in getting out of the area, and did so with a quickened pace.

He remarked that in ten days of this mission he had experienced three of the most frightening episodes in his life. "They say things come in threes, well I hope that's true because I don't want any more frightening experiences. You already know about two of these experiences, but let me tell you about the first one."
Once I was in a hotel room when someone knocking on the door wakened me. I had a hangover and was half asleep, fully expecting to see Gillian I jumped up from bed and opened the door, and heavens above, there stood one of the hotel cleaners who screamed, dropped her cleaning materials and fled down the stairs. To this day it is debatable as to who got the biggest fright, me seeing this stranger, or her seeing a naked man with his hands bound behind his back, and wearing a pair of ladies knickers like a balaclava over his face and head."

Cheng Eng laughed and laughed, as she had before when he had previously explained how this piece of fancy frilly underwear had come to be in his rucksack. She continued to laugh as they trod on their way. Because her footwear was soaked through, she was looking forward to buying some waterproof replacements. He on the other hand was looking forward to buying some lighter footwear;

mountain boots were OK for mountaineering, but far too heavy for walking in any other terrain.

Nearing the point where they thought the bridge would be, they saw before them a long grass slope that stretched as far as one could see, on it were many small pony type horses, so numerous that they had to be seen to be believed, if there was one, there was a thousand, it was an incredible site. So far they had passed through cattle country, sheep country, and now obviously they were in horse country.

What took some understanding was how they all stuck to their own areas without any fences, not once had they seen any signs of herdsmen. They had been travelling for some two hours now and there were still no signs of the road or the bridge, so they decided to have a short break and to recheck the map. According to the compass and map reading, the road should be in sight, which was strange to say the least, just where was it?

Perhaps they would have been better off following the river, but on the map it was so twisted that it looked as if it would have taken an age longer to have crossed the difficult and dangerous terrain. After a ten-minute break they resumed their journey, and after a further two miles they came across the roadway to the bridge. The road was a in a hollow and that's why they were unable to see it before and they were both so overjoyed and relieved to see the road, that they threw their arms in the air and jumped for joy, within an hour they should reach civilisation.

The road turned out to be nothing more than a dirt

track, which had been untouched for a thousand years or more, nevertheless it was a road, and he, with tongue in cheek, remarked to Cheng Eng that it was little wonder it was a weekly bus service. With the road in this state the bus had some punishment to take and by the time it had used this horrible track and eventually arrived here, it must take the rest of the week to repair it. "Perhaps this is just a better bit of the road, I have seen much worse in my country," she said. He laughed and replied,
"Well, if this is the good bit, I shudder to think what the bad bits are like."

Half a mile on they could see the bridge and hear the roar of the raging river, not long later they were standing on the bridge looking over the parapet and down into the fast flowing water, they looked at one another and their facial expressions said it all, there was no way they would try to cross other than by the bridge, the roar of the water was so loud that it drowned out all other sounds, he signalled his intentions to move on and she followed very close behind, soon they were far enough away from the river to be able to talk with one another again without shouting at the top of their voices.

They were surprised to say the least, to see in the distance a lorry coming towards them and as it got nearer they could see it was a very old looking lorry which was transporting lumber, as it passed them they couldn't help but notice the smell of the diesel exhaust fumes, much more noticeable now because they had been in a completely fume free environment all week.

They had only walked a few hundred yards when they heard the noise of another lorry, and as they turned and looked round, it was trundling along towards them, to be on the safe side they stood well back from the roadside to allow it to pass them by, but on the contrary it slowed up and stopped, the driver said something, which Cheng Eng understood, but John didn't have the slightest idea, even though he had learned numerous Tibetan phrases he only understood the odd word here and there.

He couldn't wait to ask her what the driver was on about, until she answered,

"He asked where we were going and has offered us a lift, so I said sure, we would be pleased to take him up on his offer, he says there is enough room in the cab for the luggage but only two people, but if we put our luggage in the back, there will then be ample room for both of us in the cab." He took the rucksack off his back and she took the folded tent and sleeping bag from her back and they threw them onto some bags among the lorries cargo in the back. Then they both climbed into the cab and he made sure that she was next to the driver so that she could speak to him as they went along, there was no point in him being next to the driver because there was no chance of being able to converse with him and it could be embarrassing.

As the Tibetan truck driver drove off, he was in constant conversation with Cheng Eng who started laughing. John assumed the driver had told her a joke and even if it wasn't much of a joke, she would have laughed anyway on behalf of diplomacy. Because he hadn't the faintest idea of the context of the conversation between her and the driver, he became oblivious to it, and was admiring the truck with its extra long engine bonnet, coloured olive green with thin gold lines all round it, and with gold oak leaves and acorns painted on each corner. Then at the end of the bonnet on the top of the chrome radiator, was a large water temperature gauge with an internal arrow, which pointed to the water temperature degrees in black gradations which altered to red gradations when the water temperature was too high, right up to boiling point. The reason why he found the lorry so fascinating was that it reminded him of a Christmas present he had received years ago; he had received a gift of a perfectly scaled model of an American diamond tee tank transporter.

This old lorry he was in today brought the lucid memory of it back to him, he felt certain this was a diamond tee; the only difference was that his scale model had no water gauge on the apex of the radiator, and also his scale model had a set of chrome air horns on the roof. He hadn't noticed before, so didn't know if the roof of the cab above his head had a set of chrome air horns or not, he was thinking this over when they rounded a sharp bend in the road and saw an oncoming lorry, as they passed there was the unmistakable sound of a blast from the cab roof of a set of air horns. This made his day as he was now more convinced than ever he was certainly sitting in a genuine American diamond Tee.

What amused him was how the suspension of the vehicle stood up to the punishment that was being imposed on it with the deep potholes, which weren't unlike small bomb craters, and after last night's storm they were all filled with water so in consequence there was no way of knowing what depth they were. Bumping into these holes made the lorry lurch from side to side and steadily bounce up and down, it made him think how much longer the suspension could sustain such treatment and the sheer torture it was being subjected to.

Now the outskirts of the town were looming up and the driver started to slow down, and instead of carrying on into the town took a turn off to the right, slowed down and stopped. Cheng Eng informed him that the driver was dropping them off here as he was going to a warehouse a mile out of the town. Jumping out of the cab, John climbed onto the back of the lorry and collected their luggage which he handed down to her, the driver slowly moved away and gave two long blasts of the air horns, as a parting salute to them, as he headed off on his final mile.

She told him that the lorry was loaded with rice and there were five hundred bags in all, weighing twenty-five tonnes, and it was destined for a holding warehouse. The driver had come from Mandela in Burma, a two and a half thousand-mile journey, and it had taken him ten days to complete it.

"I'm surprised it didn't take him much longer, considering the state of these roads," he said.

As they made their way into town he told her about his having a model of a truck, just like the one they had a lift in, and went on to ask her about the joke that had her laughing so much. She replied rather sheepishly,

"I would rather not say as it may upset you, and that's the last thing I want to do because I do think the world of you, and I'm just not sure how you would handle it."

He put his arm round her shoulder and reminded her of the very high regard with which he held her.

"Why! Without your company this trip would be like a six month prison sentence in solitary," he told her.

"Am I right in thinking that the joke was about me? If so you can rest assured that I am thick skinned enough not to let it bother me in the least."

She hesitated for a few seconds before giving her version of what the driver had told her.

Apparently there had been a long hold up at the border control and every lorry was being searched most thoroughly, the driver had thought this odd, because usually the check was just random when only one or two were chosen from a convoy, this time everyone was getting a going over, even private cars were having a close check. Gathering together in a group, the drivers discussed the situation amongst themselves; some thought the high profile checks were for the normal reasons of large drug consignments.

The searchers themselves would tell you nothing as they always remained tight lipped on these occasions. One of the drivers unfolded a newspaper he had taken from his pocket and pointed to the front page, the main headline story was about a hotel cleaner that had, as the paper put it- been literally terrorised to death. The article went on at

83

great length to explain all about her experience when she opened a room door and found a naked man with underwear on his head standing there. She had apparently run downstairs where she took a massive heart attack and died.

When the police arrived on the scene they had to burst the room door down because it had been securely bolted on the inside, and to this day it remains a mystery how the occupant had escaped, apparently the internal security camera had only recorded a two second sighting of the culprit, and this was hampering their enquiries. A massive search of the airports and border crossings were being conducted in an effort to catch the perpetrator, who had been nicknamed the 'knicker faced naked Houdini.' No doubt after the world famous escapologist. When she had finished explaining, she looked at his face and saw that it was drained of colour and was a ghastly sight.

"Are you all right John?" It took him a few seconds to mutter "yes."

At the same time he stopped walking, dropped his rucksack and sat on it, and covering his eyes with both hands he began to sob uncontrollably. Seeing people in the street, and with some coming towards them, Cheng opened up the map and stood in front of him pretending to study it and talking very loudly in Chinese, pretending to converse with him as to their whereabouts, she was attempting to shield him from those passing by, who seeing him could have been suspicious. Her ruse was so realistic that no one gave them a second glance.

After about ten minutes he started to calm down and with her encouragement managed to pull himself together, she wished she had not told him about the police inquiries and thought that she would have been better making up some other story. She should have known that he would have taken the news badly. After a while he donned his rucksack and moved on in silence, nothing she said would encourage him to respond, bearing in mind the shock he had just had, she decided to let him come round in his own time, so she accompanied him in silence.

As they walked on, her mind went back to the night that he had explained to her about the hotel incident, she now felt a little guilty, because to be frank, she thought the story was too good to be true, and that he had made it up to impress her, she now knew only too well that he had been telling the truth. She also remembered the occasion when he helped her by giving her brandy when she needed it, and wished she were able to do the same. By this time they were in the main area of the town, and she noticed a sign written in Tibetan which she easily translated, it read 'The weary travellers welcome resting place.'

Nodding his agreement to enter, she followed him up a long flight of steps into what looked like the interior of a Tibetan monastery with an array of small gold Buddha statues placed in arched recesses around the walls, there was one large prayer wheel in the room. In the centre of the room stood the reception desk with passageways leading from it left and right, there were some glass cases with fish tanks, which were illuminated on one side to show up the fish as they darted around in their resplendent colours.

Behind the reception desk was a young local looking girl; Cheng Eng made all the necessary booking in arrangements and was given a room key with a visitors guide to the layout of the place and information about the area. Advertising all the town had to offer, which would prove to be invaluable to them, the brochure also gave the time of the once weekly bus service, plus lots of other useful information, the complementary brochure was a hive of information inclusive of a free map with all places of interest marked on it. Further directions would not be required as they were all listed on the map.

Because Cheng Eng was speaking to the receptionist in Tibetan, he as usual hadn't a clue as to what was being said, although he sensed at one stage there was a bit of arguing going on just as Cheng Eng was given the room key. As they left the reception area and headed for the room number, which was on the key they were given, the receptionist shouted something to them.

Cheng Eng turned round and shouted back, for the very first time he saw a look of disgust etched all over her face as she shouted back to the receptionist. He had seldom seen anything other than a smile on her face and at one time he felt she was permanently smiling, except for the time she was in great pain and was crying, when the arrowhead was in her foot.

He couldn't resist asking her what it was all about; she smiled up at him, kissed him and said, "Tell you when we get inside our room." She went on to tell him how pleased she was to hear him speak to her again after being silent for so long. Going along the corridor they could see a bar with both doors open and lots of customers inside, some sat at the bar stools at the bar counter and others sat around tables in the room which was like a residents lounge, all of the customers they could see were white Caucasian westerners.

Eventually they arrived at the room allocated to them, and as usual he had to remove his rucksack and leave it in the corridor, but as soon as they were in the room she asked him for money to make an advance payment.

"I remembered where you keep it for safety, but I didn't want to embarrass you at reception by insisting you remove your boots, that's what all the shouting was about, the receptionist wanted money before she gave me the key. I made the excuse of wanting to see the room first, making sure it was up to standard before payment, and that was when the she almost accused me of being a prostitute, and that's why I became angry and demanded to see the hotel manager to lodge my complaint. Although she backed down and gave me a key, she still had a few choice words to say about me, and none of them were complementary. I was so angry that I told her to scrub out her filthy mouth with soap and water and to use some Brasso on her brass neck."

He couldn't help but laugh at her actions and expressions, and she was so pleased to see him laugh again.

After removing his boots and stockings he asked her to recite over and over again in Tibetan and to teach him to say,

"You must apologise for the slanderous insults to my wife, or I will have no choice but to lodge a formal complaint with your superiors and hopefully this will end up with your dismissal."

When he had finally memorised this, he asked her to count out the exact money for him, and handed her the plastic wallet containing his money. Grabbing the money he went straight down the stairs to the reception where he placed the money on the table and recited his well-rehearsed party piece. You could have knocked the receptionist down with a feather, she was numbed into a state of shock, he did not wait for a receipt, or any comment, but just turned and walked briskly away returning to his room, where Cheng Eng was delighted on hearing the result.

During his absence she had removed enough items from the rucksack enabling him to bring it into the bedroom. He had a shave, the first in over a week, and soon began to feel like a human being again. After they had showered they both felt much better and made their way down to the bar, bringing with them the new brochure and writing materials to make a list of the items they would require from the local store, now that there were two of them to carry the provisions they should be able to carry a few extra items, for example a hand torch and some fresh fruit like apple's and oranges, perhaps even a small-cartridge gas stove allowing them to have the occasional hot drink.

They had almost forgotten what it was like to have a

hot meal or drink and they were really looking forward to their first proper meal in over a week, which according to the timetable would be served up in a couple of hours. This allowed them some time to spend in the residence lounge to relax and put their feet up, not literally, for the first time since commencing their journey. They were now both feeling clean comfortable and relaxed, they felt like they were on another planet compared to the hardships they had endured out there in the wilderness.

On entering the lounge he handed her some money to buy some drinks while he secured them seats by the window. Being within earshot of the surrounding tables he could hear and detect at least three languages being spoken, German, English, and French, most of the people looked to be round about retirement age. After she returned with the drinks and placed a large brandy in front of him and keeping a smaller one for herself. He quietly remarked on the people in the room, saying how strange it seemed that pensioners should come on holiday to such an out of the way place as here, they seemed a bit old to be interested in mountaineering.

Cheng Eng pulled back the thick velvet curtains on the window very slightly, and pointed to a large luxury coach in the car park and said,
"There's your answer John." A large sign could be seen on the back window of the coach, which read,
'Tours to the worlds most out of the way places.'
"Ah!" said John,
"That's it, and it sure lives up to its promise by coming to

places like this."

As they sat sipping their brandy she read out some of the information from the brochure they had been given. According to the brochure this hotel had been an accommodation place for monks, a place of introduction before they took up residence in a monastery.

"That explains the décor," said John.

"Look there!" He exclaimed, pointing to a logo above the bar, "that's the same as the one on the bus, it looks as though the tour operator also owns this hotel."

"Pity you didn't know that" she answered,

"if you had known that a bus could bring you right to the door you could have saved yourself a weeks trek through the wilderness."

Stretching his hand across the table he took her hand in his, smiled and looking into her eyes said,

"But then I wouldn't have you with me, this coach is much more likely to be part of a package tour, had I known about it, who knows, perhaps I would have taken it, but I much prefer all the trials and discomfort of walking, provided you were with me, than travelling on my own in the lap of luxury."

His words impressed her and she got up from the table, threw her arms around him and kissed him passionately, not bothering about the looks of disdain she was getting from some of the company, and then returning to her seat she continued to read the brochure.

"Here is an advertisement that will interest you," she said reading out, "visit Kaskadeemus's world famous Aladdin cave warehouse, anything from a double Decker bus to a button, an Eskimo suit, to a clowns outfit. Look, it even has a drawing showing where it is," she then handed it to him. Taking the brochure he give it a cursory glance, smiled and said,

"This place is a must for tomorrow."

A few drinks later it was time for their evening meal, they were both really hungry, as they had eaten nothing since early morning some twelve hours before. Reaching their table they hoped they would be one of the first to be served as they were first to be seated. There was a menu card printed in several languages on the table, it listed the set meals for the week. This evening's meal consisted of a fruit cocktail starter, roast beef with roast potatoes and a choice of three vegetables. Followed by a sweet of syrup and ginger pudding and custard.

Their mouths were watering at the thought of such a feast, especially after what seemed to be an age, while they watched others served before them, but the long awaited starter finally arrived. After they finished their meal they were alone in the dining room except for the waiters clearing the tables. John noticed two untouched sweets at a nearby table and quick as a flash exchanged them for their empty plates.

"Ten out of ten" Chen Eng exclaimed giving him a small hand clap of approval.

"Well" he said, "it is either a feast or a famine, we should make the best of things, when we leave here it will be like six months of famine, we almost starved for a week and just look at us! I shudder to think what we would be like after six months."

Having finished their complementary sweet they were looking for either tea or coffee, but as this was only served in the snack bar downstairs they decided to go down and have a drink. Following the signs they went down the stairs, through double swing doors and into the packed coffee house, where all the tables they could see were taken, apart from one which had two vacant places, as they sat down two elderly person's at the table muttered something to each other in a foreign language and lifting their coffee, moved away elsewhere.

Looking at her John asked, "Have you ever had the feeling you were not wanted, do we have some disease that's contagious? We were the first in the dining room and yet we were last to be served." They ordered two coffees from the waiter who had just arrived at the table. "It seems" he continued,
"that we don't fit in here, we are being treated as outcasts, firstly it was the reception, dining room, and now we're snubbed in here."
"I agree" she answered,
"when I kissed you in the lounge earlier, the looks I got would have killed any thin skinned person, so it appears we are outcasts here."

He paid for their coffees, which had just been served, and they sat sipping them with delight.
"It's just a pity they are not more sociable in here as we would enjoy our coffee even more if they were, don't you

agree?" she asked.

"I couldn't agree with you more" he said,
"In fact I would feel more at home with the native hunter we met earlier than I do right now, perhaps they don't like the mountain boots I am wearing, they do seem to be looking at them a lot, they are also looking at your footwear as well Cheng Eng, they are torn and shabby and what about our clothing, we are dressed like a couple of tramps! we don't fit in here."

"Just have a look at some of the people in here" he continued, "they are dressed to kill, some of them are just dripping with jewellery, it's not my style, however I doubt if they could have existed last week like we did on meagre meals and lots of exercise."

When he ordered two more coffees, most surprisingly a most obliging waiter served them almost immediately. When they went back up into the hotel lounge and got seated they were surprised to see a band setting up their equipment in preparation for playing. As soon as the band started playing couples wasted no time getting onto the dance floor and began dancing.

Cheng Eng began giggling, and he asked her what was amusing her.

"Oh, just a thought," she replied,
"I can just see their faces if we were to go on the dance floor, you with your mountain boots and me with my dilapidated footwear."

It made him laugh, as he too could see the funny side of this. After a few drinks and some two hours later they lost interest in being spectators and retired upstairs to the luxury of a bed, and what a luxury, no more cramping together in a one-man tent.

They were exhausted and fell asleep almost before their heads hit the pillow, the overland trek of one hundred miles and the trials and tribulations of the last week had finally caught up with them, no doubt it would be a week to remember for the rest of their lives. Next morning they were both up bright and early and fully relaxed after a good night's sleep. They decided to go for an early morning stroll before breakfast but to their dismay found that the hotel exit door was securely locked and bolted. There appeared to be no one on duty, so they went into the dining room where they took the same seats that they were in last night, although they could have sat anywhere, as there was nobody else around.

"I wonder," he said, "if it will be like yesterday. First in last served, I suppose we shall just have to wait and see."

No sooner had he said that than a waiter arrived, looked at them, and returned through the swing doors, allowing the most wonderful smell of bacon and eggs being cooked to reach their table, this fairly boosted their appetite, just like walking down a high street and getting the smell of fish and chips, almost daring you to pass the shop, or alternatively on a very hot summer day meeting people licking ice cream, it's not long before you must have one for yourself.

They chatted a while and slowly the room began to fill up as other guests arrived in dribs and drabs, and all seating themselves as far away as possible from them. Some of them got served as soon as they sat down. He said to her,

"First class citizens' first and second class citizens served last." She replied,

"I reckon if you had flashed a wad of money at the first waiter, he would have accepted it and we would be eating right now, and be out of here before the crowds."

"I suppose you are right," he said,

"but we have paid enough and I fail to see why we should encourage bribery and corruption."

"I did not mean it literally," she replied,

"I would just like to see some fair treatment, just look around you, everyone has been served, and we are sitting here like a couple of lemons, I think we should take our complaints to the management."

Just then they were served with their breakfast, and he said, "I don't know about you but I shall be glad to leave this place in the morning. I can't put up with much more of this utterly deplorable treatment; I'm beginning to get an inferiority complex, it's definitely a case of first in last out, and by the look of things it will remain this way until we leave in the morning."

After breakfast they went on their shopping trip and had just left the hotel when they realised they had left the brochure with the directions to the shop behind. Cheng Eng volunteered to run back and collect it. While he waited for her return, he watched the luxury coach being parked in front of the main hotel entrance and overheard the bus driver telling passengers that the bus was heading to the Kaskadermuses warehouse, the bus driver helped some elderly passengers on to the bus and soon it appeared to be full and with a look at his wristwatch the driver went back into the driving seat and was just about to move off when a man came running down the steps waving his arms, obviously a straggler who did not want to miss the bus. The driver reopened the door to allow the passenger entry but John couldn't see whether the passenger got a seat or not.

Just then Cheng Eng returned with the brochure and both looking at it could see that their destination was a couple of miles outside of the town.

"Did you see that bus pull away?" He asked,

"well, it's taking the hotel guests to the same place as we are going to."

"I'd rather walk than accompany that crowd," she said scornfully.

"I'll second that," he replied, and they started on their walk. The journey passed quickly as it was easier travelling without backpacks.

As they got nearer to where the warehouse should be, he kept thinking they must be going in the wrong direction, because there were no visible signs of a building in sight, let alone a huge warehouse. Straight ahead, in the direction they were going, the road led into the side of a mountain and this was something neither of them had anticipated. When they got nearer they saw two huge open doors with two men dressed in sultan's outfits and holding Hal boards at the entrance and as they got to the doors their sheer size was staggering. They were gothic shaped and all of eight foot high and eighty wide, they looked about two feet thick. Each door must have weighed at least twenty tons. They were studded with huge bolt heads.

John and Cheng Eng couldn't pass the doors without standing and gasping at their truly gigantic and inspiring size, and as they stood awe struck he said to her,

"Have you noticed anything strange?"

"Yes," she answered,

"the road goes straight through these doors and there's no car park, so that means the bus from the hotel must have driven straight inside like every other vehicle."

"Well if the doors are anything to go by, inside must be enormous." He answered.

"Well let's go and see!" she said with an air of excitement. They went along a corridor similar in size to the huge doors, and lit either side by an Aladdin style light for at least a quarter of a mile, after which they entered into an area the size of many cathedrals; the height of the ceiling was at least two hundred feet.

To one side there were many assistants all very smartly lined up, and looking great in their uniforms that resembled Aladdin suits. Each group of customers was accompanied by an assistant who drove an electric car, pulling a small open seated coach for the customers.

The driver stopped as and when required at each bay, which started at bay 'A' and went through the whole alphabet.

For example bay 'A' contained small aeroplanes, acrobatic

equipment, aero engines and small parts of different types of aeroplanes.

Bay 'B' was stocked with building materials, from scaffolding to all types of materials used in the building trade. John and Cheng Eng's eyes were like organ stops as they gazed at the sheer size of each individual bay. They told their driver to stop at 'C' bay as this contained clothing. After browsing around she settled for an Eskimo suit, as this was the ideal wear for sub zero temperatures where they were going high up in the mountains. Next stop was 'F' bay where every type of fireplace, and fuel imaginable was on display, he got a small primus stove, which used disposable gas canisters, and he also got a full box containing one hundred of these.

Next stop was 'S' bay, which was where the shoes and every other conceivable footwear was kept. Nudging her, he pointed out that a crowd from the hotel were going up one of the racks of footwear; it was a miracle to have spotted them, as there were literally hundreds of alleyways with racks as far as the eye could see. To be honest you could spend a week in one bay and still not see everything held in that area.

He got himself, as promised, a pair of the strongest trainers available, while she got herself replacement trainers, and a pair of sturdy mountaineering boots. Finally they explained to the driver that they were now finished shopping, and asked to be taken to the checkout, the driver told them that the exit and checkout were at the far end, and about one hours drive away.

"Oh wait a moment," said Cheng Eng,
"I could do with a rucksack."
"Good thinking," he answered. She then told the driver who quickly spun round and drove back to bay 'L' which held a huge selection of many types of travelling cases, holdalls, vanity cases and rucksacks. Having chosen a rucksack it was back to the electric transporter to continue their journey to the cash desk. Because the vehicle moved only at a walking pace it took quite a while to complete the journey, the driver explained that this is the largest warehouse in the world and is some four miles long from the entrance to the exit. One bay was extremely large, and when they were driven past it, they both noticed the rows of single and double Decker buses and a row of old steam locomotives and railway rolling stock. He could have spent a whole day exploring this bay, but knew only too well it would have to be another time.

Eventually they got to the exit where the tourist buses were parked all ready for leaving. It was now obvious that when the buses arrived and drove into the mountain south side entrance and dropped off their passengers. They then drove on to the north side and awaited their passengers turning up in the electric transporters. That explained why there was one straight road into the mountain with no parking areas, which had baffled them both when they first arrived.

When they assembled at the check out, they thanked the driver and then went through the check out where they duly paid for their purchases and leaving the exit they noticed it was almost identical to the entrance. There was a large restaurant nearby and as they could do with a snack they went in and had coffee and cakes. They couldn't stay long as they had a long walk in front of them to get back to the hotel; having come out at the other end of the mountain they had added at least another four miles to the return journey. How fortunate it was that Cheng Eng had remembered about a rucksack for herself, he thought, because without that new rucksack there would have been no way they could comfortably carry all the items they had purchased, by the time they put the hundred gas cartridges in one rucksack it would be half full. Then there was the new footwear, Eskimo suit and the small primus stove to fit in the rucksack which would be totally full by now. So it was just as well they had the additional one for the rest of their goods.

He offered to carry the rucksack but she wouldn't hear of it and was adamant that she had to carry it as a training exercise to get into the way of it. She went on to say that if she got too tired she would let him carry it the rest of the way, but it was her intention to carry it all the way back to the hotel.

As they walked he turned and had a last look at the warehouse and said to her,

"There's one thing to be said, you could never exaggerate about the size of this store, it truly is massive."

Walking along they soon realised that they were the only ones walking as others were speeding past in cars and buses.

"Let's hope that we are not late back to the hotel as we will miss our evening meal," he grumbled.

She replied,

"It may work out in our best interests if we are late because we won't have to wait until the end of the queue."

After two hours of steady walking, during which time she refused his offers to carry her rucksack, they sighted the town but this time from the opposite end from which they had left, which meant they had to walk through the length of the town to reach the hotel and they now realised that the meal would be over by the time they reached the hotel so they decided to take a taxi should one be available. Continuing to walk he said that he could not get the warehouse out of his mind nor how such a mountain ever existed. He felt sure that if it were known to the rest of the world it would be rated as the eighth wonder and he asked her if she knew of any local knowledge of the place. "Tell you what," she said,

"you take a shot of carrying this rucksack for me and I will tell you what I know. I remember as a child my mother relating to me an old Chinese legend, which has been handed down for thousands of years." she then began her tale.

There was a mountain, which had puffs of smoke and flames coming from the top most peak. They called it Dragon cave mountain because it housed a gigantic dragon. This Dragon was nocturnal and the people of the surrounding villages placated it by leaving a horse tethered to a stone for its meal each evening. As time went on they got to the stage where there were very few horses left and the people were afraid that the Dragon would demand families for its meals.

The elders of the surrounding communities sent a delegation to the emperor for help, the emperor was sympathetic to they're request and sent along his personal bodyguard to deal with the Dragon. The bodyguard was a giant of a man, he was ten feet tall and called Kublai Khan. He carried a sword so heavy that it took two strong men to lift it, and people from miles around made a pilgrimage just to see this man.

After he had trained for a full week he was ready to tackle the dragon. When the big day came round there were some ten thousand people following behind the giant. They stopped half a mile from the mountain, while he went into the opening where the dragon slept. As the legend would have it, there was a tremendous battle, which went on in the cave and not long after a great flame came roaring from the opening of the mountain and the people fled in terror. Someone later found the giant's sword, which was twisted and burnt black. Lots were drawn to choose two messengers to return and tell the emperor about the result and then it would be doomsday. Someone suggested that they send for help from the great Buddhist leader the Dahlia Lama, so two elders were dispatched who travelled night and day to reach the monastery.

One of the two came up with the idea of covering up the smoke vent on the dragon's cave with a large bamboo mat, this encouraged them somewhat and they returned to the village with the proposal. During the return journey they discussed at length how they could make this very large bamboo mat and just who would be brave enough to go anywhere near the mountain with it. No one in living memory had ever gone near the mountain never mind climb up it. Anyway, the other elders fully agreed with this plan of action, and after a few days to allow the men to rest; a call was made for a public meeting of all the neighbouring communities.

On the day of the meeting literally many thousands turned up, so those at the back had great difficulty in hearing what was being said. Eventually a vote was taken and they got a one hundred per cent backing for the operation. Because of the urgency involved the very next day the mat was ready including long ropes for each corner, twenty of the older elders volunteered to carry the mat up the mountain. By noon the next day they had the mat in position ready to cover the smoke vent, however, they had not allowed for the tremendous heat and the many sparks from the smoke stack, and just before they managed to complete the job, the mat burst into flames and their operation was a total failure.

Quite naturally the elders did not wish to return to their homes because of their failure but to their surprise however, they were greeted like national heroes, for they were thought to have been incinerated by the dragon. Heroes or not, a solution to the original problem still had to be found.

A new plan was derived where they would steal

horses from neighbouring countries in an effort to feed the Dragon. One day while they awaited the return of the young men with stolen horses, a stranger rode into one of the villages. He was a giant of a man, and was riding on a massive horse the likes of which they had never seen before. Because the stranger was able to speak Chinese, he could converse with them. He told of men from a far away land who were building a great wall to protect the people who lived on the other side of it.

He had come directly from the emperor to give some advice to this community regarding their problem with the dragon. The stranger spent much time investigating the dragon's actions and behaviour, and eventually derived a very cunning but intricate plan to kill it. It involved a workforce of two and a half thousand people, and it took them many months intensive effort but eventually they managed to kill the dragon as it returned to its mountainside retreat. As the story goes, during the Dragon's agonising struggle and rage, it melted the mountain centre and in its final death struggle it blasted a hole right through the mountainside and to this day it is still believed that is the reason for the great cavity, and openings, within the mountain, which form Aladdin's cave.

He had been so engrossed in her story that the miles just seemed to fly by. There was now no need for a taxi as they had arrived at their destination. In fact they had almost missed the hotel entrance. As they had suspected they arrived a bit late for the start of the evening meal, so they went directly to the dining room, leaving their luggage on the floor next to their feet at the table where they sat. The looks they were receiving from the other guests were less than complimentary. This really upset Cheng Eng and he had to console her by reminding her that they would not have to put up with it after tomorrow as they would have bid the place good riddance by that at time.

As the guests left the dining area, all of them without exception, put their noses in the air as they passed their table. One man in particular really annoyed them because as he passed them he deliberately kicked their rucksack and said in as loud a voice as possible,

"I ask you ladies and gentlemen of culture, what kind of people would bring that into a hotel dining room, riff-raff, I tell you, total riff - raff."

It took John all his time to keep his composure so he pretended he hadn't heard what was said. He had to restrain himself from getting up from the table and confronting this person. After the other guests had left the dining room he said to her,

"It's a good job Big Tom wasn't here, he wouldn't have put up with that kind of behaviour. He would have taken him by the scruff of the neck and closed his loud abusive mouth once and for all, make no mistake. Not only that but Tom would have insisted that this ignoramus got down on his hands and knees and made a public apology".

While waiting to be served he went on to explain some of big Tom's exploits, which were many and varied. Eventually when they did get served, they were alone in the dining room and they felt much more comfortable without the stares and snide remarks.

"These people could do with learning some manners and show some respect for other people," reflected John, "there is a saying 'spare the rod and spoil the child.' These days, even parents are not allowed to administer any form of punishment for misbehaviour, this encourages those young people to get into further trouble, sometimes even much more serious trouble, what are your views Cheng Eng?"

Looking across the table at him she said. "I am totally in favour of corporal punishment, being a school teacher I have the experience of knowing how very disruptive some pupils can be, believe me, your hands are tied behind your back and boy do they know it, and use it to their advantage. Having finished their meal they left the waiters to clean up, and collecting their luggage went on to their room, retiring for the night early because they were both exhausted after a very tiring day. She asked if he minded if she missed breakfast in the morning as she felt she could not put up with any more of the other guests ill manners. He answered by telling her that it sounded like sweet music to his ears, and he was only too happy to agree.

Next morning they were both out of bed and up at the crack of dawn. They had showered, packed up and had left the hotel while most of the other guests were still in their beds. They were both exhilarated to get out of that hotel and into the morning fresh air. They still had a number of provisions to purchase and surprisingly enough still had some room in their rucksacks to hold them. They had plenty of time so they went for a stroll to await the market traders and shops opening.

He hoped to purchase two airmail letters and send one to Ruby and the other to his parents, he had fully intended writing to them from the last town, but because of the unfortunate experience he had in the restaurant the envelopes were used for another purpose altogether. By this time the sun was up and it was a beautiful morning as they watched the traders' set-up their stalls. They noticed an open cafe and decided to have breakfast there, being such a beautiful morning they decided to eat outside and were pleased to see there was room at a table out in the sunshine.

Cheng Eng ordered breakfast, getting coffee first, they sat sipping it and leisurely watched the world go by them. They thoroughly enjoyed their breakfast that morning and both were feeling very contented and in no way out of place here, as they had in the hotel. Finishing their breakfast they were almost reluctant to leave as they had enjoyed the time together so much, however, they needed supplies, so off they went on a shopping spree.

Among other things, they bought fresh fruit and vegetables, some dried cereal and then, yes, he remembered the two airmail envelopes. The idea was to write his two letters and send them from the post office next door to the café. By the time they were finished shopping it was noon, and although they were a good half-mile or so away from the cafe they were in earlier, they decided to backtrack and return there for lunch. It was certainly worth it as the meal and atmosphere were delicious; they were fortunate enough to secure the same table that they had in the morning. Again they were reluctant to leave, they knew only too well that it would be a long-time before they were back in civilisation and sitting down and being waited upon. Who could blame them for savouring and enjoying their last few moments of home comforts? reluctantly they both got ready to leave. He posted his letters in the post office and they continued on their way out of town. On reaching the town's outskirts they stopped for a final look back and wondered how long it would take them to return. One thing they were sure of, on their return they would seek alternate accommodation, they vowed never to return to that hotel again.

During their walk, each hour they had stopped for a break to relieve the weight of their rucksacks. They had been walking for some four hours and they were very tired so they decided to stop for the night. Now that they carried water supplies it made things much easier as they were able to set up camp wherever they wanted, rather than next to water. He had added on the map, features such as exact distances between each stopping off place, and restricted each camp to a point as near a prominent landmark as possible.

Watching him do this she asked him why go to so much trouble. He told her that at each site they set up, before they left he would place four cornerstones to mark the position of the tent, and in the centre would be a much larger stone, and under that centre stone he would bury some food supplies, and a gas canister. He further explained that when they re-visited each site on their return journey, the supplies would be there waiting for them, it also saved them carrying supplies up the mountain and back again.

She had listened with rapture, and exclaimed, "That's a brilliant idea! and it also explains why you bought so much dry cereal and a hundred gas canisters, I must admit I was also baffled why you bought a large roll of cling film, but now I understand." They soon had the tent up and proudly stood watching their new miniature stove easily boil the water for their eagerly awaited evening hot drink. They had a routine now, just before they went to sleep he would tell a story, and the next evening it was her turn.

There was also a morning routine, packing up the tent, sleeping bags etc. having breakfast, mostly cereal and placing the marker stones in readiness for their return. He scooped out two handfuls of soil making two holes. In one, he placed a handful of cereal, two teaspoonful of coffee and half a handful of dried vegetables, each item was wrapped separately in cling film. In the other hole he buried one of the gas canisters, a large flat stone then covered the holes so that the contents were well and truly out of sight.

They had not travelled far when she asked why he kept turning round and looking back at the campsite, he told her that he was putting a row of indicating markers in the ground so that they would have no problems finding the site on their return; he intended to do this at each site as they left. She watched him cut ten straight branches from a nearby tree and strip the leaves from them, he then sharpened each end to a point and put a split in the other end to which he tied a thin strip of white cloth, he used an old travelling shirt to cut the strips from.

Taking a bearing from a local land mark, he took one of the pointers and stuck it into the ground; next he took a note of its location in his book and told her that he would do this at each tenth of a mile from all the camps. She thought this navigational system was marvellous and ingenious and from then on she readily assisted him to do the same as they broke camp each day. It took them a full month of hard slogging to reach the mountains and they knew that the average of twenty miles a day they had been making, would now be out of the question and that they would be lucky to make five miles a day in this treacherous rough terrain. In fact it was so bad in some areas they were only able to travel two miles a day. In addition, the higher altitude they were now travelling in exhausted them, and they had to stop for a break every few yards.

Another factor was the intense cold and particularly the wind chill. Cheng Eng of course was as snug as a bug in a rug, in her Eskimo suit, while he on the other hand was feeling the cold even through his thermal mountaineering clothes. They were six weeks into the expedition, and only a few days from their objective, when they were almost forced to abandon the whole operation.

They had been walking between two vertical and narrow mountain faces when the path they were following ended abruptly. Before them lay a sheer drop, lying on his belly he crawled to the edge and had a look down, he could see at a glance that his longest rope would not reach the bottom. With the sheer rock face at either side of them, there seemed no way out of the situation. Any climbing here would be extremely dangerous and this was the last place in the world to sustain a broken limb. They decided to camp here for the night and have a fresh look at the situation in the morning.

All night long his mind was so involved with the crisis that he was awake most of the night, while Cheng Eng was sound asleep. Although he felt totally shattered in the morning, he was up at daybreak searching for a place to tie a rope to, eventually finding a small tapered crack in the rock face, this gave him an idea. He would tie a knot on the end of the mountaineering rope and bang the end into the crack as tight as possible. Even if it did move, the knot would act as a retainer as it was too big to pull through the crack. So far so good, he then lay on his belly and looking down the overhang he fed the rope down until there was no more slack left and just as he had surmised it didn't reach the bottom. During the night he had thought of just such a situation and had evolved a theory of how it could be overcome. Tying both rucksacks onto the end of the rope would give them a few extra feet, which might be all that was required, he was excited and eager to try out his idea.

He awakened Cheng Eng and explained the situation

to her, she was more than hopeful; and had another suggestion, which he hadn't thought about. The idea was to roll the tent up and use that along with the rucksacks and again this would give another few feet of extension to the rope.

So after a very hurried breakfast, it was time to test the theory out, he pulled the rope up and tied on one rucksack, and then the second. Cheng Eng had just finished rolling up the tent ready to tie it on as well when she suggested that it might be better to tie the tent on firstly and then the rucksacks, that way you could stand on the rucksacks to untie the tent from the end of the rope, whereas standing on the tent would give you very little extra height. He readily agreed and untied the first rucksack and replaced it with the tent then he added the other two rucksacks.

Taking up his familiar position of lying flat, face down, he slowly fed the first rucksack over the edge followed by the second then the tent and lastly the loose rope. When the slack was all taken up he saw the last rucksack still wasn't touching the ground under it, however from his vantage point it looked as though there was only a shortfall of a matter of a few feet. The rope would have to remain here until they returned. He told her that he knew only too well the risks involved in having to go down it but explained they had little choice and had to take the risk because he certainly didn't want to abort the expedition after getting this far.

She agreed and was quite willing to take the risk but

insisted on firstly kneeling down to pray, so he knelt down and joined her in a silent prayer. As they both got up they stood and held each other in their arms and kissed. He said, "Keep your fingers crossed I am going now," and without any hesitation abseiled over the overhang and down he went, out of sight.

She lay on her stomach watching him, and let out a huge sigh of relief when she saw that he had reached the last rucksack and was almost on the ground, she could see the dangling rucksack was almost at waist height, so it was a great consolation. There was still the problem of getting up to untie the tent and the other rucksacks. However, the most important thing remaining at the moment was to help Cheng Eng make her descent. He had explained and demonstrated to her what to do and how to go about it, just as he had been instructed by the mountaineering instructor back home in the Lake District.

He held his breath, as she started to make her descent, and watched with bated breath as she slowly abseiled over the overhang and then made her way down to him. He dared not blink his eyes, as he was so intent in watching her every movement. Slowly but surely she made her way down and what a relief it was to him as he held her by the waist and lifted her off the last rucksack and let her down gently to the ground. She was trembling with a mixture of excitement and fear. He held her in his arms and congratulated her for making a safe descent. With his reassuring words her fear soon left her and she regained her composure once more.

He untied the lowest rucksack and then helped her stand on his back to reach the other bag and the tent, this operation was tricky but successful and he reminded her that it would have to be done again on their return. Having packed up, they were soon on the move again, however he couldn't help looking back at the dangling rope and worrying about what would happen if they should come across a similar situation, because he now had no rope left.

Now that they were in mountainous terrain where the ground was either rock or frozen solid, he had to derive another way of arranging camp markers. What he did was to mark each area with strips of cloth torn from an old tartan shirt, and rather than bury the provisions he just left them on the surface where they could easily be found even if they were covered with snow. In addition to numbering all the campsites in his book, he gave each campsite, which had no particular landmark a feature name such as 'Hanging rope site' representing last nights camp.

On another occasion they had camped under an overhanging rock canopy, which had huge icicles hanging from the top of the rock down to the ground. They had really enjoyed this site, because of the way it was constructed it had sheltered them from the bitter wind. It was a foregone conclusion that he called this 'The hanging icicle campsite.'

There were many named sites, such as 'Shepherds crook camp' so named after a rock in the shape of a shepherd and his crook.

One in particular they would both remember, was the

'Howling wolf site,' their night there had been a sleepless one, because of the wind blowing in between a rock crevice, it sounded just like howling wolves, and depending on the velocity of the wind, it either sounded near or farther away. Their prayer in the morning included a wind free night on their return. As they were now into the end of their seventh week in the mountains, they had now only two days supplies of rations including gas canisters left. So things were now in a critical state, if they couldn't locate their objective, i.e., the two peaks of similar height with a smaller one in the middle, within the next two days they would have to admit defeat and abandon the mission.

They both studied the map and compass bearings at great length, they were spot on and exactly where they should be. The mountain ridge high above them would be an excellent observation look out post, but it seemed like an almost impossible task to climb up to that ridge, it looked like an insurmountable obstacle directly in their path, however, it was never the less a challenge which had to be overcome. Painfully, step-by-step in a zigzagging route they made their way up the nearly sheer slope. It took a long time, and it was nearly dark by the time they reached the ridge.

He was first to the top with her close behind, gripping the ridge with both hands, and with an almost superhuman effort, he pulled himself up to the top and looked over. He stared in disbelief; it felt as though his heart, and time, had stopped for there, straight in front of him were the two mountains with peaks of the same height with the smaller one in the middle. It also had a flat plain of snow down the front of the middle mountain, and exactly as he had seen in his previous visions, there was the green splash of colour in that flat plain of pure white snow.

He was overwhelmed with excitement and shouted out

"Look it's there, it's there! just as I have seen it so many times. I just knew it existed!"

Cheng Eng equally excited, scrambled up to see it for herself, and she seemed every bit as thrilled as he was. In his state of utopia he grasped at his binoculars, and inadvertently let go of his grip on the ridge. In a flash he was off and starting to slide headfirst and face down, his hands clawed into the rock face, frantically grabbing for a grip. The friction caused a burning sensation. Was he dreaming? Was he asleep? This was what he had experienced many times in his nightmares but unfortunately this time it was for real. He could hear Cheng Eng's screams of terror, the only reality in the nightmare, things were happening as if in slow motion, almost frozen in time.

His foot hit a solid mass, which twisted him round so that he was now falling head first, almost at the same time he landed on a small ledge, which broke his fall and stopped him dead. It happened so abruptly, he felt as if he had been compressed down to half his size. In spite of the pain and discomfort, with his heart doing overtime and trembling with shock and fear, he was still alive, that was an instant consolation. It was essential to get back up to the ridge as it was getting darker by the minute. Looking up he could see Cheng Eng was making her way down to him. He shouted,

"Stay there, I'm coming back up, there are some ledges to get hold of, and I should make it OK." She immediately retraced her steps and obeyed his commands. He took a few minutes to pull himself together and to take stock of the situation he was now in.

Slowly he clawed his way back up the ridge, and after what seemed like an eternity, he rejoined her on the top, they cuddled each other as best they could in the circumstances, each with one hand clinging on to the ridge and the other arm round each other's waist. He noticed tears running down her cheeks and she was sobbing so much that it was most uncomfortable trying to hold on and at the same time console her. It would be difficult to decide as to whom got the biggest fright, him losing his grip and sliding down, or her witnessing the whole affair. However time was pressing and it was getting darker by the minute, so after a few precious moments of consoling each other and having to change hands gripping the ridge, he explained that it was now essential to get over the ridge and set up camp.

He went first and with her help managed to get over the top and drop down to a ledge, which was conveniently at waist height, from there it was now a gradual slope down as far as the eye could see, in the now darkening visibility. He lost no time in helping her over the ridge to where they started to set up camp right away, because by now it was too late to go any further.

After setting up the campsite he got his binoculars out and focused on the green splash in the white snow on that far away distant landscape, it now appeared much brighter, almost luminous, with the mountain background area being dark, as he focused on the centre he could see quite plainly the different shades of green, darker in the middle and getting much lighter the nearer the edge he looked.

By this time Cheng Eng had prepared their evening meal, and accepting a plate from her, and getting tucked in, he thanked her and handed her the binoculars. After a while looking at it, she asked him if he had any idea why this particular area of snow should be coloured green, and what size of area was it covering. He said that being so far away it was very difficult to estimate and quite frankly it was anybody's guess; however in his opinion it was a very large area. He had no idea why it was coloured green, perhaps it was caused by radiation, but this was just speculation. One thing was for sure, it must have been there since time immemorial, because it had been mentioned in an old Tibetan legend that goes back thousands of years.

Later as they sat sipping a coffee, while in their sleeping bags. He told her about the encounters he had with the ghostly voices and the paranormal situation that surrounded the green snow and how the premonitions he had so far had all come true. He told her all about the haunting nightmares he had and how he had been compelled to search for and find this spot.

She listened to him spell bound and suggested it would have been great to have been able to celebrate the finding of the green snow. He agreed, and rummaging in his rucksack, he held aloft the very last bar of chocolate covered Kendal mint cake, and shouted with elation and triumph.

"Yes, we shall celebrate!" he then handed her half, and they tucked into a celebration feast, before sleep overcame them. He awoke next morning before Cheng Eng, and right away he studied the green area through his binoculars, it had lost its luminescence, which did not help him estimate just how far away it was; it looked about two miles away, as the crow flies. However they would have a flat plain of about four miles to travel going down into a valley, and then a slope up to the Green snow, making it about eight miles away. Cheng Eng arrived with the welcome news that a cup of coffee was ready for him, they returned to the tent and had breakfast there, sheltered from the biting below zero wind.

They broke camp and headed off towards their objective, after the usual routine of marking the camp etc. He felt quite pleased with his choice of name he had marked in his book for last night's camp, 'Sharp ridge site' quite appropriate he thought, rubbing the aches and pains he had acquired when he had fallen. As they walked he remarked to her about the inhospitable landscape and said, "It's little wonder that this place has remained a secret for so long, at least we have proved the legend to be fact and not fiction."

"Well," she said "someone was here way back in the mists of time, otherwise the legend would never have been written."

"I agree," he replied,

"what's worrying me a little at the moment is the quote I read in an ancient book which read

'Never never go, to the green snow,'

Red for stop and green for go,

No go near the bright green snow."

She stopped in her tracks with an expression of fear and terror etched on her face, she gripped his arm and said,

"I don't want anything awful to happen to us, let's turn back now, after all, you have found it."

"I will tell you what I can't do," he answered,

"I can't just leave now, after what we've been through, I must at least take some of the green snow back for laboratory analysis. I will never have peace of mind until I discover why that one area alone should be coloured green. If I leave you the tent and provisions would you wait here for my return?"

Throwing her arms around his neck and with tears in her eyes she sobbed, "I'm coming with you."

Holding her close until she stopped sobbing he kissed her and holding her hand led the way forward towards the green snow and it's great, as yet, untold mystery. They reached the bottom of the long gradient within an hour, and then it was across the valley and the long climb up to the snow covered plateau, it was a blessing to be out of the sub-zero blizzard wind as they made their way up. After a few yards they were feeling tired and exhausted, so they decided to have a rest, especially now they were once again exposed to that terrible wind.

They had both no sooner sat down with their backs to the wind, when it seemed in an instant a terrible blizzard blew up. There had been a clear blue sky only moments ago; now they couldn't see a yard in front of their faces in any direction. This was nothing new to them as they had experienced this type of weather before. They both knew there was only one thing to do and that was to stay where they were, however long it lasted. To wander off in these conditions could mean signing your own death certificate.

Sitting with their backs to the terrible conditions they ate their rations consisting of a mixture of dry cereals and vegetables. Now that the snow was building up so much on their backs, it was simply a matter of putting their hands behind their backs and collect handfuls of snow and use it to quench their thirst. They restricted warm drinks to first thing in the morning and last thing at night. Due to the prevailing atrocious conditions they had come to an agreement that they should restrict themselves to half rations, because they could be marooned here for as long as this storm continued.

They both sat in silence, as there was little point in talking, the wind was so ferocious there was no way you could be heard above its howling. Two hours had passed before Cheng Eng shouted. "I hope this isn't an omen to warn us not to go any further, and force us to turn back."
He shouted back that he didn't think so. Incredibly as it

may seem the blizzard stopped as suddenly as it had started and the cloudless blue sky returned overhead, however the gale force wind was as strong as ever.

When they attempted to get up they got a surprisingly nasty shock, try as they might, neither of them could get up from their sitting positions, their frozen snowed-up rucksacks had stuck firmly to the ground, to say that they were in a predicament was an understatement. His army knife was in a pocket of his rucksack, and he couldn't get to it. This meant he couldn't cut the straps of the rucksacks to relieve them, as luck would have it he did have the little gas stove in a pocket where he kept it to enable his body heat to stop the gas freezing. One resolution was to detach themselves from the rucksacks, and then try tugging the frozen rucksacks to free them from their present positions. After shuffling out from the rucksacks they encountered another problem, their bottoms had both adhered and frozen to the snow where they had been sitting for the last two and a half hours. Luckily they were able to move their legs and feet, because they had kept them tucked up with their knees close to their chests, and only occasionally moving their feet. They couldn't budge no matter how much they pushed and pulled at each other. He said "I have heard about pranksters who put super glue on a toilet seat, and whoever sat on it couldn't move, but there was always someone around to come to their rescue."

"But we have no-one to get us out of our predicament." she replied.

"we are getting nowhere trying to push ourselves straight up from our sitting positions, why don't we try rocking from side to side?"

They had very little energy left, the atmosphere at this high altitude left them breathless, however they gave it a try, and both started swaying from side to side in a pendulum movement until they were exhausted. She burst into tears and said, "We're doomed, we are doomed!"

He put his arm around her to try and console her and said, "Within an hour we shall free ourselves from these rucksacks, trust me I have a plan." Choking back her tears she said, "I wish with all my heart that you are right, and that it can be done, but I think you are saying that just to calm me down."

"Not at all." He replied "I have a plan of action which I am confident will work, it's our one and only chance of survival, so bear with me, and I'll explain." He then went on to explain that to free themselves meant getting out of their top layer of clothing, and getting back in again, as quickly as possible as they would be unable to survive out of their mountain top gear for more than just a few minutes before dying of exposure.

"What we must do," he said, "is this, as soon as I get out of my top and bottom suit, with your help, I will put the lighted gas stove to the outside part of my trousers where they are stuck to the ground. While I'm doing that, you must take off your gloves and using the heat from your hands, heat the seat of my trousers to free them."

They wasted no time in carrying out his plan, and it worked in almost military fashion, within minutes it was all over, he was free. She held him close to her and her body heat soon stopped his violent shivering. .Next it was her turn, with their previous experience it took even less time to free her and get her temperature back up and out of the danger area, but no matter how they tried they were quite unable to move the frozen rucksacks. After discussing the situation for a while they agreed the best plan of action was to empty each rucksack and place the small stove in it. They carried out this plan, firstly on his rucksack and within five minutes he had it free, next they tackled hers. This time it only took a few minutes to enable it to be lifted from the ground, they were both glad that it took very little time because they were down on their hunkers, as both were afraid to sit down in case they became stuck again.

The storm and defrosting had held them up for four hours but now they were ready to move, the going would be rough because of the fresh fall of snow, so they would be satisfied if they could reach the base of the mountain and set up camp there tonight. They travelled on for two hours, only stopping for the occasional break by turning their back to the gale force winds. Although he was positive that they were in the area of the green snow, there was no sign of it to be seen, he swept the area time and time again with his binoculars, visibility was now excellent, the sky was blue and indeed the sun was shining, but still there was no sign of the green snow.

Handing the glasses to her he suggested that she look

for the green snow as he was becoming frustrated, putting the glasses to her eyes and focusing them. She looked for ages, scanning all around the area, but eventually had to admit defeat, there was no sign of it anywhere. They were now both most despondent, and were beginning to wonder if they had seen an optical illusion from their base camp yesterday. Although they were fairly sure that they were in the area of the green snow they had to move on and search for a suitable place to camp for the night, they were very lucky because almost by accident they came across an empty cave, and this would make an excellent camping area; there would be no need for the tent as the cave was bone dry inside.

While she dealt with the priority of making a hot drink and serving out the half rations. He took his torch and went to explore the interior of the cave. It was a natural cave in the form of a large semicircle. He soon made a very interesting discovery, about fifty yards into the cave there was a man made corridor about two yards wide and three high, it went in for about ten yards and then terminated in a face of solid rock. On closer examination he could see the very tool marks on the walls where they had been chipped away. What on earth, he thought, brought mankind to such an out of the way place such as this, twenty eight thousand feet above sea level and then cut out such a perfectly shaped cavern within the cave only to stop after ten feet, were these ancient people prospectors looking for veins of gold or other precious stones?

Before he could make any further discoveries he

heard Cheng Eng shout, "Tea up"

"Coming!" he replied. Ah! he thought, makes a welcome change from the usual coffee. When they were both sitting comfortable with their tea and warm gruel, he told her of his find, and suggested that since there were still a few hours of daylight left. They should climb a further one thousand feet above their present position to enable them to survey the whole of the snow covered Plateau beneath them in the hope of finding the green area, and because they would be returning here later, there was no need to take their rucksacks. He took his binoculars, sketchpad and torch.

Even without the rucksacks, climbing was not easy because of their breathing difficulties due to the high altitude. After gaining a few hundred feet they reached a very suitable vantage point and right away he started searching the area with his binoculars and giving her a full commentary. He could see their footsteps in the snow right up to the entrance of the cave, and also 'Sharp ridge' mountain site, which was almost straight across from their present position. Later she also had a good search using the binoculars, but she like him, could not see any sign of the green snow.

Totally baffled by its disappearance, he came to the conclusion that, like a luminous watch face, perhaps it could only be seen properly in the dark, it was after all pitch black when they last saw it. They decided that the only way to prove, or disprove, this theory was to wait where they were until nightfall in the hope of being able to see it again.

Later on, their return to the cave in the dark should be no problem, as they would quite easily be able to see their return path, with the aid of the torch. He sat and sketched in his notebook while waiting for darkness to fall. The wait was really quite comfortable because where they were sitting they were sheltered from the icy wind.

As time passed they took turns in using the binoculars to scan the surroundings, nothing happened until dusk when a small green dot of snow was spotted, the darker the night became the greater the green area increased, they were both jubilant. It was pleasing to see that they had been proved correct without any shadow of a doubt. She held the torch allowing him to see as he sketched the details in his book.

Being finished here, they made their way back down to the cave. The descent was slow and laborious because it was now pitch black, about half way down they stopped for a well earned rest. Suddenly they both saw something that had not been visible from above, the green snow was pulsating, changing from a light green to a more brilliant green, especially in the centre, which he estimated would be about one hundred metres in diameter.

For what seemed an eternity, they stood mesmerised and awe inspired by this sight before them. By the time they had arrived back at the cave they were quite unable to see any of the green snow and they were pleased that they had climbed to the higher vantage point earlier. All this walking and climbing had taken its toll and they were both very tired so they climbed straight into their sleeping bags for the night.

John was wakened by Cheng Eng shaking him and telling him that she was very frightened and could not sleep she couldn't quite explain the reason for her fear, but felt she would rather sleep in the tent outside the cave. Half asleep he took her in his arms and tried to console her, by saying, "It is far too late dear to put up the tent tonight why not try a couple of paracetamol tablets, I'll get them from the first aid kit."
He picked up the tablets and handed them to her along with a drink, they obviously helped her settle, because she was still asleep in the morning when he arose.

It was late morning before Cheng Eng wakened, normally the light from the morning sun would waken her but being in the cave meant it was darker for longer. The morning sun could not shine through it like it did in a tent. After breakfast they packed their rucksacks and were ready to move when he remembered that he had not shown her the man made cavern in the cave. She had shown an interest and had asked him last night if she could see it before they left. Armed with the torch they set off and he was soon showing her the chiselled rock and the tool markings on the walls and ceiling, on reaching the end of the rock face they inspected it very closely. Whilst commenting on the mystery of why it should end so abruptly. He noticed something rather peculiar on the ceiling very close to the end of the corridor, shining his light on it they were amazed to see a near perfect round circle about one foot in diameter, for all the world like an inspection hatch. It looked such a perfect fit that he doubted he could get a razor blade into the gap where it fitted in the ceiling. He thought it was little wonder he missed it the first time he was here.

They were both very excited with this discovery and began to make plans to open it.

"Its edges must be tapered to hold it in position," he said, "a bit like a cork in a bottle."

They had been looking at it for so long now that their necks ached being stretched back so far, rubbing his neck he said, "If only these walls were able to talk what a story they would have to tell. I am convinced there's something up there, I can't talk for you, but I am not leaving here until I find out."

She replied that she was just as curious as he was and suggested that if she stood on his shoulders she would be able to reach up and try to push or lift it open. He readily agreed and bent down to enable her to step on to his shoulders. Stabilising herself against the wall with her hands she slowly straightened up to a standing position, this was just the right height to enable her to use both her hands to push up and attempt to open the stone bung.

"Right," she said, "Here goes!" and pushed up with all the strength she could summon, but she could not move the circular stone bung, trying not to show his disappointment he said, "We might have to abandon trying to open it, unless you take my knife and go round the join to see if grit or dust is wedged in it and causing it to stick."

"Wait, lets give it one more try," she said, "let me rest my arms for a minute, then, if I hold my arms up straight with the palms of my hands flat on the bung, you bend your knees down, then very quickly straighten up, the extra force may free it."

"And if not we shall try with the knife," he agreed,

"just let me know when you are ready." When she was ready, he straightened up quickly and instantly felt the impacting strain on both his shoulders.

The stone bung opened and instantly all hell was let lose, a small skeleton with a cloak around it fell through the now open hole, Cheng Eng fell over backwards screaming in terror, he dropped his torch which went out when it hit the floor. It was now darker than the darkest night, what little daylight there had been coming in from the mouth of the cave had suddenly been blacked out, there was a loud rumbling sound followed by a thud, and very noticeable was the most obnoxious smell in the air.

Cheng Eng was lying on the floor screaming hysterically. Her screams were amplified and echoed within the enclosed space of the cavern and he was on his knees frantically searching for the torch in the darkness. His hands shook and he was trembling all over and had broken out in a cold sweat. He had never been so terrified in his whole life, his heart and head were pounding ready to burst. His throat was dry and he almost screamed aloud as he felt he was going to choke, when instead of finding the torch he grabbed hold of the skeleton's leg. A cold shiver ran down his spine and he felt sick with his gruesome find.

Giving up looking for the torch he scrabbled about on his hands and knees over to where Cheng Eng was still screaming, and coming up against her foot he touched her and said,

"It's me, it's alright it's only me." He doubted very much that she could hear him above her screaming and sobbing. Very gently he lifted her head in his arms and cuddled her in an effort to console her. "Are you hurt?" he asked but she continued to sob and she held him to her like a drowning person clutching at a straw. There was no way she would let him go.

"Hush now, it's ok, we will be alright you'll see."

He whispered as he tried to sound as if he were in control, but doubted very much that he succeeded. He was at his wits end with all sorts of thoughts whizzing through his mind, the most worrying was that they were now trapped. Something had obviously sealed the entrance to the cave, if they were sealed in, then their air supply would be limited and it would only be a matter of time before they suffocated to death. However, he knew that there was little that could be done until he quietened her down, drastic action had to be taken to stop her sobbing, so he shook her time and time again, at times quite violently, and shouted to her to snap out of it, then he continued very quietly.

"We've both had a shock, a once in a lifetime shock, but you must pull yourself together Cheng Eng, the longer you keep this up the less time we have to conceive a survival plan and put it into action." Enough was enough, he stopped shaking her and instead kissed her many times, and thank God, it worked a treat, she stopped crying almost immediately.

He didn't know whether to cry or laugh when she asked him if her fall had made her blind, she obviously was not aware that they were now sealed in. Very gently he explained the situation in full to her explaining in great detail that as far as he knew the round bung in the roof had been booby trapped and had set off a rock fall which had sealed the entrance to the cave, and that was the reason for the darkness, and no, she need not worry, she was not blind!

She was very quiet for what seemed ages but when she finally did speak, she caught him by complete surprise when she said,

"From what you say dear it sounds as if we are trapped in here with little hope of escape, well if I'm going to die I'm going to do so on my terms."

With that said, she pulled him to her and undoing his clothing she made her intentions very clear. He was quite taken aback by this and couldn't quite understand how she could turn from being hysterical one minute to extremely romantic the next; being in total darkness was known to bring an increased sense of closeness, but this close?

He may well have been baffled, but being a man he returned her passionate embrace, and soon the world and all its problems seemed so far away. Later, much later when they untangled from their lovers embrace they knew that should their life end now then they would take with them the memory of their wonderful moments together. Almost apologetically he brought them back to reality when he started looking for the torch again in the hope it had not been broken beyond repair when it fell. Although they had some matches in one rucksack they were most reluctant to use them and would only do so as a last resort. He knew the flame would rapidly exhaust what little air supply they had left. He got down on his hands and knees and searched on the ground for the torch. She meanwhile fumbled through the rucksacks in search of their matches just in case they had to use them.

Every time his hand came in contact with the skeleton a shiver ran up his spine and gave him the creeps. He was sure that he had searched most of the floor but had still not found the torch. She on the other hand had been much more successful and shouted over to him that she now had the matches.

Striking the first of the matches they were able to take stock of their situation and could quite clearly see that it was snow, and not rocks that had fallen and blocked the cave entrance.

Cheng Eng built up the rucksacks and putting on her all- weather gloves, she started clearing away the snow from the top of the cave mouth. He retreated to the back of the cavern and lit another match and looked around desperately trying to find the torch, for it had to be found. Things were definitely not going his way regarding the torch, then he had a brain wave. The only place the torch could be and the one place he dreaded looking for it must be under the skeleton's cloak. So closing his eyes tight he wormed his hands under the cloak feeling left then right and bingo! There was the torch, he gripped it tight and pulled out his hand as fast as a rocket.

Unfortunately he was able to feel that it was incomplete and that the batteries and the front lens were missing. There was nothing else for it, he had to have another search under the cloak even although it was both frightening and sickening to do so. Only then did it occur to him how silly he had been to close his eyes in the total darkness. He supposed he gained some psychological benefit from it but that was all. Nevertheless he was able to quite quickly reassemble the torch in the dark and to his delight it worked first time when he switched it on.

Turning away immediately from the cavern he went over to see how Cheng Eng was doing at the cave entrance, and was delighted to see that she had scooped out an area of the snow to just about as far as she could reach.
"You have done well, why don't you take a rest and I'll take over for a while," he suggested. She took off her gloves and with difficulty helped him put them on, small as they were. He then began scooping out the snow which was quite easy but he was sure that he would manage even better with his own gloves on, so he asked her to look for them in his rucksack. Later wearing his own gloves he managed to dig enough snow out to bring daylight back into the top of the cave entrance. Although he was still unable to completely break through to the outside he could not stop thinking about the other danger they were in and

his concern was the warning in the book to keep well away from the green snow.

Meanwhile she gave him a drink of water and it was just what he needed, for it is a well-known fact that fear can dry up the mouth. He explained to her that he was unable to break through by himself but he asked if she minded shuffling her way into the tunnel and pass the snow backwards away from him until he broke through to the outside which would clear the way out for them.

She agreed and standing on both rucksacks he lifted her up into the tunnel. They continued working away for about twenty minutes. By that time he was totally exhausted so they gladly took a five minute rest, after which he had another go at trying to knock his way through the end of the tunnel and into the outside world, but again without success. They were both at their wits end now and decided to have a hot drink, even although they would be using up valuable air by using the stove. The hot sweet drink revived their energies and they began to give serious thought about other alternatives to get out of that cave. There may well be an escape route through the circular hole in the roof of the cavern; first problem however was actually getting high enough to get through the hole.

"I know how to get up there," said Cheng Eng. She then explained that if they completely emptied all the contents of the rucksacks, they could fill them with snow, drag them over to the hole and build a snow ramp. While I am filling one, you could drag a full one over, empty it, and bring it back, by that time I will have another one filled, making it an on going process until the ramp is completed."

They lost little time in getting the rucksacks emptied and putting their plan into action. The snow was an unlimited supply of material and it was no wonder that in a very short time a ramp of snow had been constructed. Then came the big decision, who would go up first. He volunteered, so armed with the torch he went up the ramp and very nervously put his head up through the opening and shone the torch cautiously round trying to see if there were any more booby traps, then he gasped and said

"Jeepers, Creepers! This is massive up here and it's full of things."

"Things! What things?" she enquired fearfully from below.

"I don't know what they are!" he gasped "but I could have a better look if you can give me a push up?"

She steadied him and helped him up until he disappeared right through the hole in the roof.

When he was inside, he bent down and grasping her hands he managed to get her up beside him, very slowly and deliberately he shone the torch along the walls, it was like a museum without the glass cases, the contents within this vast space was an archaeologists dream. It was filled with artefacts of a long lost civilisation and of a time long since relegated history.

Who were these people who had gone to so much trouble to hide and preserve their valuables? Not only to hide their treasures, they certainly had made sure their valuables were not disturbed, nor indeed stolen when they arranged the booby trap to seal the vault. Cheng Eng's eyes popped out like organ stops as he shone the torch around illuminating one section of the wall. Which showed a huge painting, all done in the brightest of colours. Instinctively she wanted to rush over and inspect it but he urgently restrained her and reminded her there could be more booby traps up here.

"We might get right up to it, to admire it, when the floor area we were on could suddenly drop us into an abyss or something. We must exercise extreme caution and be suspicious of everything until we are sure it's really safe." Pointing the torch and shining its light on a bamboo ladder which was laid alongside a wall just a yard away from where they were standing, he said "See that ladder? that very ladder was most likely pulled up here for the last time many thousands of years ago possibly by the last surviving people, who would then have put that stone bung in place and then sealed it with candle wax, and that's the reason why it was air- tightly sealed. "How do you know that," she asked?"

"Well, one of the first things I noticed when I put my head through the hole was this half burnt candle." he said, and shone the torch on it so she could see it was unlike any candle of today. It had a bamboo collar near the base with a spout so that the melting wax, which collected in the collar, could be poured out, then he shone the torch on the round stone bung and showed her there was a seal of wax all around it.

"I wouldn't have noticed that John full marks to you," she said. "I would be interested to know if there is anything else you can explain to me about this strange case?"

"Yes," he replied. "There are some more interesting points, had we both come in here immediately we forced an entry, we would both have been poisoned and be lying here dead now, that was the intention of the ancient people who constructed this vault. I must take my hat off to them, here we have people with none of our modern day technology what-so-ever, yet their security aspect couldn't be improved upon, except for one fatal flaw, assuming that we manage to get out of here alive."

"What was that then?" she asked.

He replied immediately, "Seems to me the one flaw was that the sealer of the vault sealed his own death warrant. Of course he knew he would soon die because he most likely volunteered to be the eternal guardian. However as fate would have it, when he died he must have fallen over and his body rested on the sealed bung, and when you lifted the bung the skeleton fell out. Do you remember there was a pungent smell when the lid was opened? Well, that was a poisonous gas that had been trapped and hermetically sealed up here for all those thousands of years. Not only that, the keeper of the tomb burned candles to use up all the oxygen. If you look over there, he shone the torch on a dozen or so half burnt candles.

We should thank the lord you took such a fright and fell down, there's no doubt it saved our lives, if that hadn't happened we would have both come up here and died exceedingly quickly." He decided to test the air by striking a match and explained to her to keep an eye on the flame for if it flickers rapidly and grows smaller then they must retreat immediately, he struck a match and handed it to her to hold and they watched as it burnt evenly along its full length, indicating it was quite safe to remain. Lifting the ladder he placed it on the floor in the direction of the painting, and explained to her that the floor or indeed the ceiling, could conceal a trap, I have still to work out how the avalanche was triggered.

Before they attempted to walk on the ladder he inspected the ceiling above it and to their amazement they found another identical round stone bung.
"It would be really interesting to find out what's up there," he said, "but we shall never know, for there is no way that I am even going to think about it. I'm all for a quick look round here to see if we can find anything to help us to escape, that is our first priority."
Lighting a match she followed him as he gingerly crawled along the ladder stopping regularly to check the floor for any signs of a trap, all went well and they reached the picture on the wall, and standing on the side of the ladder as a security precaution, they examined the picture in more detail. When they had first seen it from a distance it appeared to be a picture hanging from the wall, however on closer examination it could be seen to be actually painted on the very smooth wall. She lit another match and was able to observe the picture from a side angle which made her gasp.

"It's a picture of the legendary giant bird."

Squinting his eyes he stared at the picture as close as he could but had to concede that he could not see the bird.

"Let me show you," she said, "I know you don't understand so let me explain."

She moved in front of him and got closer to the picture and holding the torch she excitedly pointed to a large brown domed circle and said, "There it is," and she traced with her finger round a ring of robed men all with long hair who were encircling a large bird. She then went on tracing out the many other figures and salient points of the picture to him.

So far he had not understood anything about this picture because as far as he could make out the drawing depicted an ancient civilisation trying to attack a fortification. Shining the torch further up the wall he saw something which really astonished him, there before him was the picture which had been branded on his mind, the two mountains with peaks off similar height and the smaller one in between and there at the base of the smaller mountain could be clearly seen the outline of the actual cave entrance, he pointed to the spot and said,

"Yes that's where we are right now." The more he looked at the picture the greater the feeling of foreboding he had. There was no disputing that this place held the key to some great mystery.

It was totally uncanny and anyone who believes in the supernatural, then this was the place to be. They moved on a little further and had a look at some of the artefacts, which were neatly leaning against the walls. They were still moving with extreme caution and were still using the ladder to walk on, however as he pushed it in front of him he accidentally knocked over an earthenware jug, which incredibly did not break. He crawled along the ladder very cautiously to study the spilt contents, and stared in disbelief he then called to her to come over and have a look at what he had found,

"If I'm not mistaken," he continued, "these are nuggets of pure gold."

Scooping up a handful of them he offered them to her, saying, "These are definitely gold, feel the weight of them." She chose an average sized one about the size of a pea, which after inspection she handed back. He very carefully gathered up the scattered nuggets and returned them to the jar. The lid of the jar had a very interesting design in the form of an inscription upon it, these symbols were very similar to those of the present day and Cheng Eng was able to decipher them.

She read aloud, "Gold is bright, but this gold will never see daylight." As she replaced the lid, he said, "Never was there a truer inscription written, and I can see there are many jars like this, which no doubt all contain valuables, but I think we will leave them alone."

Moving on, they came to a large collection of bamboo poles and gathered two of them. One with a large diameter and another of a smaller diameter that fitted inside it. Their idea being to use them, telescopic fashion, and push them through the snow which was blocking the cave entrance and allow them an air intake.

"I'll tell you what," he said, "let's collect them on the road back, if you hang on here I'll climb over the poles and see what's on the other side."

When he got over the poles he could see many more of the large containers, and all had lids on them, again with inscriptions. He examined the contents of the nearest two, one was full of rice and the other had dried herbs, he put a large handful of each into his pockets being fully aware they were almost out of their own foodstuff.

Moving his torch around he could see many different things some of which he didn't recognise and once again he decided to leave well alone. Resolving to leave them undisturbed because of the dangers involved and there was also the problem of time, which was rapidly running out for them.

He was in for another shock when he saw over to his extreme left, many skeletons piled up to the ceiling and still wearing their fancy robes. Not wanting her to see them he quickly scrambled back over the pile of bamboo poles and back to where she was. He went on to explain to her all that he had seen, apart from the gruesome find of the huge pile of skeletons.

Collecting the two poles they cautiously made their way over to the opposite wall intending to make their exit that way. Before they could reach the exit however, they encountered a huge bundle of thin bamboo canes all bound together with what looked like leather thongs, on both ends of each cane was a narrow sharp head with serrated razor-sharp edges and constructed with what appeared to be bone and certainly not stone. They were obviously spears of some description but why be double ended?

There must have been a reason for it but the two of them were certainly baffled, lying next to this pile was a smaller bundle of these nasty looking spearheads, probably used as replacements; they were also tied with leather thongs, looking at the spears very closely they went on to speculate as to their use and in particular their peculiar double-ended design, but neither of them could come to any firm conclusions.

The next items they came upon were a culmination of specially shaped stone tools of every conceivable design some appeared to have been used while others were mostly brand new. They would have liked to spend a little more time examining them but were most conscious of the fact that they were very close to the other sealed up hole in the roof, and neither of them would have been in the least surprised if these instruments were booby trapped in some way, they also knew that these ancient people had gone to great lengths to protect their property. "Who knows what is up there," he said, "that bung could be holding back a million gallons of water just waiting to be let loose and drown all intruders."

She laughed and suggested he was getting paranoid and that they had better move on quickly.

The next group of items they could see by the torch light, on the floor, were rows of unused candles stacked up high for about a yard along the wall, in front of them were candle holders all exactly the same as the one beside the tomb guardian. In front of them was a row of small stone bowls each containing what looked like dried moss and to one side of the moss there were bowls filled with some black powdery substance. Finally beside each bowl were neatly laid out diamond shaped stones, although they were roughly made, each was highly coloured and different from its neighbour.

"What do you make of them?" Cheng Eng asked.

"I could be wrong" he answered, "but I think they are ancient man's fire, a bit like today's matches. Looks like they would have used the stones to create a spark to light the powder and moss, from which they could light the candles."

"Why don't you give it a try?" she said, lifting a bowl and two of the diamond shaped stones and handing them to him. He very soon got the hang of it and striking the two stones together sent a shower of sparks into the bowl from which there was a small puff of smoke followed by a flash of fire as the moss ignited, it gave off a lovely smell, not unlike that of lavender.

Spotting a very large bowl, he heard her gasp when his torch lit up the inscription on its lid. "It's dated," she said, "it's dated 25,000 years ago," she continued excitedly, "Quick! Shine the torch on the wall picture again, yes that answers it all," she said after studying the picture.

"Hold on a minute," he said, "slow down a bit you have lost me, what are you on about?"

Looking at her he could see she had great difficulty

in containing her excitement. She took a deep breath and explained. "Look at the picture on the wall it shows snow only on the very top of the mountains, that would be correct way back then but since then the climatic change has given us snow almost half way down the mountains."

"Sounds logical," he agreed, while having a look in the large container. It was full of rounded stones ranging in size from that of a hens egg to that of a goose.

She said, "I know what they are for, they fit in the end of these long poles just like on the picture over there. I well remember my grandmother explaining to me how the warriors used these poles to propel stones up to ten times as far as they could throw them by hand. I didn't quite understand how at the time, but now I do."

They were now at the open hole in the floor, he dropped down to the cave and after collecting the two hollow poles from her he helped her down beside him, as they moved from the cavern and through into the cave they both stopped and stared in disbelief, for there right before them at the cave mouth where they had been digging only a few hours ago, was a large opening into the outside world. When the reality of the situation finally got through to them they hugged, kissed and danced for joy, it was their way of expressing their great joy with the miracle that they were no longer going to die.

They agreed on a course of action, while she was repacking the rucksacks he would return the poles along with the skeleton and the bung, to their original position. Whilst agreeing with him she mentioned that it would take him some time to gather up the skeleton to enable its replacement. "Anyway, she said, better you than me for that job."

Returning the items, he used the same precautionary measures as before, although he felt sorely tempted to drop the poles and run, before he left he could not resist having one final look at that magnificent wall painting completed so long ago. Here was probably the most expensive and valuable picture in the world and many times more secure than those present day ones with all their sophisticated alarm systems.

He was suddenly brought back to reality by her calling out. "Are you all right up there John? I'm packed and ready to go." "Yes!" He shouted back, "I'm fine I'll be with you soon." He crawled back along the ladder to the tomb entrance and replaced the ladder exactly where it had been, he came back and collected the robed skeleton and only then when handling it in the light was he able to inspect it more fully, it was dressed in a beautifully made one piece outfit fashioned from a soft animal hide and dyed in a lovely purple hue. He had nothing but admiration and respect for those early Tailors. After finally replacing the bung as best he could, he rejoined Cheng Eng who was waiting for him and ready to go. Soon after they had squeezed through the narrow gap and had travelled about five hundred yards from the cave, there was a most tremendous roar.

The very ground shook beneath their feet and they both turned and looked on in terror as a mighty avalanche of snow completely covered the exit they had just left and within seconds there was absolutely no sign of the cave's entrance. It was frightening to think that just a few minutes before they would have most certainly been sealed in that cave for life, had he taken just a little longer looking at the cloak covering the skeleton! She was the first to break the silence when she said,

"You know John, this story is so fantastic, if you told anyone about it and what has just happened I think they would be inclined to think we would be telling them a tall story and dismiss it, as being beyond the realms of possibility."

"It's really uncanny," he replied, "I wonder just what is up there above that second bung hole. I wonder if we have been under constant surveillance, very strange how we got an escape route supplied and then sealed again as soon as we left, perhaps it's the work of ancient supernatural spirits, who saw that we did not steal even one gold nugget and were merciful towards us and allowed us to escape."

Continuing on their journey he felt that now that they were far away from the cave it would be safe to tell her of his frightening experience when he found the room full of skeletons, when he had finished with his graphic explanation and missing out no detail however small. She said that she appreciated not knowing about it until now, as it is quite enough to frighten the wits out of her now, never mind being told while she was there next to them.

It was midday now and still light, there was no sign of the green snow, further evidence that it was not noticeable until after dark. He reckoned on reaching 'sharp ridge camp' by nightfall, provided they did not encounter any more blizzards or other hold-ups. Walking was comfortable, as the wind, which was light, was on their backs and helping them along. They were feeling great and almost had a spring in their step. "That reminds me," said John, "you promised to explain the story your Grandmother told you about the giant bird we saw on the wall painting."

"Ah! Yes!" she said, "as soon as I set eyes on the painting I knew right away that it depicted the story of the giant bird, which came to our land way back in the mists of time. It was round with no apparent wings; just a huge round bird, which caused a reign of terror in all the land. It would swoop from the sky and grab people with its talons and they were never seen again. Some urgent decision had to be reached regarding action to kill this creature. So three Hundred warriors were gathered and they went on a hunting expedition to hunt down the bird. When it landed they intended to surround it and bombard it with stones, not one person returned from that hunting expedition, but the big bird was also never seen again.

These hunters were the most efficient soldiers of their time and if the methods they used were practised in today's modern armies and using modern weapons. I am sure they would be the most efficient military force in the world.

Cheng Eng said it should be possible in this day and age to have specially designed vehicles, which would be fitted out with a high standard of technology with hydraulics, computers etc. It would have laser shields making it almost indestructible and making most modern tanks obsolete overnight.

"All very well," he replied, "but such a machine would never go on sale on the open market. Its use would throw the worlds economy into turmoil, this world requires oil, coal, gas etc and their use keep millions of people in employment. Someday the world's natural resources will come to an end but hopefully they will still have the sun. It's easy to see why early man worshiped the sun and the picture on the wall confirmed that these people were sun worshipers."

They had been walking now for four hours and they were down at the base of sharp ridge mountain so they stopped for an hour's rest, when they were sitting comfortably he took some of the old grain from his pocket and gave her half. "These grains are a bit old, he said, "I got them from the cave."

"Not to worry" she answered "I'm hungry enough to eat an ox." John did his best to make the ancient grain sound palatable but considered at least it would still retain some food value. "It may taste like eating old straw," he said. "I can't wait to get back to civilisation and get our first real meal in six months, a large steak, chips, peas Lancashire puddings with gravy."

"Ok, you've got my mouth watering," she said, "I'll just have to use my imagination."

They popped some of the rice into their mouths. It

didn't stay there long as they had to spit it out because it was so hard it was like trying to eat gravel. They then tried some of the dried herbs and found them most palatable. It was soon time to start their four-hour journey to their camp but they were both so drowsy and tired that they fell asleep just where they were. How long they slept was anyone's guess. He woke with a start when Cheng Eng was throwing her arms around and shouting "Get off me you brute"

He rubbed his eyes again because he couldn't see anything, so what an earth was she shouting and going on about. Jumping to his feet he couldn't believe what he saw, a few feet away was a sun drenched beach and laid out on the sand under a palm tree was a beautiful young, brown-skinned woman wearing a grass skirt, and very little else. She had long black hair down to her waist, and wore a garland of flowers over her shoulders which did not hide her young firm looking breasts. She turned her head towards him and smiled, then she beckoned with her hand for him to come and join her.

By now his mind was oblivious to Cheng Eng's shouts He couldn't resist the urge to go to the young woman as she beckoned. Like steel to a magnet he tried to reach her however as he quickly approached she appeared to be going further and further away. So he started to run, his last recollection was just as he got to her, she whacked him on the head with a huge wooden club.

After that, nothing, until he was being violently shaken again and again. Opening his eyes he realised it was night time and could just make out Cheng Eng leaning over him saying, "Are you alright? I've been here for hours trying to revive you. You have been out for hours after running head first into that rock face there. I saw you do it but I couldn't help you as I was fighting off a monster of a man who I had to push into a ravine."

"A monster man you pushed into? a ravine?" He asked, "there's nothing like that around here."

"Oh yes there is," she replied,

"I saw him fall over when I pushed him and I saw him lying dead at the bottom of the ravine. I'll show you when it's light."

He had a headache, the mother of all headaches, he had suffered many a sore head, but nothing remotely as bad as this, and placing his hands up to his forehead he felt a large dressing. She informed him that he had a nasty gash on his forehead; she had cleaned the wound as soon as she could, but it was quite a considerable time after the incident before she could get to the first aid kit because she had fallen down in a state of exhaustion after battling with the monster of a man.

"Well." he said, "we'll see about the monster man in the morning, we'll still be here, because there's one thing for certain. We can't make a move until daylight and the way my head feels right now if it's not any better by daylight I won't feel like going anywhere. My head feels as if it is being subjected to a hundred hangovers all at the same time and my throat is parched dry. I'm dying for a mug of coffee or tea but there is no chance of that until we get up to sharp ridge camp where our provisions are."

Cheng Eng offered to go and get a cup of water for them both; she took the torch with her over to the rucksacks, and returned a few minutes later with two mugs of water in one hand and the torch in the other, and after accepting a mug of water he propped himself up and drank the whole lot in one go. He then asked her if she could do him another favour by getting a cloth, soaking it in cold water and bathing his forehead,

"No problem!" she said putting down her mug.

Later with the wet cloth she gently bathed his forehead, and round to his temples. He thanked her and said she would make a good nurse because she had that special sympathetic touch, she explained that she had done a first aid course, but that's as far as it went.

"After I pushed the monster man away," she added,

"I arrived to find you out for the count, the first thing I did was check your pulse rate and then I knew you would eventually come round but you concussed yourself by running into that rock face. I just couldn't understand it, I thought you were chasing after something."

"I was," he replied,

"when I wakened up, you were shouting while throwing your arms around, and screaming at something imaginary, I couldn't see what you were trying to thump, I was coming to your assistance when I saw this most beautiful woman beckoning to me, the closer I got, the further away she seemed to be, so that's why I started running towards her, last thing I remember was getting up beside her, then she lifted a huge wooden club and smashed it onto my forehead.

"Well how nice of you John," she replied sarcastically, "I think you got your priorities all wrong, rather than assist me, you discarded me for someone more attractive to you, she snaps her fingers and you go running to her."

"I know how it looks to you, and yes, my actions were totally out of order and inexcusable," he said, "but we both suffered the effects of being blown out of our minds on drugs."

"Drugs?" She retorted, "are you mad? What are you on about?"

"Yes drugs," he repeated, "and I know the source, remember when we both ate a handful of what we thought was centuries old dried herbs? and soon after we both fell into a sound sleep? Well they were herbs all right, quite an illegal herb, drugs in other words. The effects of the drugs when we awoke made us hallucinate and become quite fearless. There is a drug problem today among our young people, but just think of what it would have been like twenty five thousand years ago, it is believed they gave these drugs to their troops before going into battle to make them totally immune to fear."

"Well now, all that you have said certainly ties in," she said, "and makes sense, but it was so real, it seems impossible to believe it was all a dream, but now the more I think about it the more sense it makes. I would normally be scared stiff at the very thought of meeting a monster man and yet when I did meet one I had no fear whatsoever, it's

153

just difficult to accept that it was all just a figment of our imagination."

"Never mind," he said,

"its over and done with now, let's cuddle up close and try to get some sleep and look forward to a fresh start in the morning."

He was the first to awake in the morning and was delighted that his headache had gone; when Cheng Eng wakened he asked her how she felt. She yawned and replied, "I am raring to go and I'm ready to climb up to sharp ridge camp for a welcome mug of coffee and some food."

"I'll second that," he replied, "but before we go, are you quite satisfied there is no monster here?"

"Oh yes, I'm perfectly happy with the situation now and I accept it was all a drug related fantasy," she said with a smile.

As they climbed towards the campsite, they found the going very tough and were forced to take a break every twenty-minutes or so to get their breath back. It took them fully five hours to reach the camp by midday. The journey had taken so much out of them they decided to rest up there until the following morning, before moving on to the next base camp. During their hours of rest, he tried to find the cave mouth using his binoculars but was quite unable to do so, the avalanche had done a good job by keeping it well hidden until the next thaw perhaps.

He was delighted to observe an eagle feeding its young in a nest high up on the mountain, even using his binoculars he was unable to get a close enough view to recognise the breed. Whatever kind it was, it surely could fly and must have covered many miles in search of food for there was very little, if any, suitable food in this barren wasteland. After they had their meal and a hot drink, which they both thoroughly enjoyed they were able to set their tent up in a sheltered area away from the biting ice-cold winds, and although it was only midday they went to bed and slept right through until very late evening.

It was dark when they wakened and after another refreshing hot drink they sat at the tent door with the binoculars watching that vivid spot of green snow which was getting much brighter as the night wore on. They took turns each with the binoculars. They discussed between them at length all that had happened just recently, and the only conclusion that they could fully agree on was that a supernatural power was at work.

"Just a pity we hadn't thought of bringing back something from the cave to prove our point, you know, perhaps footwear or the like," he said,

"I remember years ago as a boy my father showed me an old Roman shoe which he had found while digging a ditch. The shoe was later dated as two thousand years old and the leather was as good as new."

"Oh no," she replied, "I'm so glad we took nothing and left things as we found them. I fear had we disturbed or stolen anything we would still be there, remember the relief we felt when we were freed."

They spent many hours talking and having their final

look at the green snow, being well aware that they would not be in this area in the dark again. Next morning she prepared breakfast while he explained a theory he had regarding the big bird, perhaps it had been captured and held down from flying with many heavy stones.

The next six weeks of retracing their steps from campsite to campsite in all weather conditions took their toll and they arrived back in civilisation worn out, dishevelled, scruffy, and dirty. Their first priority was to find suitable accommodation and it must posses a bath or shower. Cheng Eng had asked directions from a resident and had been directed to a place called 'The weary travellers resting home'

"Well it is aptly named," he said. "Let's hope it has comfortable beds I've almost forgotten what it's like to sleep in a real bed, oh! and I hope they have some suitable shaving facilities as I'm desperate to get rid of this beard of mine."

She started to laugh and told him that if anyone should look at his passport they would take him as an impostor. Keeping their eyes peeled they eventually found the place they had been directed to, crossing the street they approached it but were immensely disappointed to see that it was only a café They were both feeling very dejected and depressed almost to the point of tears and it took all their efforts to keep control and not to curse their luck. They looked around in vain for an entrance other than the one leading into the café. Deciding that at least they would get a meal they made their way in and sat down. A small solidly built waiter approached the table and accepted their order from Cheng Eng who spoke his language.

After a fairly lengthy wait he arrived with their order of boiled rice and mixed vegetables. She thanked the waiter and got into a conversation with him, after which he bowed politely and left. She noticed John's enquiring glance, so she explained to him that the waiter had said enjoy your meal.

As they were finishing off their meal she said to him, "Would you like a surprise?"

"What!" He replied, "another one? I thought I had my share of surprises for today but go on then surprise me."

"Well," she said, "I asked the waiter just now to recommend a place to stay and would you believe it, he puts people up here."

"Indeed that is a surprise," he said, while looking under the table then added. "I am looking under here for the bed. This place is so small I can't see where the bedrooms are and I don't mind telling you that if this place does not have a bath then I am off to pitch the tent up at the edge of town."

It was now just after four in the afternoon and other customers were coming in and ordering afternoon coffee. Although John and Cheng Eng had thoroughly enjoyed their meal and the added luxury of sitting at a table after such a long time roughing it. The presence of other customers made them feel embarrassed, when they noticed how well dressed the strangers were and remembering just how scruffy they were.

Nevertheless when the waiter returned to clear the table. She asked him for coffee, John suggested that when he returned with their drinks. She should ask him details of the accommodation and not to forget to enquire about a hot bath and also what day the once a week bus departs.

They had decided to take the bus, saving themselves an eighty-mile hike back to the town where she worked.
"You know dear that when we get back to your place of work, we must part company," he said. "For I have many flights to catch to get home from there. It will be one of the saddest days of my life when we part and I am so thankful to have had you with me throughout this expedition."

Cheng Eng with tears running down her face and choked up with emotional sorrow whispered,
"I wish we could be together for ever and ever." He realized that he had upset her prematurely in mentioning the unenviable parting that had to come. As they finished their drinks he handed some money to her as payment for their meals and lodgings, which she handed to the little fat waiter. Who proceeded to pull aside a curtain beside a window behind them. He then pressed a button on the wall and a door slid aside revealing a very narrow staircase, so narrow in fact that the rucksacks were unable to fit in to it. John thought surely this must be so narrow it should be in the Guinness book of records. Reaching the top of the stairway they could see at the end of a long narrow corridor the one and only bathroom beside the room they had been given.

Walking along the corridor could only be done single

file and it reminded him of his younger days when the corridors in trains were every bit as narrow, the passengers could only pass each other by turning sideways. Entering the bathroom they were both in for a very pleasant surprise. The room was very large and fitted out in beautiful mosaic patterns of tiles. The bath itself could only be described as king size and was supported by cast iron legs with fancy claw shaped ornamental feet. "My," he exclaimed, "I'm sure this is the biggest bath I have ever seen and look here! Look at the sign on the end of the bath, it say's 'Shanks, made in England' it's amazing to think this has come all the way from England and it's obviously been here a while, long before that stairwell was built that's for sure."

Really excited now, she insisted that they have a look in their room. The room was small and very basic, it had neither toilet nor washbasin, just two single beds a chair and an old wardrobe. However to them it was sheer luxury compared to their tent, so they decided that it would do them just fine but there was a problem with the rucksacks and how to get them into the room. Looking from the window he could see the street below and believed that with a rope he could pull them up one at a time.

Returning downstairs they asked the little fat man, who was shaped like an apple with legs and arms, where the toilet was, he told them it was at the opposite end of the corridor to the bathroom. He also gave them permission to use their rope to get the bags into their room. When he explained to them the charges, they were in for another

159

surprise, because one week's board here was less than one night in the snobbish hotel they had used on their last visit. He also told them the bus was due to leave town in two days time on Friday.

They carried their rucksacks out into the street underneath their room window. John made his way upstairs with his mountain rope, while she remained with the rucksacks waiting on him dropping down the rope, by the time he dropped her the rope from the window a large crowd of spectators had crowded round her and all seemed extremely amused at this spectacle before them. Slowly but surely and inch by inch he manhandled the heavy rucksack up to the window where his problems really began, it took quite a bit of huffing and puffing to manoeuvre the bag through the window. There was a loud cheer from the spectators when the bag finally disappeared through the window.

The next bag, which was Cheng Eng's, was much lighter and smaller than his and took half the time to get it into the room. There were no cheers this time as the spectators had all drifted away, and the show was over. Shortly after she had rejoined him in their bedroom, they could hardly wait to get their smelly clothes off and to soak in that lovely bath. Two hours later at eight o'clock they reluctantly emerged from the giant size bath, which they had shared together. They had no words that could describe just how wonderfully refreshed they were now feeling. They felt like members of the human race again and not some dirty smelly animals. Both had changed into clean clothing and John looked twenty years younger now that his beard was off.

At nine O'clock they decided to try downstairs for a coffee before retiring for the evening. However when they slipped the downstairs door aside, they found the dining room in total darkness, returning to the bedroom they made their own hot drink using the little gas stove which had served them so well in the wilderness. They sat sipping their hot coffee and discussed their current clothing situation, he said he was quite prepared to sell off most of their mountaineering gear and purchase new more suitable clothing as he didn't fancy continuing in heavy mountaineering boots. She laughed and said,
"I totally agree with that action, I have had enough of this Eskimo suit and to be frank I hope I never have to wear one ever again."

Both of them were in agreement that although their trip had been a once in a lifetime experience that they would never forget, for now they were quite sure they did not want to climb any more mountains ever again. He said,
"When you consider how we met and all the adventures we've been through together, it cannot be coincidental. I believe that some supernatural power is in control of our destiny and to quote the holy Bible God moves in mysterious ways his wonders to perform."
"You will get no argument from me on that John," she replied,
"from the moment we first met I have felt the hand of providence guide my every action and that's why I find it

so difficult we have to part."

"You know Cheng Eng that I feel exactly the same way but we must have some sense of reality and when the time comes we will have to part, and talking about reality. I do hope the photographs we took on our journey turn out, otherwise we will have no way of convincing the press and other media that we have uncovered proof of the ancient saga of the green snow and the giant bird."

4

Fear the Green Snow

John lay awake and watched the morning light slowly penetrate all the corners of their bedroom. He also listened to the morning chorus of his native Scottish blackbirds as they sang their hearts out in greeting the new dawn. He glanced down at the sleeping girl beside him and remembered the turmoil of both of their minds when they thought they must part forever at the end of their long trail of discovery.

Now he was back in his native land and in his own home and with Cheng Eng beside him. She lay on her back breathing through her mouth and her slightly parted lips showed the gleaming white of her young teeth. She stirred slightly, shifting to her side and the covers came off her shoulders. One milk white breast was now exposed to his view and he noted the fine tracery of small blue veins showing beneath the white skin. The areola was a pale reddish colour topped with a small pink nipple.

John passed his thumb over the flaccid looking nipple and watched it instantly firm up. She stirred again and groaned in her sleep and feeling guilty, John pulled the covers over them both and cupped her breast in his hand

163

under the covers as he did so. He then lay there, enjoying the bird song outside in their garden.

Almost asleep he became aware of the voices once more. Voices which did not appear to come from human throats but from the flitting shadows which skipped through his brain. At first the voices were completely incoherent then suddenly John heard the words they were chanting clearly.

"Never never go,   to the Green Snow
Red for Stop and   Green for Go
No Go Near the   Bright Green Snow"

John gasped when he realised the words the voices were chanting were identical to those he had read in the ancient book. He sat up, bolt upright and shook his head violently to stop the voices but if anything they only became louder.

"NEVER NEVER GO,   TO THE GREEN SNOW
RED FOR STOP AND   GREEN FOR GO
NO GO NEAR THE   BRIGHT GREEN SNOW

He let out a yell of fear which instantly awoke Cheng Eng. She sat up and John's eyes told her of his great fright. She gripped his head and pulled it down on to her bare breasts and the voices stopped immediately.

John sobbed uncontrollably for some time as she cradled him in her arms, before he recovered sufficiently to tell her what had happened. She made no comment and for once she was showing a stronger temperament that he had not seen before. She lifted his head in both hands and kissed him on the mouth. His mouth clung to hers and shifting his body on to her he lay between her thighs and gratefully penetrated her. He began to thrust in and out of her body with a greater urgency than he had ever done before. He also found himself going faster and faster and trying to go deeper and deeper into her body. Whether it was caused by his fright or not, the sex act between them that morning was the best they had ever experienced. Afterwards totally worn out they both fell into a deep sleep.

He was again the first to awaken and he lay thinking of their last days spent together in Tibet. He remembered wanting to give her a present that might remind her of him after they finally parted company. He decided to give her his Binoculars, then something more valuable later on. He could actually recall the exact words he had used on that occasion.

5

Thoughts on the Universe

"Would you to be kind enough to get the binoculars from my rucksack beside you?" John asked and she obligingly handed him the glasses. He took up a position at the open window and then gave her the glasses telling her to focus on one of the stars.

"Look at them," he said, "there are billions of them, it is known that there are more stars in the universe than there are grains of sand on earth. I want you to imagine while you are looking at them through the glasses, that one of those planets had life on its surface so long ago in time, that our planet was part of the sun. On the planet you will be looking at, their day lasted a thousand years and their night was also a thousand years.

Life evolved to cope with that, everything flourished and was active in the thousand years of light, but when the thousand years of darkness fell, everything went into a state of hibernation. The Bible tells us that a blink of God's eye is a thousand years, so it is quite possible that millions of years ago there were people with technology well in advance of anything we have now. Letting you look at the stars is the best way I can explain my theories to you." She was totally fascinated by his explanations and was delighted when he gifted the binoculars to her. "I will treasure these for ever," she said, "and when I look at the stars through them I will ever remember our time together." She threw her arms around his neck and gave him a long and passionate kiss.

After the necessary toiletries and washing up, he went to bed. She was still looking at the stars when he bid her goodnight. In the morning he had shaved and was relaxing on top of his bed while Cheng Eng still slept. Today, he was thinking would be a day where there was no rush, they could take their time, sell their obsolete camping accessories and just have a general look around. He lay there thinking what would be going on thousands of miles away at home in Langwathby and how Ruby would be coping with the twins and her self-employed business. He knew that it was going to be difficult parting from Cheng Eng whose companionship had proved to be of incalculable value during the now completed mission.

What kind of gift could he buy her to show his gratitude? He knew the binoculars he had given her were quite inadequate even although she loved them, so he must be on the look out for something more appropriate. When she eventually did wake it was almost ten 'o clock and after she dressed and washed they prepared to go downstairs for breakfast. She told him that she had spent half the night looking at the stars and was convinced that there must be life on other planets. "I got such a buzz from looking at them, I want to take up astrology seriously and I am going to study and take it up professionally. I feel it will be much more interesting than teaching, and that's all thanks to you."

When they arrived at the downstairs café all the tables were taken except one, as they sat down at the vacant table she started to giggle and whispered,

"Did you see these people's faces, they must be thinking that we appeared out of nowhere just walked right out of a wall, there is no sign to be seen of the door when it's shut and as you know it is silent in opening. One minute they are looking at an empty table then all of a sudden we're sitting at it."

He laughed, as he too could see the funny side of it, they were both still laughing and giggling when the little tubby waiter came to take their order and as usual she was left to do the talking. She spoke with the waiter for some time and as soon as he had left she explained to John that she had asked him if he knew where they could sell their rucksacks and other items. He had recommended Aladdin's cave, and had gone on to give full instructions on how to get there.

She couldn't get a word in sideways to tell him that they already knew how to get there, since that was where they had bought most of the gear in the first place.

"Well you can't fault him for being friendly," he replied, "tomorrow we must make an effort to have an early breakfast, because the bus leaves at ten, when the waiter comes back find out what time he starts breakfast and when he shuts up shop at night. If we sell the stove then we won't be able to make our own hot drinks any more. I'll tell you something I found very odd last night, I didn't hear a sound, I would have thought the other residents would have made some noise, don't you?"

"To tell you the truth," she replied. "I think we are the only ones here. You would never think this place is anything other than a café. We almost moved on, didn't we! I doubt if we would have enquired about a bed if that stranger I asked had not recommended it to us, mind you I still think it's peculiar that we were not required to sign any register, so there just might be more going on here than meets the eye, however time will tell."

"Maybe he has tax problems or something like that, and only takes in the occasional boarder on the side," he replied.

Just then the little waiter brought them their breakfasts of eggs bacon, sausages and all the trimmings, John could hardly take his eyes off his plate, even when Cheng Eng followed the waiter over to the counter. This was the first real breakfast they had had in months and he got tucked in, not even waiting for her to return. When she did return she explained between eating her meal that the café is open from six in the morning until six at night, but as they are boarders they only have to call the waiter by pressing a bell on the counter, which he had pointed out to her, and they would be served until ten at night.

In the morning they had to go through the procedure of lowering the rucksacks from the window to the ground and just as a few days before, they drew a large crowd of onlookers. There was a bit of a mishap when he burnt his hands on the rope when he lost his grip and it slipped through his hands, allowing the bag to drop to the ground with a thud, narrowly missing those below. He spent ten minutes running his hands under cold water to lessen the pain.

When he joined her outside she had already made arrangements with a taxi to take them to Aladdin's cave and return four hours later for them. It would be fairly expensive but well worth it, considering the walk they were being saved. With some difficulty they managed to get the entire luggage and themselves safely in the taxi and off they went and arrived after about a ten-minute drive. They paid the driver, who according to his name badge was called Ackmeed Singh, and arranged for him to return to the exit end of the cave for them.

In the store they were directed to the stock room and there an assistant instructed them to put all the items for sale on a long wide conveyor belt. Then an elderly man carrying a clipboard inspected the items and took note of the ones they were prepared to buy. He accepted all of the goods and then gave Cheng Eng a carbon copy of his notes along with directions of where to collect payment. Having collected their money they went on a spending spree, she bought herself a full rig out including a dress, blouse, jersey, and shoes.

He bought himself a suit, shoes, and shirt. He also spotted just the very present to give to her by way of a thank you for all her help. It was an astrologer's telescope with an adjustable tripod stand. He said, "It would have been nicer to give you this as a surprise, but surprise or not I'm sure you will get endless hours of enjoyment from this."

"Why John I'm delighted," she said. "I can hardly wait to try it out, and with the binoculars there should be nothing holding me back now."

On their departure they found Akmeed and his taxi awaiting them and he immediately took them back to the café. Later while they were enjoying a meal the little fat waiter asked them if they had received a good price for the sale of their goods. He also asked them if they would like to be wakened in the morning. They graciously refused saying that they were normally early risers and should be up in plenty of time for their ten o'clock departure.

However it would be most helpful if he would recommend evening entertainment for them. The waiter explained that in the town hall they had traditional dancing each evening, the dancers wear traditional costumes and each dance tells a story.

"A bit like your ballet dancing," explained Cheng Eng.

Because it was a cloudy sky, and she would be unable to do her stargazing they decided to attend. After changing into their new clothes and feeling great they went downstairs for a coffee. The café was empty so they were served right away, she asked the tubby waiter how they would get in tonight should they be late back. He told them just to press the doorbell outside and he would arrange their entry, he then gave them directions on how to get to the dancing. It was only a few minutes away and they had to wait in a queue waiting for the doors to open, after a short while they started slowly shuffling forward and slowly but surely they edged their way nearer the open doorway. They paid their admission fee at the door and just managed to get a seat in the hall, which was filling up fast. After a while there wasn't an empty seat to be seen In fact it was so full there were people squatting down on the floor and on the walkways, however there were many seats in a balcony area upstairs and they were empty. The reason why soon became apparent, they must have been reserved and soon they were taken up by European tourists, and it looked like there were busloads of them.

As soon as everyone had settled down, the lights went down and the stage curtain opened, an English speaking compare arrived and welcomed everyone. Particularly the foreign visitors, it was obvious they were getting preferential treatment. The show started off with twenty female dancers all wearing traditional, beautifully coloured costumes, which appeared to be made from a silk material, which shimmered and sparkled in the multi coloured lights. Their performance was fascinating and riveting, and they were so precise with their dancing rhythm, it had been a pleasure to see them. Alas all too soon the two-hour performance came to an end.

When the curtain closed, the audience showed their appreciation by hand clapping, which seemed as if it would never end. The compere then requested that all remain in their seats to allow the European guests to leave first. He then informed the English-speaking tourists that their coaches were waiting outside. Piped music was played for about ten minutes to give them time to get out and on their busses.

While walking back to their lodgings they talked about the wonderful evening and the great time they had there. When the little fat waiter answered the door of the cafe they excitedly thanked him, and told him of their pleasant evening. Over coffee they discussed what seemed a peculiarity which was the little fat waiter seemed to be a one-man show. He seemed to do everything himself. "Perhaps he has someone working in the background." She said.

"He must have, for there is no way he can get up that narrow staircase to make the beds etc, unless of course he uses a ladder," said John laughing. They stopped talking about the tubby waiter, because he arrived at the table offering them a nightcap in the form of a bowl of fresh fruit and even although they were not hungry they were glad to accept it and give the business to the waiter. Afterwards they were glad they had done so because it was beautifully presented and they thoroughly enjoyed it. By this time they were ready for bed. She had hoped to do a bit of star gazing but was disappointed because of cloudy skies.

Next morning she was up bathed and dressed before he wakened at around eight thirty. Just as they were ready to go downstairs for breakfast he started raking through his pockets and was almost frantic. He realised he had left his passport in a side pocket of the rucksack he had sold to Aladdin's cave warehouse. She tried to calm him down and told him to leave it with her as she would go and see the fat waiter for his help. She explained the situation to the waiter who was extremely helpful and went to telephone for a taxi. She immediately returned to explain the situation to John.

Shortly after, the taxi arrived for them and soon they were speeding along on the road to the warehouse. On arrival they were fortunate enough to make contact with the youth who had dealt with them the day before and as luck would have it. He remembered them and was able to tell them that the rucksack had not been sold but had gone to their cleaning, come renovation department.

He invited them in and preceded them into the storeroom, which was piled high with all kinds of objects. He stopped beside a man made mountain of clothing and other items. To say they were disappointed would be an under statement as they thought there would be nothing easier than collecting the rucksack. Undeterred the youth obtained a ladder and scrambled to the top of the pile and completely out of sight.

Sometime later a rucksack dropped down without any warning and landed almost at their feet but unfortunately it was the wrong one. So they shouted up to him that their bag was a green one, and not coloured blue. John offered to come up and help since he knew exactly what the bag looked like. His offer of assisting in the search was refused. The youth shouted down to him that it was too dangerous for him to come up on top and that he was not insured for such actions.

John and Cheng Eng took turns in holding the ladder steady against the pile of clothing. Opposite them was another great pile of items, mainly books and magazines. While she held the ladder John had a look at the books. He was astonished to see one written in English called, 'Know your stars' and scooping it up and flicking through the pages he could see at a glance that it would be an excellent present for Cheng Eng. He handed it to her and she had a look at it while they awaited the assistant finding the bag.

She really liked it and saw several chapters that interested her immensely. She could not put it down and was still reading it when another bag was thrown to the ground and this time, thank goodness, it was the one they were after. John very quickly extracted his passport from the pocket. He was also surprised to find that he had left a rather tidy sum of money in the same pocket and remembered he had hidden it there for emergency reasons after he had soaked it in the pool all these months ago, quickly pocketing the money he told her to let the assistant know that he had recovered the passport.

The youth threw down a rope and asked them to tie on the two rucksacks, which he then pulled up and made his way down the ladder to join them on the ground. She spoke with the youth for some time and although John couldn't make out a word they were saying. He could tell by the youth's facial expressions that all was not well. She soon put him in the picture, apparently she had asked the youth if she could purchase the book but he said that because it wasn't priced he was unable to sell it.

"That's ridiculous" John said. "Let me have a go at him, what's his name anyway?"

"You'll never guess in a thousand years!" she replied, "translated into English his name is Toothache."

He laughed and said "That can't be true, come off it!"

"Well that's what he told me," she said, "He said his mother suffered more toothache than childbirth pains when he was being born and that's why she called him that."

"I know what I'd call him," said John, "a pain in the neck, try flashing a few of these notes at him." He took the roll of notes from his pocket and peeled a few off giving them to her.

She then took them over to the youth and started haggling and showing him the notes in her hand and as John watched he noticed that it had worked. Toothache quickly took the notes from her and pocketed them, while at the same time she had a big smile on her face. Because the book had not been paid for officially it had to be smuggled out under John's shirt. He was most reluctant to go through with this as he didn't want to be caught as a shoplifter.

The very thought of this made him cringe but because of her desire for the book he agreed to go through with it, just this one time. He spent a terrified time going through the checkout and after what seemed like ages, they were outside and able to get into the taxi which was waiting for them. The taxi took off at breakneck speed and arrived at the café about nine fifteen, which gave them half and hour to get their breakfast, collect their things and get on the bus. The taxi driver readily accepted their invitation to have breakfast with them by way of expressing their thanks for all his help. The tubby little waiter was on his toes and served the breakfasts in record time. They were so satisfied with the meal, that they gave not only the waiter but also the taxi driver a hefty tip to show appreciation for the extra effort and help they had been given.

When John returned with their entire luggage from upstairs, they said their farewells and returned to the taxi, which took them to the market bus station. Where the bus was waiting, after boarding they were told it wouldn't be leaving for ten minutes, so he decided to have a look around for suitable presents to take home to his wife, the twins and his parents. She said she would remain on the bus to keep their seats and make sure the bus didn't leave without him.

He was unable to find any suitable gifts but did end up buying some oranges and grapes thinking they would come in handy on the bus journey. The bus was full when he returned and he told her about being unable to find any suitable presents but suggested he would have plenty of time later on as he intended staying for a few weeks at the hotel where she had lived and worked as a teacher. The mission he was on originally was for a full six months duration he explained. So he intended spending the last three weeks remaining in Tibet.

After a while he began shuffling around in his seat and then remembered, the reason for his discomfort was the book which he had under his shirt. It was poking into his back and was most uncomfortable and with him being in a public place. He was most unhappy about being unable to retrieve it until he got off the bus. The bus driver started the engine and the well wishers waved their goodbyes. The passengers did the same as we moved away. During the journey, she suggested that while staying at the hotel he could write a novel about the legendary green snow which she thought would make a great novel.

He answered laughingly, "It takes me all my time to write a letter let alone a book but I suppose I could manage it if I put my mind to it. With the money I might make I could pay back Ruby's uncle Reg who sponsored me to the sum of ten thousand pounds." She said, "One thing I would ask, whatever you write in your book please on no account mention the cave and its hidden secrets. Because if that gets around it would soon be robbed and stripped bare."
He replied by saying, "I'm so pleased at being able to escape, it will get no mention from me, its secret will be safe."

The bus trundled along the road very slowly because of the many potholes. On the journey his mind turned to thoughts of the book he could write. He felt he had to include Cheng Eng in it but what would his wife Ruby back home make of it, and would Cheng Eng lose her job? Taking compassionate leave under false pretences?

It was a problem that would have to be ironed out eventually. He knew however that this problem was trivial compared to the wrath he would have to face from his wife and particularly his mother. Both of whom were such pillars of strength and God-fearing women. The thought of being back home in four weeks time made his conscience trouble him considerably. After a slow bone shaking three-hour journey, the bus arrived back at the original hotel. Disembarking from the bus, it was great to stretch their legs again after the one hundred mile journey and also with great relief he retrieved the book from its hiding place under the back of his shirt.

6

Parting is Such Sweet Sorrow

Later when they discussed the situation about them parting company she started to cry and putting both arms around his waist she said

"I can't bear to be parted from you, I know you are married but I am devoted to you and love you more than anything in the whole world, can't I come with you and get a job near you? So we can keep seeing each other, because my life will be an empty vacuum without you."

He was stuck for words, he had to say something to console her and quickly too, for the situation was extremely embarrassing, with her standing sobbing her eyes out in public with so many onlookers, hurriedly placing his luggage on the ground he held her in his arms and whispered in her ear,

"I love you and I will take you back home with me. I could never be at rest if I had gone home without you." Now completely oblivious to the onlookers he gave her a long and passionate kiss. He returned to reality when an elderly lady passer by tripped over his luggage and let out a cry of alarm and pain. Within seconds and as if by magic, a large crowd gathered around and although he could not understand what they were saying it was very obvious that they were hostile to him as a foreigner.

Cheng Eng was quick to grasp the situation and went immediately to the lady and talked with her for a while and soon found out that she needed neither a doctor nor hospital treatment because, apart from being a little shaken. She was ok by this time the crowd had dispersed, the excitement was over for the day. He felt very guilty that he had been responsible for the accident and felt the least he could do was to take the old lady to the local cafe for refreshment. They assisted her over to the cafe and seated her comfortably. She accepted a drink and seemed to perk up soon after. Seeing a taxi rank nearby he thought it prudent to arrange to have the injured lady taken home, so while Cheng Eng went off to arrange the taxi, whose driver agreed to call for them in about ten minutes time. John spent a most uncomfortable ten minutes or so with the old lady. He was literally twiddling his thumbs, because the only way they could communicate with each other was with a look and a smile. When Cheng Eng returned he excused himself and went off to the market stalls for a few necessary items.

He returned just as the taxi arrived for the old lady, they sent her on her way with a generous sum of money and a lovely bouquet of flowers, along with a large basket of fresh fruit, which he had purchased at the market. The old lady was delighted and it was pretty obvious by the way she accepted the cash she was very poor. She waved at them from the taxi until it was out of sight. After about ten minutes walk they arrived at the hotel. Where the receptionist made such a fuss; she was obviously pleased to see Cheng Eng again and almost immediately enquired as to her father's health,

Cheng Eng thanked her and explained that he was slowly recovering. They booked in separately at the reception and Cheng Eng was given a room on the ground floor while he was on the second floor. They both went to her room first where she prepared coffee for them; while he with a great flourish of showmanship handed her the book he had gone to so much trouble over. She immediately started to read it and was so engrossed in the book she barely noticed when he left for his own room, he tapped her on the shoulder saying,
"I shall see you in the dining room when it's time for tea." Barely lifting her eyes from the book she nodded acknowledgement.

He decided to make a start on writing his book and realising he just had time to purchase writing materials before the shops shut. He slipped out of the hotel and sprinted to the shops. He had timed it just right, because after he had purchased the necessary items including paper, pencils etc, the shopkeeper closed up for the night. When he returned to the hotel he resisted the temptation of going to Cheng Eng's room and showing her his writing materials, instead he made his way directly to his own room, which was identical to hers both in size and furnishings. He immediately made use of the facility for making a hot drink, which incidentally, were also identical. He had an hour to pass before the evening meal would be served, his mind was in a turmoil regarding the book he was about to write, and about the reception he would receive when returning home with Cheng Eng in tow. It also bothered him that he had changed his mind about his original thought that in the cave under the green snow, was a giant bird, he now firmly believed that the wall painting depicted not a bird but a spaceship of some description. The time passed very quickly however and he went down to her room to find her still lost in her book. Closing the book when he arrived, she too was surprised that the time had passed so quickly.

Over their meal they had a long discussion and she agreed wholeheartedly to be included in his book. She agreed with him to a slightly lesser degree regarding his theory on the spaceship. She mentioned her intention of going back to work at the school the next day. Saying she would tender her resignation and work the last three weeks while he was still in the country. Later on in her room when they decided it would be dark enough to see the stars. He started to set-up the telescope, while she opened the curtains for the first time and gave a cry of despair. There before them was a view of a brick wall. The wall of the adjoining building to be exact. They decided to try his room to see if the view was any better there and they were not disappointed for they had a clear view of the stars.

Between them they decided that she would move into this room with him and quite unnoticed by anyone they managed to slip her bed and bedding up to his room. She left a note informing the staff where her bed was to be found. It was a beautifully clear night and the stars could be clearly seen. He wasted no time in setting up the telescope and as soon as it was set up, she very quickly looked through the eye glass and started adjusting the focus.

"I'm so disappointed," she said, "no matter how much I adjust this eyepiece I'm unable to see anything other than what I think is a black hole, it's just total blackness."

He couldn't control himself and broke out in laughter. Much to her annoyance as she could not see what was so funny. Until he pointed out that the lens cover was still on the front of the telescope. She immediately saw the funny side and while laughing said. "My, I'm so glad, for a minute I thought I had gone blind in that eye. To be serious though, I'm glad that we didn't buy a `pig in a poke." She soon had it focussed properly and he was surprised just how much she had picked up from the book, in the comparatively short time she had had it. They took turns stargazing with it, sometimes almost fighting over it well into the small hours.

When he awoke in the morning she was still fast asleep. He preferred not to disturb her so he went for breakfast and on his return found her still asleep. He started work on his own book and after what must have been two hours, she finally wakened. "Good morning sleepy head," he said, "you are awake just in time for lunch."

"I'm still very sleepy," she replied. "But I should be OK after I take a shower.

Later on he responded to her request to lather and

wash her back. One thing led to another and before long he was in the shower with her. The antics they got up to in the next half an hour were definitely not stargazing. Although arguably just as exciting and tiring. Their timing was impeccable; they just avoided being caught in the act by the room service staff who entered their room just as they were leaving to go out for lunch.

It was a lovely sunny day when they left the hotel. It was also very warm so they took a leisurely stroll to an outdoor café. Where they ordered a three-course meal, during lunch he told her that he had written six pages of his book and hoped she would give him her opinion on it. After lunch they took a walk to the open-air market where he hoped to buy some presents to take back to his family at home.

They were both very interested in a statue of a man on a horse they saw in the town square. Both thought it was very realistic looking. She had a look at the inscription chiselled in the stone and told him it had been erected in the memory of Genghis Khan. His name translated from the Chinese was 'Precious Warrior' and he was among the youngest warriors of all times and was actually a tribal chief at the young age of thirteen years.

He was ruthless towards his enemies and was renowned to have conquered half of the then known world before he died on the eighteenth of august twelve twenty seven. They enjoyed a leisurely walk back to the hotel and because the weather was so nice they spent the rest of the day sitting on the hotel verandah. The weekend passed very quickly and soon it was Monday and he was on his own as she had gone back to teach at the school. His book writing was coming on fine, now that he had the time to concentrate on it. He was anxious to have enough completed to submit it to a publisher.

The last three weeks of his stay passed very quickly probably because he was so busy with the book. On the morning of his last day, they remembered to return her bed back to its original bedroom downstairs. After breakfast they planned to pack up and then get a taxi to the airport. He was a bit concerned at the volume of luggage she was bringing with her and although she left some at the hotel he hoped they would get on the plane with all that they still had. Their flight had to be diverted because of inclement weather and they would now be going to Bangkok international airport in Thailand. Where they would have a two-day wait for a connecting flight to London.

This presented no problem to them as they were in no hurry and it gave him some more, much needed time to work on his book. After a couple of hours wait, they boarded their flight. He spent the duration of the flight adding to his book while she spent the time reading hers. It interested him to note that some passengers totally disregarded the guidelines they had been given regarding their seatbelts and unfastened them long before the plane came to a halt.

It reminded him of people standing at traffic lights; some would rush over the crossing, putting their own and other people's lives in danger. Before the plane had stopped the aisles were full of passengers trapping John and Cheng Eng along with other law abiders. Eventually they disembarked and made their way through customs straight to the airport restaurant, where he picked up a car hire brochure and they had a look at it over coffee.

They decided to hire a camper van for the next two days and get out of town into the quietness of the country, because of the licence conditions and the fact that only he had a licence. They were obliged to leave not only a large deposit but also their passport as security against theft or damage. They were sternly advised that any damage to the vehicle would result in the forfeiture of their deposit.

They didn't have long to wait before the vehicle was delivered to them. The driver took his time in explaining the workings of the fridge, cooker etc and then appeared to be in a hurry to be off, so when he was about to leave they asked him to hang on a bit until the outside of the vehicle was checked for damage and it's just as well they did because they found a very badly scratched front-wing. They were able to get a local taxi driver who was nearby to confirm the damage and he left them his name and address and as a double precaution.

They took a photograph of the van driver beside the damage, this left only one shot left in the camera so they asked a passer by to take a photograph of them together. He then took advantage of the developing service offered within one of the airport shops and arranged to uplift them on his return in two days time. They then returned to the motor home and after a run round the car park he was confident enough to take to the main road.

Making use of the map provided they were soon through the town and cruising along in the country area, as the miles flew by he became much more accustomed to the gears and handling of the vehicle. It was completely different to anything he was used to driving, having a diesel engine it was very slow and sluggish compared to his high-powered petrol powered sports car at home.

7

A Busman's Holiday

When they stopped in a suitable lay by for the night he had been driving for about six hours and it was now very dark. They were both tired and in the peace and quiet of the countryside they soon fell asleep. When they awakened late the next morning they were both very hungry indeed, as they had not eaten anything since leaving the airport yesterday. Priority number one now was to purchase some provisions since they had completely overlooked this the day before. Looking at the map they could see that a populated area was only about half an hours drive away, so off they went heading in that direction.

On reaching the seaside town it was naturally enough extremely busy being such a beautiful day. Many of the visitors were European and American. If the car's registration plates were anything to go by. After a bit of touring around they managed to find a parking place large enough for their long vehicle and as luck would have it, just across the road was a restaurant.

He was delighted to find that the menu was in English. So for once on his journey he was able to see what he was about to order. Following a welcome and most hearty breakfast they were ready to look round the marketplace. They felt it more sensible to leave their vehicle where it was and just walk to the shopping area, which was quite near.

Window shopping in this town was great fun as everything was quite different to what they were used to One shop that really amused them had its name in large English letters above it's door 'Benji's clocks and watches.' Curiosity got the better of them so in they went to have a look, before them lay a bewildering selection of clocks and watches of every conceivable type, from a large antique grandfather clock to a very delicate ring watch.

It struck him that his problem of what to buy for his relatives back home would be solved by purchasing them each a good quality watch, he also got Cheng Eng to choose one to her liking. Later when paying for the goods the assistant inquired about his hometown and during the ensuing conversation the assistant told them that he had come here on holiday from Birmingham ten years ago but things were so good here. He was quite satisfied to remain here forever, they were no sooner away from the shop before she put on the new watch and was so delighted with it she threw her arms around his neck and kissed him in appreciation and thanks.

After about an hour of wandering about they decided to go down onto the beach, so they bought some sweet items so they could have a picnic. They only just managed to find a spot on the crowded beach where they could sunbathe. The heat was almost unbearable so that after an hour without any barrier cream they decided that was enough and moved off to the shade of a tree, where they sat down and enjoyed their little picnic. Being so relaxed and content in the pleasant surroundings they fell asleep, and only awoke in time to see the sun go down, and what a beautiful sight it was. It was now quite dark and the area seemed to be coming alive with the opening of nightclubs casinos etc, as they made their way back to the restaurant next to where the van was parked. The restaurant was open and rather full, they did manage however to secure a table under an alcove in a corner.

It looked as if it would take a while getting served so with her agreement. He nipped back out to the van with the groceries they had bought and returned with his writing pad and materials to continue with his book. It was just as well that he had, for it was at least another thirty minutes before they were served. Over coffee he continued to write knowing only too well the lights in the van were battery operated and would be a bit dull to enable him to write. Not that Cheng Eng objected, since she couldn't keep her eyes off her new watch. She was so proud of it she flashed it around for all to see, about three coffees and two hours later they realised they were the last two customers, as soon as they left they could hear the door being bolted shut behind them and out went the lights.

Because they wanted to see the scenery on the return journey. They camped just where they were. On the main road for the night to make sure the return journey would be in daylight the next day. They were soon to pay for this decision, because the noise of the traffic and the lights from headlights of passing cars kept them awake most of the night. Adding to this, the fact that they had slept so much during the day meant that they only snatched a few hours sleep before the morning traffic awakened them.

He managed to do a bit more writing and she had a walk before the café opened and they had breakfast. Getting out of the car park was a bit of a headache because the vehicles next to him had parked up close giving him very little room to manoeuvre. Eventually they made it without damage to any vehicle and they made sure their return journey was slow and leisurely. They stopped once for a meal of fresh fruit and a coffee. She wrote to her parents telling them about her return to England, to take up a new teaching position and promising an updated letter after she settled in.

As for John she would quite understand if he did not approve of her telling lies about her working and teaching in England but she felt that she had a good chance of getting a job fairly quickly in London. However she confessed to him that she would prefer to be near to him so they could keep seeing each other regularly. He said that he was hardly in a position to judge, bearing in mind that being married with twins he knew it was wrong having a relationship with anyone other than his wife, but he had grown so attached to Cheng Eng that he also couldn't stand the thought of them not seeing each other on a regular basis. He was holding her hand over the table as he told her this, and she knew he was serious.

After their coffee break, she found a post box and

posted the letter to her parents. She then walked back to the motor home and they continued their drive to the airport. Instead of driving through the heavy traffic of the city of Bangkok. She had charted a route to the airport round the outskirts and even though this was a much longer route it was preferably better than driving through the heart of the city.

Because their flight wasn't due for departure until one 'o clock in the morning they had lots of time to spare, as long as they checked in at the airport for midnight. The usual procedure was to check in for your flight one hour before departure. After a few more stops to refuel the motor home. They had passed through some lovely rural countryside but were now only a few minutes away from the airport. It was getting dark and the traffic was dense as they were now off the quiet rural roads and had joined the extremely busy roads.

In fact they were now on the busiest road in Thailand, so he had to concentrate more on his driving, but full marks and to his credit, they arrived at the airport intact. After negotiating through some horrendous traffic. He parked up the motor home and said
"The first thing we must do is collect the photographs, and then have an evening meal in the airport restaurant." He locked up the motor home and they both made a beeline for the airport shop where she exchanged the official slip and payment for the many films which they had left for processing. She wanted to see them there and then but he said, "No, lets sit down for our evening meal and we can

both look through them at our leisure." Nodding in agreement they moved over to the restaurant. They arrived to find they had to wait in a queue for a table, as it was crowded to saturation point. However the queue was continually on the move and within half an hour they managed to grab a table, she remarked that it was just as well they had time to spare.

As soon as they sat down she opened up the folder to look at the photographs, which she thought had come out well. She carefully studied each one and then passed them on to him for his comments. Each photo told its own story, like the one when they had sat down with their backs to the blizzard and finished up frozen to the ground. The exact spot where this happened was photographed along with all the other incidents on the journey.

"Wow, this photo could be worth a fortune!" She shouted, passing it over the table to him.

His eyes stood out like organ stops, it was a picture taken in the dark with a ten minute open camera shutter exposure and it was the only one to come out properly from the several he had taken. The other camera shots were taken with the camera shutter only being open for a minute or so. This ten minute exposure was the longest the camera shutter had been left open. It was taken in the black dark from high up in the mountainside. Well above the secret cave entrance which was now completely and safely concealed by the avalanche. The photograph was exceptionally good as it showed the snow with its dark green centre, not only that it clearly showed up the various lighter shades of green from the centre outwards.

"You know, you could be right," he said,

"this picture could be worth a fortune. It goes a long way towards proving our story, and the legend about the green snow." Just then a waiter arrived, and leant over the table to take their order. John hastily pocketed the photograph, the fewer who knew of its existence the better. John had a quick look through the rest of the photos after the waiter left with their order.

He could not find any sign of the picture he had taken of Cheng Eng at the entrance to the cave. He even went to the trouble of holding each negative up to the light in an attempt to find it. He asked her if she had seen it but she said she had not it and was just as mystified about its loss as he was. "I just don't get it," he said, "I've counted the negatives and there are none missing. There are three blanks but these were the ones taken at night. There's a lot more going on here than meets the eye.

I'll go so far as to say that I'm now totally convinced that there is a supernatural power at work. It's far too uncanny for all that's happened to be all coincidental. Also when I consider the premonitions I was plagued with over the years and the fact they all came true. I shudder when I think about the cave now but still wonder what great mysteries are hidden behind that second bung?"

Because they were both starving they were pleased when the waiter arrived with their meal. They ate in silence and finished in record time. Over a leisurely cup of coffee, the conversation returned to the subject of the photographs.

They were both very pleased that the majority of them had turned out well. Particularly the last one taken with the taxi driver beside the damaged motor home.

"Good golly," he exclaimed, "it's later than I thought, quick take this money and pay the bill. We better return the motor home before we miss our plane." Pocketing the photos he said quietly, "Tempus Fugit"
"That's a new one on me," she exclaimed, "what does it mean?"
"It's an old saying which is not used very often nowadays. It's Latin and means 'Time flies'," He replied, as they walked to the cashiers department.

She liked the old saying so much that to his embarrassment, she repeated it out loud time and time again. Cheng Eng paid for the meals, while the cashier's facial expression showed she thought she was dealing with another mad tourist. Not that it made the slightest difference to Cheng Eng, because she only stopped repeating it when she was confident she had it memorised and by that time they were outside.

They made a Beeline for the airport and the vehicle hire reception area. On arrival they were disappointed to find the reception deserted, with the exception of a rather irate American couple. The man told them that they had been waiting for about twenty-five minutes.
"Yip we sure have been waiting now for a good old time, sure thing a good old time," said the American woman in her unmistakable southern drawl. "This is desperate," replied John, "this firm owes us money and worse still,

holds our passports which we need for our departure flight in two hours time."

Just then a young man came rushing to the reception area with a ring of car keys in one hand and a fistful of paperwork in the other. Opening the service centre hatch and putting the paperwork and keys down, he arrived at the counter full of smiles saying.

"First please, can I help you?" John took a step back and pointed to the other couple indicating that they were before him. The elderly American gentleman stood forward and said,

"Yea son of a bitch, we been waiting ages, for sure. We have a car booked by prior arrangement under the name of Jenkins, Lincolnville, Nebraska, USA." The service attendant answered in English, "Yes Sir, one moment please." He tapped the information into his computer, then he made a phone call. Replacing the receiver he advised them their car would be waiting for them opposite the airport terminal taxi rank in five minutes time. Without as much as a word of thanks the couple turned on their heels, collected their baggage and strode off.

After explaining that they were returning a vehicle they too were directed to the taxi rank where an official would be holding a clipboard and would attend to them. The attendant went on at great length to remind them that their deposit would be forfeited in the event of any damage having been done to the vehicle. John and Cheng Eng looked at each other for both of them were in no doubt that there was a sham going on here. As they left the office he said to her, "You can bet your bottom dollar they will blame us for the damage done previously to the vehicle, it's just as well we have proof it happened before we hired the van."

When they arrived at the taxi rank the official had just finished with the American couple who were driving off very slowly. The man then started to inspect the returned van with the aid of a powerful torch and what a meal he made of it. Starting at the back of the vehicle he worked his way toward the damaged area at the front and then right on queue. He put on a great show, which was no doubt rehearsed many times, when he found the scratches on the paintwork. Throwing his arms in the air and then pointing to the damage he shouted that they had lost their deposit.

"Is that right?" Said John, "we shall soon see about that!" Handing him the photograph they had taken at the time they hired the van. Clearly showing the damage, he said, "Have a look at that. I have the names and addresses of witnesses who can prove this photograph was taken before we hired the van. You are a chancer and a con man, no doubt you've tried this many times, and taken in many innocent tourists, but not any more, because I'm going to the police."

Whether the thought of going to jail, or just being put out of business affected the inspector they did not know, but he suddenly turned pale and started to tremble, and this time it was surely not an act. In a very humble voice he said that he was very sorry and had made a mistake and would make sure they got a full refund.

"Yes you will," replied John, "I insist you accompany us to the desk just to make sure." It was just as well he did so, because the second half of the act behind the counter was not prepared to return their passports, until his associate had a quiet word with him. Later on John thanked Cheng Eng on her ingenuity regarding suggesting taking the photographs, Otherwise they would never have had their money returned from the crooked hire company.

They had timed things just right, as information had just come over the address system to say their flight number had to assemble at gate four. They had enough time, so decided to buy a holdall to transport the telescope, tripod, binoculars and other items. However this was not their day, as even this simple act turned out to be a bit of a disaster. The shopkeeper must have got out of bed on the wrong side this morning because she was most unhelpful and almost threw the holdalls at them and was most reluctant to let them try out different sizes. Perhaps she objected to removing, and returning the packing that was in the bags.

In the end they settled for one, which was slightly smaller than they would have liked but make do and mend John thought as they joined the boarding passenger group once more. The check in staff were very efficient and soon everyone was on board and belted up ready to go.

Throughout the journey John and Cheng Eng passed the time by either reading or writing. After the plane had stopped for refuelling in the Middle East. They both fell asleep and awakened only as the plane touched down at London airport. From there, they hailed a taxi to Regent Park Hotel. They confirmed at the reception that there was room for them, and booked in for three weeks for bed and breakfast. Leaving their luggage behind they followed the receptionist's directions to the nearest bank to change his currency back into British money. He arranged to return within two hours to pick up his payment; this would give them time to have a mid day meal. At the bank again they had to wait in a queue for the foreign exchange desk, but they did not have long to wait before they were served.

Because it was such a nice day they bought some fruit and cakes so they could have a picnic lunch later on. They returned to the hotel paid for their stay and then just dumped their belongings in the room, leaving them to be sorted out later, and went straight over the road to picnic in the park. After they finished their meal they went for a walk and just by chance they came across a pickup point where they could take a round London trip in an open deck bus. Shortly after a bus arrived, and they boarded it along with some other waiting tourists. The bus moved on quite slowly with a courier giving a running commentary on all the points of historical interest. As they wound their way through the streets of London they were both mesmerised and fascinated by the sites they were seeing, they enjoyed it so much they decided to go around a second time, and much to their surprise they were not charged for this second tour.

After the tour they went window-shopping to some

of the largest shops which the rich and famous frequented, not that they intended buying much as it was more of a visit of curiosity. The time passed so quickly they were soon caught up in the rush hour as shops began to close, and they were lucky to get a taxi back to the hotel in time for their evening meal. It had been a long day, so after a most enjoyable meal and a few drinks in a bar later, they retired for the night. In the morning over breakfast she suggested she should look for a job, and reminded him that she still held an international students work permit which allowed her to work part-time. So after breakfast they parted company, she went off in search of work while he went off to the park and continued with his book writing.

It was a dull and rather dreary day although not particularly cold, but sitting and writing for two hours was enough for him, so he decided to go for a hot cup of coffee in a nearby cafe he had noticed yesterday. From the outside the cafe looked rather ordinary, inside was a different matter altogether, it was charming and had a wonderful atmosphere; it was one of the very few genuine coffee houses which ground its own coffee from the vast available varieties. The coffee tables were a feature in their own right, they had round marble tops which sat on what looked like old treadle sewing machine stands with ornately designed fancy scrolled metal work. Ah, thought John, what a lovely place, I must remember and bring Cheng Eng here one day.

His thoughts were broken by the appearance of a lovely young waitress wearing a black and white uniform, who asked him what brand of coffee he would prefer. Being quite ignorant of the many brands, he said that he would settle for whatever she recommended. She suggested their own make and also recommended a homemade coffee cream cake to accompany it. He looked up, smiled and said, "Why not!" He went back to working on his book while waiting to be served. He found the coffee most enjoyable, and with a couple of spoonfuls of brown sugar added was one of the best cups of coffee he had ever tasted. The cream cake was delicious and out of this world, it just melted in his mouth. It was little wonder that this cafe was packed full. He had already made up his mind to call here daily, be it rain, hail, wind or shine.

He would be here for his cup of coffee. Later back in the park, he was seated and busily writing his book when an elderly gentleman using a walking stick and wearing a trilby hat sat down next to him and after a little while asked him if he was a tourist, and where he came from. John had no choice but to close his writing jotter, as there was no way he could concentrate on writing and hold a conversation at the same time. The elderly man explained that he had been a professional soldier and told him all about his exploits during the Second World War from Dunkirk to North Africa to Sicily, Italy, and Germany and then out in Kenya, Malaya, Korea, Hong Kong, Singapore and Northern Ireland.

He had served in all of these countries and explained in great detail all the hair-raising experiences that had happened during those times. He went on as though it had happened yesterday and not over half a century ago. He told him that he was eighty-eight years old and lived alone in a pensioner flat within walking distance of the park, which he walked through everyday of the year no matter the weather, it was his daily ritual to do this.

As he was listening, the thought suddenly flashed through John's mind. That if he were offered back to the elderly man's flat he would have to use a plan of diversion to avoid that. He realised the man was a very lonely old man, who desperately required to partake in conversation, but if John encountered such people everyday he would never get his writing finished.

The old military man then went on to ask what John did for a living, so he explained all about his work, which was a bit tame, dull, and monotonous in comparison to the ex- military man's career. Never the less the old man seemed to be genuinely interested and asked him what had brought him to this neck of the woods.

This put him in a bit of a dilemma, whether tell the truth which would be hard to believe, or to make up a story which the stranger might find easier to swallow. After a pause he decided to tell the truth, as he didn't have the heart to tell him lies, that way whether the old man believed him or not, his conscience would clear.

Starting from the very beginning he explained everything step-by-step; and to his amusement the old man was spellbound. At one 'o clock in the afternoon it started to rain and he was only half way through his story, so he invited the old man to accompany him to the coffee house where it would be dry, and over a coffee he could finish explaining the rest of his story. The old man picked up his walking stick got up from the bench, and said,

"Lead on, I'm looking forward to this, I very seldom frequent cafes as I just have my army pension and I like to be totally self-supporting. I still cook all my own meals you know! I never eat out."

By now the few spots of rain had turned into a downpour, and by the time they reached the coffee shop it was a welcoming retreat. There was one vacant table, so they grabbed it before it was taken; it was as it happens the very same table John had sat at only a few hours ago. He gave the same waitress a repeat of his previous order, but doubled up. When he started to relate his story from where he had left off, the waitress served up their order. Without interrupting his story telling he shoved the bowl with the brown sugar over to the old solider who helped himself.

Between munching on the coffee cream cake and sipping coffee, he continued with his real life story, which the old soldier appeared to listen to with great fascination. The old man commented on the cup of coffee and coffee cream cake and said "This is a great day, I will remember it for the rest of my life." By the time John had related all his exploits to the old soldier they had downed another three cups of coffee, time had passed so very quickly. He felt guilty about occupying a table without ordering anything else so he explained as kindly as he could that he would have to go home. The pensioner gave his name as Walter McArthur and suggested it would be nice if they could meet again before John had to leave London in three weeks time.

"Tell you what Walter, they call me John foster, why don't we meet here each morning about ten-thirty and we can have a chat?" The old soldier thought that was a good idea and replied, "Right John, I shall make every effort to be here in the morning, good bye for now" and they went their separate ways in the rain.

By the time John got back to the hotel he was soaked through and so was Cheng Eng when she returned soon after. They spent most of the early evening either reading or writing and then discussing their day's activities, when she got an opportunity, she told him that she had a job interview at ten thirty next morning with The London School of languages.

Although they had tried to dry their clothing over a radiator they were still damp when they wore them to dinner that evening. They sat through their meal feeling extremely uncomfortable but they were determined it was not going to spoil their evening. So they decided to order a taxi to take them to the nearest cinema. They would have preferred to have walked but it was still raining very heavily.

They arranged with the taxi driver to return for them in two hours time after they had seen the film now showing, which had the unusual name of Fried green tomatoes. As they climbed the cinema stairs he looked at her and said, The film looks a bit iffy, I only hope it's better than its title, I suppose we shall just have to wait and see."

As it so happened they both fully enjoyed the film, which had as it's main feature 'The whistle stop café' When the film finished they had about a five minute wait before the prearranged taxi whisked them back to the hotel, where they had a late evening drink before retiring for the evening.

Next morning after breakfast he wished her well with her job interview, as they parted and went their different ways. The weather was beautiful and a complete contrast to yesterday and he really enjoyed sitting in the park writing his book. Understandably for a military man the old soldier arrived spot on at ten thirty, and he was not only disciplined in his time keeping but also in his whole demeanour. His shoes were polished to such a degree you could almost see your face in them.

Looking at them John had a humorous thought that Walter must be related to a French polisher. After the usual greetings and niceties of the weather, they made their way to the cafe where John ordered the same as they had the day before. Walter insisted that he paid for today's refreshments indicating that it was his turn to do so, appreciating the fact that the pensioner had his pride John readily agreed and suggested that he would pay tomorrow.

During the half-hour or so in the cafe Walter more or less gave a repeat performance of the story he had told yesterday. He was so accurate right down to the very finest detail that he convinced John that he was in no way exaggerating, and his exploits must surely be true. Finishing their coffee they agreed to meet at the same time the next day and said their farewells. Being such a nice day the park was now extremely busy and John had a problem in finding a seat.

Later on while fully engrossed with writing his book he was interrupted by a couple of cheeky youths who seated themselves down next to him and asked him what he was writing about. He answered them rather gruffly by telling them that it was confidential, and to do him a favour by letting him get on with it. Perhaps this was not the wisest way to deal with the distraction but the park was crowded and offered some protection. Thankfully the youths made nothing more of it and moved away with nothing other than a few choice words, which were obviously not complementary.

Throughout the afternoon he had no other distractions other than an elderly couple that sat next to him and conversed with each other almost non-stop for about an hour. About five O'clock in the afternoon Cheng Eng came running up to him and said excitedly that she had got the job and was to start right away. Gathering her in his arms and sweeping her up in a circle he said,
"Well done, good for you: let's have a coffee to celebrate." Considering the time however, they made their way back to the hotel and had their coffee over their evening meal.

During the meal she explained all about her interview and examination etc, she even went on to explain what she had for lunch. "And!" She said, "not only that, but I have subsidised accommodation laid on for me and I've told them I'll move there in three weeks time. I've been told that my students will include Civil servants who are directly involved in working with illegal immigrants." He was truly delighted for her and that evening before retiring they celebrated with a bottle of champagne.

For the next two weeks the routine was the same. She went off to teach at school while he continued with his book writing, apart of course for the weekends when they spent more time together. When Cheng Eng was introduced to Walter in the coffee house she was so intrigued by his tales that she often asked him to repeat them.

John however had heard them so often he could almost repeat them word for word and it took him all his time to appear interested. By the end of the second week he had completed his book and spent most of the third week searching for publishers or other agents. The trouble was they did not believe him and thought he had written fiction rather than a factual work.

In the evening when he was telling Cheng Eng, he was very despondent and downcast, "One editor even went into a fit of laughter, and suggested I have a vivid imagination, do you know what? He even had the audacity to inspect the photographs with a magnifying glass and then said they were forgeries."

"Oh I do wish I had been with you," she said, "perhaps a second witness would have been a help."

"I doubt that very much," he replied, "his mind seemed to have been made up, and that was that." She tried everything she could to cheer him up and encourage him but even her suggestion to accompany him the next day was refused.

"I would just love to prove them wrong," he said.

On Sunday morning the three of them were in the café enjoying a coffee and Walter was again relating some of his War exploits, when an elderly rather well dressed looking gentleman asked in an American accent if he could sit next to them. this appeared to be the only vacant seat. While Cheng Eng was engrossed with Walter's exploits, John and the stranger got into a conversation and as it transpired the American said he was a journalist for the national geographic magazine and was over here concerning some freelance work he was doing for NASA. "My that sounds interesting," said John, and went on to ask him what his work involved.

The journalist said that most of his work was top secret and was mainly to do with the placing of objects in orbit around the earth in an effort to safeguard earth's natural resources. He intimated that he would love to tell him more but the official secrets act prohibited him from doing so. The journalist then asked him what he did for a living, so he explained everything right up to being in London and about his work being turned down by a publisher.

The American journalist's eyes lit up and he asked if there was any chance of seeing the book. John was delighted and replied, "Certainly it's in our hotel room which is only ten minutes walk away, if you want to see it why not come with me now?" The journalist answered "Sure, there is no time like the present and I'm most interested." With that they excused themselves and made their way out of the coffee house, leaving old Walter still relating his war time exploits to Cheng Eng who was quite happy to be a patient and understanding listener.

On the other hand John was happy to get a respite from old Walter's repetitive hair-raising wartime adventures. Within minutes they reached the hotel and he handed the journalist the large jotter, the man sat down on the edge of the bed and started to read it. In the meantime John busied himself by making some coffee, but emphasized that it would be nowhere as good as that from the coffee shop, it would be bottom of the league compared to that.

The journalist was so intent with his reading that he was oblivious to anything being said to him. John felt like he was talking to himself, so he decided to stay silent. Even when he put a cup of coffee down and said, "There you are, a cup of coffee," he got no response and he sat and watched the coffee go cold. Half an hour passed before Cheng Eng made a welcome return and said, "Oh Boy! was I glad to get away from old Walter. I thought I'd never get away and envied you, when you had an excuse to leave."

John explained in a whisper that the American was a journalist for NASA and was in London to attend a convention on space exploration. He went on to explain about the topics that were to be discussed at the convention.

By now it was one `o clock in the afternoon and she whispered to John. "Isn't it about time we had lunch?" He whispered back "I'll second that motion but what will we do about him? Should we invite him to join us for a bar lunch?" The journalist raised his head and said excitably, "Son of a gun, this book you have written is dynamite, how that editor turned you down, I'll never know, in all my years of experience. I have never read anything quite like it. It's truly riveting. This book will make you a wealthy and famous young man no doubt about it, I'll stake my reputation on it, that's for sure."

"Well," John replied, "you've done wonders for my morale, which was totally deflated when I was turned down by the publishing editor." The American journalist then said "make no mistake about it, that self same editor will rue the day, that's for sure." He then got up from sitting on the edge of the bed and said, "Can I take this to continue reading while at lunch?" John replied promptly "No problem!" They left the hotel to go two hundred yards along the street where the trio went in for a pub meal.

While waiting to be served the journalist got stuck back into reading the book, while John and Cheng Eng chatted together. John reckoned it would take the reporter about nine hours reading to finish the book, so not being prepared to hang around this long. He let the journalist retain the book and made arrangements for its return the next morning. He was well aware that he knew very little about the journalist, but felt that he had little option other than take a chance on his honesty.

8

Publish and be Damned

It was Monday morning and as he waited to cross the road on his way to the coffee shop. He couldn't help notice the awful smell of carbon monoxide from the dense traffic, which was crawling along bumper to bumper for miles. Walter and the journalist had beaten him to the coffee house and had a coffee waiting for him. He murmured a grateful thanks but he knew he had little chance of getting a word in edgeways as Walter was in full flow with his battle exploits. Some time later, after Walter had departed. John and the reporter could discuss the situation regarding his book.   After they were seated comfortably back in the pub the journalist said he had been in touch with his boss at National Geographic and he seemed keen to meet John to make arrangements for publication, and as it happened, he would be in London tomorrow on other business and was hopeful of meeting him in the morning. Naturally John was delighted and was only to happy to say so.

"I wonder what he will make of this photograph," he said, handing it to the journalist,

"That's the green snow I mention in my book," he continued, pointing out the area on the photograph. After studying it for some time the journalist exclaimed,

"Sure thing man he's just gonna love this, this picture could make your fortune young man, guard it with your life." He also told him not to worry about its authenticity because if need be it could be tracked and the area photographed by satellite, and then there would be absolutely no question about it being faked.

It was agreed that the reporter and his boss would call on John in the morning at his hotel. This suited him just fine since he would not have to go looking for the editor. They parted company with a handshake and he returned to his hotel to safely store his book and pictures. The rest of the afternoon he spent looking at ancient Egyptian relics within the nearby London museum and later just by chance, whom should he bump into on the hotel steps but Cheng Eng returning from her work. "Hi," he said cheerfully,
"have I got news for you." She replied, "that's good, I've had a great day also but let's wait till we are seated in the lounge bar and we can discuss it together."

During supper they had plenty to talk about. Firstly she explained that she had been chauffeur driven from the school to Heathrow airport. Where she had spent the day working as an interpreter between asylum seekers and the immigration authorities. "They must have been pleased with my effort," she said, "because they offered me a full-time job with them."

"How did they know to get into in touch with you?" he asked. "Well to be frank John, I don't know, it's quite a mystery to me, anyway I told them I would think about their offer, getting driven around is rather tempting," she answered with a smile. "The best bit of it though, is the characters you come in contact with and some of the stories they tell would make your hair curl."

They both had a good laugh when she recalled the antics and some of the tales she had been expected to believe and they spent a rather pleasant evening exchanging the happenings of the day. Then after a few drinks they retired for the evening. Next morning he was late in wakening and only just managed to get dressed before his guests arrived. After the introductions where over, they went down to the comfortable lounge bar to conduct their business. The editor in chief had a quick inspection of the book and the photograph, and said that subject to him reading the book overnight he would be along at noon tomorrow with a contract, which would be around $100,000 for the sole rights to the book and a further $10,000 for the photograph.

It seems that he mistook the look of total astonishment on John's face for that of a refusal. Because he quickly offered to increase it if it was not enough. Taking a few long deep breaths, John regained his composure somewhat and with a very dry throat said that the offer was more than generous and most acceptable.

After some more small formalities, which to be frank he wasn't interested in, they left with the promise to meet again tomorrow. Pulling himself together as best he could he wandered over to the coffee house and was quite glad that he had missed Walter, because he felt he just couldn't

214

listen to him and his war exploits today. Sitting with his coffee he had time to think things over. It was a good feeling to have a lot of money, and even after he had repaid his uncle Reg the £10,000 he owed him, he would still be left with more than a normal lifetimes earnings.

No doubt there would be even more to come, with television interviews, documentaries, lectures etc. Financial worries would surely be a thing of the past. On the other hand, he did not have a clear conscience, he was aware of breaking God's Ten Commandments. An old saying came to mind 'A contented mind is a blessing kind, better by far than a purse well lined'

He still had to face his wife Ruby back home, and had already made up his mind to be truthful regarding his affair with Cheng Eng. He was in such turmoil that he almost wished old Walter would arrive and take his mind off the inevitable. After a while, he could stand it no longer so he went out and spent the remainder of the day visiting in the maritime museum and the tower of London before returning to the hotel to meet Cheng Eng.

This evening's chat over lunch was more like confession time because he told her all about his fears of returning home to his wife and his twins. He even told her how he could not live with a lie and that he would have to explain his infidelity. "Try not to feel like that my darling, we have been over this so many times, you know I will always be waiting for you," she said while hugging him.
"You are my life and no matter what happens I will stand by you." Her obvious sincerity touched his heart as he said.

215

"Oh forgive me Cheng Eng, I know I should not be going on so, but the thought of our parting is almost unbearable. If things don't work out at home I shall be straight back for you." The tears in his eyes were most genuine. In an attempt to cheer him up she changed the subject and told him that for the time being she would no longer be working with immigration but would be called upon when necessary. The height of the conversation of course was the subject of his book and of the vast amount of money he had been offered. By the time he had explained all about it they were ready for bed. Next morning he was up at the crack of dawn and in plenty of time to have breakfast with Cheng Eng before she went off to work.

He was so excited about the visit from the editor that time seemed to drag. He had an hour to go but it seemed like eternity. Although he wasn't one for reading newspapers this morning he was quite happy to make use of the hotel's complimentary copy until his business associates arrived.

On their arrival he was given a contract and advised to scrutinise it and if necessary make any alterations before signatures were given. It was a lengthy document and not surprisingly it took him about an hour to read it through. It made reference to things like percentages payable should a film be made of it, which all seemed fair and above board, so he finally signed it.

Arrangements being that the money would be paid directly into his bank. All the formalities being finished they went for a celebratory lunch.

Some future plans involved an expedition by nuclear physicists and other experts to the area of green snow as soon as the appropriate governments gave permission. They indicated that John could come along as their chief guide. "I'm sorry gentlemen but one trip there was enough for me." He said, "So reluctantly, gentlemen I must refuse." Eventually the meeting broke up and he went to Waterloo station for a train timetable up to Carlisle, from there it would be only a short bus journey to Langwathby. He purchased a ticket for the train leaving at ten 'o clock which should be in Carlisle for about half past two in the afternoon.

On the road back from the station he bought a bunch of flowers and a large box of chocolates as a small parting gift for Cheng Eng as this would be their last night together. She was delighted with her gifts and it helped her get over the thought of their parting the next day. Rather than have their tea at the hotel he wanted to make sure they had a night to remember, so they dined at a very posh west end hotel, then ended their evening out with a visit to Covent Garden Opera house.

Their evening finished in one of extreme passion which resulted in them being late in awakening in the morning. Missing breakfast they had a mad dash by taxi and arrived at the station with five minutes to spare, within minutes he was on the train and on his way, with a tearful Cheng Eng waving goodbye from the platform, in return he waved back until she was out of sight.

Even although he felt depressed at their parting he

decided to go for breakfast in the hope that it might cheer him up but it was all wishful thinking because as the train sped northwards. He could not get her out of his mind and he could not shift the uncanny feeling that he would be back for her soon. The train ran to its timetable and within the hour he had arrived home by bus. The bus stopped right outside his parent's house.

Entering the open door, he greeted his mother with "Surprise, surprise look who's home!" She was obviously surprised to see him and putting down her knitting she got up and greeted him with open arms. Instinctively he knew that all was not well and asked her what was wrong. She started to cry and through her sobs she told him about his father's death through a heart attack three months ago. They had tried everything to contact him with the news.

"Perhaps it's just as well we couldn't find you," she said. "There was nothing you could have done, the doctor did his best but even he could do nothing to help other than make sure your dad's last moments were peaceful and painless."

After a while they ceased their sobbing and sat down, he in the armchair that had always been his fathers.

He asked about the twins, thinking they would be here with her but she said that they were up at the farmhouse. This seemed strange to him but he let it rest but he had a feeling she was not telling him everything. Later as he sat finishing off a most welcome meal his mother had prepared. He asked her how she was managing financially and let her know that he was now financially able to help her. She said that she would manage fine on her widow's pension, which was enough to keep her head above water. Later she explained that after his father's death she was unable to cope with the children and his wife Ruby had taken on a full-time helper and that's who was looking after the twins right now.

"The children are really grown up now, you'll see such a difference in them since you left, why don't you go up and see them now?" his mother asked.

"No, I'll wait till tomorrow I'd like to visit dad's grave first," he replied, "another day is not going to make any difference."

Later when they had finished clearing away the dinner dishes he accompanied his mother to the nearby graveyard behind the church and then to the Foster family grave, which was surrounded by posies of beautiful flowers his mother had left daily. An inscription on a headstone read John Foster born 10 th April 1940, died 5thAugust 1998.

Nearby was a little monument, which had been erected and maintained by his work mates from the water board.

By this time John was quite unable to control himself and all the thoughts about how he'd let his mother down by not being here when she needed him got the better of him and he went into a bout of uncontrolled sobbing. It was hours later back in his mother's house over a cup of coffee that he was able to pull himself together, and explained to her all about his exploits and adventures, including all the details of Cheng Eng and Gillian. They conversed right into the early hours of the morning before fatigue overcame them, forcing them to retire to their beds.

He got up first thing in the morning and had the fire lit and the table set by the time his mother got up. After breakfast, while his mother washed up he went for a walk round the garden. The vegetable garden had been his father's pride and joy and although it had not been touched for three months it was still a great tribute to him.

Everything was so neat and tidy and there was not a weed to be seen. The forty years attention his father had given to it was very evident, even in the shed his tools were all clean, oiled, painted and laid out ready for use. There were seed boxes, which were spotlessly clean, all lined up waiting to be used in springtime.

Looking at these mementoes he could envisage his father standing near and this made him feel so very sad, yes he would miss his father very much. The noise made by his mother chopping firewood at the back door, brought him back to reality; "Hang on mother," he said, "Let me do that, I'll chop the kindling for you."

He spent over an hour chopping and stacking the firewood neatly beside the back door; this should keep her going for a good while, he thought. He filled her coal scuttle before having the cup of coffee which his mother brought out to him. He asked her if she would like to accompany him on the hours walk up to the farm to see the children.

"Why not," she said, "It's a nice morning, however, I'll put my coat on just in case it turns cold."

He waited until his mother came out and locked the door, before jumping down from his perch on the dyke and following her on the long walk ahead through the village and then up the farm road. As they walked along his mother said, "In the six months you were gone, three new families have moved into the village," and she pointed out the houses they had moved into. There were also two houses in the village with for sale signs in their gardens.

9

East West Hame is Best

After leaving the village behind, they hadn't gone very far before a land rover slowed down and pulled over beside them. It was owned by big Tom the farmer and his manager was driving it. He offered to give them a lift to the farm, which they gladly accepted as it saved them a good twenty minutes of walking. When they drew up in the farmyard they both got out and the manager offered John's mother a hand out. One of the first things John noticed was a beautifully cleaned and polished sports car parked near the front door of the farmhouse. The chrome was sparkling in the morning sunshine.

Before they reached the front door, a young girl, who was a stranger to him and who must have seen them approach, came out and said, "Good to see you, come in." "This is my son, the twin's father," his mother explained by way of an introduction. The girl smiled and shook John's hand saying. "I knew right away at first glance, I could see the family resemblance come in and see the twins. They are playing in their play pen, they have just had their breakfast and have been washed and had their nappies changed." Seeing them again for the first time in six months. He couldn't believe the difference in them, they had grown astronomically. They recognised their grandmother right away but now John was a total stranger to them. His first reaction, after getting over the initial shock of seeing how much they had grown, was to get down on his knees and play with them through the spars of the playpen. They could now stand up by pulling on the spars and hanging on for dear life. They certainly looked very happy and contented; there was no doubt about that.

While he and his mother had been entertaining the twins the girl had made coffee for them, so they sat down with their coffee and some biscuits. He could see through the window that overlooked the lawn, and saw a clothes line full of baby clothes hanging out to dry. The lawn was cut short and it appeared to have had a manicure and the flower borders were looking so good it was obvious they were being well maintained by a gardener. He asked the baby sitter if she knew where Ruby was working at the moment. She replied by saying she didn't know exactly, but did know it was somewhere in the Penrith area.

After the coffee and biscuits he said he fancied a walk up to Big Tom's farm but his mother said that she would rather stay with the twins and would wait here for his return. On the way he stopped to admire the conduit pipe archway which Alan Little, the electrician had made many years before. The pipe work was now all hidden with highly scented sweet peas, thanks to the part time gardener.

As he made his way out of the farmyard and into the fields, he couldn't help noticing that the old broken down decapitated field gates, had been replaced with new galvanised ones. Even the old fences had been replaced with new ones. Since the farm manager had taken over there had been an outstanding visual array of improvements that had taken place and not before time. Big Tom had been unable to cope and had let the farm get run down and into a state of decay over the years. He thought how nice to see things being restored to their formal glory.

Although he was surprised to see these changes, he was in for more surprises when he reached the farm. All the buildings were gleaming white, almost as white as snow they had been recently painted with Snowcem and even the yard had been brushed spotlessly clean. He shook his head slowly as if to shake himself awake, surely this can't be the same farm he last saw only a matter of months ago.

The back garden had also undergone a marvellous transformation, from an overgrown unkempt wilderness to what could almost be described as the Garden of Eden. He was full of admiration for the work carried out by the retired professional gardener who worked here part time.

After a while he decided to return home the long way via the ridge of high east field where he would visit old Sam's resting place. It took him about twenty minutes to get there as it was quite a climb up to this high point. The area of the grave was fenced off and was tidy. All the flowers, which had been in full bloom during his previous visit, were now only dying leaves.

He sat down right where old Sam used to during the lambing season and stayed for what seemed like hours, surveying the lovely countryside and drinking in the wonderful peaceful sounds of the birds. He could make out the Curlews and peewees above all the others. For a while he was at peace with himself and God. It was a far cry from the hustle and bustle of the rat race in London.

On his return home he had a look at the two seater MG sports car, which had been his pride and joy before he gave it to his wife Ruby. He was still admiring it when he heard his mother calling to him that his dinner was on the table ready for him. Sitting down to his fish and chips, bread butter and tea, on his own, he surmised that the others had eaten before him and no doubt the old faithful Aga oven had been used to keep his dinner warm. When he sat down in the living room he gave thanks for the meal, which he had enjoyed so much, yes he sure had missed home cooking. He tried to play with the twins but they would have none of it and they started to cry when he attempted to lift them up. He was still a stranger to them and no doubt it would take time before they took to him, so rather than try to lift them he got down on his knees beside them to play.

Some hours later he was still playing with them when his wife Ruby returned from her work. The moment she saw him he saw a look of surprise, or was it shock, on her face. He got up as quick as he could to greet her with a loving kiss and cuddle. She seemed not to respond and her attitude to him was quite defensive and cold, at least that's how he felt, perhaps he was wrong. He let the matter drop, putting it down to his stiff back and knees having been on the floor for so long. Anyway she probably has had a hard day at work he thought. As the evening wore on things improved very little because after she had had her tea his wife joined his mother in playing with and nursing the twins. Later on when the baby sitter had prepared a bath for the children, Ruby had gathered the children in her arms and prepared to take them upstairs. He was in for a shock when she turned and said to him. "Just let me know when you and your mother are ready to leave and I'll give you a lift home." Perhaps he had misunderstood, so he answered. "No need for that, you have just come in from work, if you give me the car keys I'll run mother home."

"Look John," she said, "let's get something straight right away. You are welcome to come here as often as you want to see the children. You are their father and I suppose have a legal right to access but under no circumstances will you be allowed to stay here."

He sat there speechless; his mind was in turmoil had she somehow found out about his adultery with Cheng Eng? Just then the baby sitter returned and announced that the twins were now settling down in their cots. Ruby said, "I'm just running John and his mother back down to the village, I'll be straight back so I won't be long." Then she put both her arms round the babysitter's neck and pulling her close kissed her full on the mouth and said tenderly, "I will be back in a few minutes."

Now it was all too plain to see why he was surplus to requirements. This young girl was not just a nanny for she and his wife appeared to be in a full-blown lesbian relationship and were lovers. No wonder his wife had been so cold towards him. Yes it was quite a shock to him but at least it was now out in the open. There was nothing more to be said, so he beckoned his mother and they left the house. If it had been left to him he would have walked home but his mother was glad to accept a lift from Ruby, so he followed her into the vehicle.

Not a word was spoken during the journey, apart from his mother thanking Ruby for their lift. When they got home he set to lighting the fire that had gone out, while his mother prepared a pot of tea. As they sat talking together, he confessed that he was devastated and wished he had never left, considering all that had happened during his absence. She tried to console him by telling him that these things would have happened anyway whether he was away or not and he should certainly not feel guilty about it.

"Ruby confessed to me about their relationship long before you had gone away, I had promised to remain silent and no matter what. I could not have broken your heart by telling you." His mother seemed to relish the opportunity to talk and she was able to share with him many of the intimate details that had troubled her, especially since her husband's death. She had been so terribly lonely and until now had no one to confide in.

They spoke very frankly and at great length, he reminding her about all his exploits with Cheng Eng and before they knew it, morning was almost upon them. His mother went upstairs to bed while he just lay down on the couch but he was soon up again as his mind was far too active to allow sleep. He just didn't know what to make of the situation, his wife rejecting him for another man was one thing but for another woman?? This really did confuse him, for there was no way he could compete in these circumstances, perhaps it was just his pride that had been hurt. He kept himself busy with things like stoking the fire, setting the table etc, until his mother came down in the morning.

As she went to make their breakfast he told her that he had not slept a wink all night, but had decided to return to London right away. "And I want you to come with me for a week's holiday," he said. "It will do you the world of good to get away for a wee while." His mother was a bit reluctant at first but his persistence paid off and she eventually agreed. "Right," he said suddenly cheering up. "You pop upstairs and pack a few essentials and I'll have a light breakfast waiting for you." His mother looked at the grandfather clock and agreed they would have to hurry since the bus left in three-quarters of an hour. When she went upstairs he timed himself, fifteen minutes is all it took for him to prepare and lay out poached eggs, fresh toast and a pot of tea.

Although they left in a hurry, as she locked up, his mother had the presence of mind to leave a note pinned to the door for the milkman and Ruby, explaining she would be away for a few days. As they joined another couple at the bus stop he suddenly remembered that the spark guard should have been placed in front of the fire. Rushing back to the house he just made it in time, and boarded the bus gasping for breath.

Eventually when they arrived at Carlisle railway station and after he had purchased their tickets, they went for a coffee to pass the hour before their train arrived. The time passed quickly and it wasn't long before they heard the announcement over the public address system that the intercity express to London was now arriving at platform two, then calling at Lancaster, Preston, Manchester, Sheffield, Nottingham and London.

As soon as the train came to a halt, they moved along the platform to a quiet spot and climbed on board and chose a seat to their liking next to a window. He had just put their luggage on the racks above their seat and was seeing to his mother's comfort when he noticed his friend Martin pass the window. Obviously he had just departed from the train, he couldn't resist giving him a shout and they were able to talk for a few minutes before the train set off.

"That was Martin, mother," he said, "remember, the person I bought the MG from, quite a coincidence to meet him here, don't you think?" As the train sped on its journey, the lack of sleep the previous night caught up with him and he was soon fast asleep, only to be rudely awakened an hour later when an announcement was made advising that the dining room was now open.

Yawning and rubbing his eyes he apologised to his mother for having fallen asleep. "Oh my dear son, don't apologise, I've had a wonderful time looking through this window," she said. "I never imagined a train journey would be like this." They made their way along to lunch and when they finished and were ready to return to their seats his mother asked him how long the train would be stopped for in the next station. "Normally just for a few minutes" he answered, "why do you ask?"

His mother looking round to make sure no one was listening, whispered that she had to go to the toilet.

He only just managed to suppress his laughter, his parents had never had much money and his mother had never been on a train before. Far less be aware that toilets were available on board. Taking his mother's hand he led her along the corridor and explained the workings of the toilet to her before returning to his seat. How ironic he thought, here am I a rich man and able to give my parents everything they never had before, and my father is not here to share with us.

Later as he watched his mother peer with amazement through the window. He could see that this was one great adventure for her, she had never been farther a field than Carlisle, just a matter of miles from her home. If she was amazed and spellbound now, what was she to make of London? The train came to a stop and they stepped onto the platform at London station. His mother was almost swept away in the fast moving crowds. Because he was carrying two cases he had difficulty in guiding her along to a quieter area but eventually they made it to the taxi rank.

In the taxi his mother gave a sigh of relief and wondered why everyone was in such a rush.

"You'll get used to it mother, it's just the way they go about things down here," he said smiling. He had already instructed the driver to take them to the Regent Park Hotel. Feeling that having spent three weeks there, it would be very suitable for his mother, although there could be some awkward moments if the staff recalled him being there with Cheng Eng. However as luck would have it the receptionist did not know him and he managed to book a double room without any embarrassment.

When they entered the room, he gave his mother first choice of bed and said, "This is your holiday, so all arrangements will be made to suit you."
His mother had already sat on the bed next to the wall and bounced on it a few times. "This one will do just fine," she said while looking round the room with pleasure written all over her face.

He was pleased for her and was glad that he was able to take her mind off her grief, it gave him a sense of pride to be able to make his mother happy. "Do you feel up to a walk?" He asked, "it'll do us good to stretch our legs after sitting all day."
"Feel up to it! you cheeky young scamp. I am not old and past it yet you know," she joked with a twinkle in her eye.
"Right," he said, "only joking, let's go to the park, it's just down the road and I'm sure you'll love it."

Holding his mother's arm they walked slowly through the park and he was right. She was in her element and being a flower lover was thoroughly enjoying the beautiful displays. What a pity he thought, that my dad's not here to share this with her. Later after about an hours walking they were enjoying a seat, with a view overlooking a duck pond where some swans were eagerly eating up bread thrown to them by some nearby children.

He suggested calling to meet up with Cheng Eng and they could all go out for their dinner to some nice hotel. His mother thought this was a good idea and she readily agreed. On arrival at the international school of languages. He left his mother in the cab and told the driver that he would only be a few minutes and to wait. Knowing that Cheng Eng would have finished teaching he went straight to the hostel where he was confronted by the door's security system, which required a room number to be punched in but not knowing her room number he wasn't sure what to do. Then he saw a number with caretaker next to it, so he quickly pressed the appropriate buttons. He was taken by surprise at the speed of reply.

He introduced himself and said he wanted to contact Cheng Eng and would be more than pleased if the message could be passed on. There was a bit of crackling from the loudspeaker on the door and then quite clearly he was told to input the numbers 347 which he did without delay. She answered almost immediately. "John darling, come on in" and he heard the click as she automatically unlocked the door. "Hello, are you there?" he asked timidly, the way you do when talking to a machine. "Yes I'm still here," came the reply. He then explained that he had a taxi waiting and wanted her to come down.

"Sure thing, I'll be down in a minute," she replied, and true to her word she arrived promptly. She was absolutely delighted to see him and for some strange reason did not appear surprised. She threw her arms around him and showered him with kisses. What a wonderful welcome he thought, a complete contrast to that uncompassionate abrupt greeting from his wife yesterday.

He broke away from her embrace after a few moments. He grasped her hand and guided her over to the waiting taxi telling her that he had a surprise passenger for her to meet. After the introductions he was pleased to see that they took to one another right away and in a short time they were talking away to each other as if they were old time friends. He decided it would be just as well to return to their hotel for their meal, at least he knew they would get good service there.

They were not in the least disappointed because they had a most enjoyable time, the meal was excellent and the fellowship really did them a power of good, although there were moments of sadness when the position regarding his father was discussed. He was not sure how to approach the matter regarding his wife and her female lover and rather than mention the subject in front of his mother. He took the opportunity later when he walked with Cheng Eng to get her a taxi when she was going home. He told her everything, making sure that he missed no details. "Oh dear that is dreadful," she replied tearfully. "What a terrible shock for you."

With that she consoled him in her arms, he clung to her as if his life depended on it and would have remained there with her had it not been for the arrival of the taxi. He just had time to offer her some money to pay for the taxi, however she would not accept it from him stating that she had sufficient money now she had a job.

"Yes I know you have," he said,

"but I am inviting you over to the hotel every night this week so that you can share in my mother's holiday."

She was about to continue with her protest but could see that the taxi driver was anxious to get on his way, so she reluctantly accepted the money and bid him goodnight while promising to come along the following evening.

On his return to the hotel he found that his mother had already retired for the evening, so he got into his bed as quietly as he could so that he would not disturb her. Next morning during breakfast he laid out his plans for the day. However when his mother heard of the proposed boat trip on the river Thames she was a bit apprehensive and reminded him that she did not travel well on boats, and not only that, she could not swim.

He chuckled and teased her saying that she was not going over the Pentland Firth in the St Ola in wintertime to Orkney. The trip on the river Thames would be like travelling on a millpond by comparison. "It will be all right," he reassured her, "trust me, I'll do nothing to spoil this week for you. I want you to have a holiday with good memories to take home with you."

What then started out afterwards as a leisurely walk in the park progressed into a two-hour marathon. They were enjoying themselves so much that they completely lost track of the time. Not that they were tired, because they had regularly rested on the park benches while surveying the wonderful scenery which surrounded them. It was such a lovely day, the sun shining and not a cloud to be seen.

They also appreciated it being so much milder here than they were used to up in Scotland. He felt truly happy and contented and it felt good to see his mother obviously enjoying herself so much. He was beginning to realise that the simpler things in life appeared to bring about the most contentment. His peaceful meditation was about to be shattered! was someone calling his name or was he just imagining it. "John, John." Yes someone was clearly calling his name, even his mother turned to face the caller.

Too late he was out in the open with nowhere to hide, he couldn't believe it, of all the people to meet it had to be old Walter. The way he reacted you would have thought that John was his long lost son. He was obviously very pleased to see him and grabbing his hand almost shook his arm off with his warm welcome. John had to put on a bit of a show and make out that he too was glad that they had met again, mainly for the sake of his mother.

After introducing his mother, he invited Walter to join them for a coffee, and whenever there was the slightest chance of a listening ear, there was no way Walter would refuse. Sitting in the cafe John switched off. He had heard old Walter's stories on more than one occasion, so his thoughts were elsewhere. Walter on the other hand, could hardly believe he had such an attentive listener and was in full flow with his war stories.

At one stage John glanced over at his mother and it was plain to see that not only was she an attentive listener, but she seemed mesmerised, even awe- struck by the stories she was being told. Later, much later, when he managed to drag his mother away with the promise of them meeting here again in the morning, as soon as they were out of earshot he gave a great sigh of relief and was on the verge of apologising for her boring evening, when she really surprised him when she said. "What an interesting gentleman, you do have some really nice friends."

He thought surely she must be joking, but no, she was not. She seemed truly interested in Walter and said so in a most complementary manner.

He couldn't resist pulling her leg a bit and said, "He lives on his own in a lovely little flat and he's very active and goes for walks every day." As they walked on, his mother put her nose in the air in a mock sense of indignity and said. "I have no idea what you are talking about, I'm sure."

They both burst into laughter, in fact they laughed and joked all the way back to the hotel. From there it was a short taxi ride to the quayside for their afternoon boat trip. They had a while to wait before the trip commenced, so mainly in an effort to pass some time he sat on a bench and ate a beef burger which he bought from a nearby stall. His mother had politely refused his offer of one; she had no intentions of bringing on a bout of seasickness.

They both enjoyed the boat trip down the river and the courier kept most people interested with his running commentary and pointing out items of interest, such as the House's of Parliament. After they had disembarked on their return, he asked his mother if she had enjoyed it.

"Yes I did son very much, but to be really truthful I feel much better now that I'm back on dry land."

As they walked back to the hotel he kept his eye open for a taxi because his mother had told him her feet were killing her. He could see no sign of a taxi, but did see a sign for the underground. "Tell you what mother, how would you like a ride on an electric train?" He asked, whilst guiding her down the stairs and into the subway station. Among the rush of people he kept a firm hold of her arm, especially when they stood on the platform next to that black gaping hole of a tunnel.

There was a real danger of being jostled and accidentally knocked onto the track. He knew this was a new experience for her and was not in the least surprised when she stepped back when a train approached. Firstly there was the rattling noise which preceded the train which became louder as it came nearer but perhaps the most disturbing feature to the uninitiated was the great blast of air pushed out of the tunnel by the train as it exploded into view alongside the platform.

The instant it stopped the automatic doors slid open and people poured out, almost like salt from a salt-seller. They managed to get a seat, and he had to laugh at his mother's attempt to see out of the windows. All she could see was darkness and occasionally long lines of dirty cables which seemed to flash by endlessly. However soon the rocking and swaying lessened as the train burst into and stopped at Regent Park station, which was where they wanted to get off. They stood for a while on the pavement giving her a chance to get her bearings. The look on his mother's face said it all. She had been to Hell and back but had survived.

He was sure of one thing, her sore feet no longer bothered her! On their return to the hotel they were soon freshened up and made their way down to the dining room where Cheng Eng was waiting. Their time over the meal passed quickly and his mother brought Cheng Eng up to date by telling her all about her days activities.
"Did you know?" Cheng Eng asked, "that the vast majority of the world's population has never ever seen a car, never mind any other form of transportation?"

They had just finished their meal when the receptionist came over to advise that the taxi he had booked earlier had arrived. He thanked the receptionist and asked if she would tell the driver that they would be there in a few more minutes. He looked at his mother and explained that this evening's treat was a visit to a west end theatre. As soon as his mother had retrieved her coat they got under way. After the evening out they dropped Cheng Eng off before returning to the hotel in a taxi.

Next morning his mother reminded him to meet up with Walter. As they walked round the park he told her that he had not forgotten. Although secretly he wished he had and could think of a thousand things he would rather do than listen to a repeat of old Walter's exploits. They arrived at the coffee shop to find Walter smartly dressed waiting to open the door for them. John's mother was impressed by his good manners as Walter also pulled a chair out for her and pushed it back towards her as she sat down.

He then insisted that today was the day he should pay for their refreshments and went on to ask her if she was enjoying her stay in London. John was happy that the subject had changed today and was pleased that he wouldn't have to listen to Walter's memoirs once again. He was content to let them converse together while he stayed silent. He had just finished his last piece of coffee cream cake and drank the last of his coffee when he felt someone tapping on his left shoulder, and turning round he was startled to see the American journalist standing there, looking really troubled as he said to John

"Thank the Lord I have found you, we must go where we can speak in private. I have important and highly confidential news for you." Rising immediately from his seat John asked. "May we be excused for half an hour?" Walter answered for them both saying, "No problem your mother is in good hands." When they were outside John asked. "What is this all about?"

"Wait until we are out of earshot" the Journalist answered, "Then I'll tell you."

They crossed the road and went into the park. As soon as they were sitting on a bench with no one around the journalist said. "Boy have I got news for you, remember you gave me a theory about the green snow being possibly radioactive? Well an expedition team went to investigate and that was the first check they made."

"After getting the necessary guarantee from the

Tibetan authorities NASA lost no time in arranging for the advance team of scientists, including all their supplies to be dropped at night by parachutes over that area. They all wore white suits and all the equipment they had was also white for camouflage as there was no way of knowing if there were any unfriendly patrols around that area." John interrupted. "During the time we spent there, no one, not even a footprint was seen apart from our own."

"Let me continue," said the journalist, "The aircraft mission was successful, and the scientists working with the most advanced equipment found the area of green snow to be dangerous and highly radioactive. The readings went right off the scale. It was just as well they were wearing protective suits.

Further tests carried out ascertained that a circular metal object almost one hundred feet in diameter was lying about thirty feet below the surface. Data from a core bore confirmed your assumption that it had been there about twenty-five thousand years. Other evidence came from researchers who uncovered some old Tibetan quotes taken from ancient books written by Monks and going back thousands of years. When the researchers translated them into English. Oh! wait a minute, I can't quite remember exactly what they said word for word."

He opened his briefcase and took out a fax sheet. "Here it is, you read it." He handed it over and John read aloud,

'Red, like the erupting volcano means keep away, it cultivates fear,

So by no means ever go near;
Green is for safe pastures, where contented cattle graze,
where couples can walk happily hand in hand,
To survey the flowers and the peaceful land,
There is an exception to this green rule
and he who ignores it would be a fool,
never, never go
to the green snow.
Ignore this warning if you like,
But the end of your life is certainly in sight. "

John started to tremble and the colour drained from his cheeks. The journalist asked if he was all right? He could barely speak but he managed to stutter, "It's not only my life which will end prematurely but poor innocent Cheng Eng, we both walked over that highly radioactive snow. Not once but twice and now we shall both pay the penalty of death."

By now he was in a shocking state and let the fax sheet drop from his trembling hand, tears ran down his face and in a trembling practically incoherent voice he said. "How am I going to tell her? How?" Putting both hands on his forehead he started to sob great loud gasping sobs. The journalist put his arm round his shoulder to console him and said,

"Look on the bright side, both of you will be given the best treatment that money can buy, it won't cost you a cent."

In his time of grief he let it all out. Telling the journalist all about the bad news he had received when he first arrived home. His father's death had left him feeling downhearted and saddened. Now he was devastated and muttered that he wished he had stayed in Tibet. A gust of wind had blown the fax sheet away and as the journalist went to retrieve it from where it had caught on a nearby bush. He noticed a small group of spectators gathering around. Gripping John by the shoulders he gently shook him and said, "Come on buddy you must pull yourself together, look at all these people staring at you. I'm sure they think you are a drunk or a druggy. Let's get out of here." He took John's arm and steered him across the road into a public house.

In the pub John downed a double brandy and was sipping his second, when the journalist reminded him that he had promised his mother he would be back in half an hour. The journalist suggested that he could break the news to Cheng Eng if John wanted him to do so. The brandy was having an effect on John and he was managing to pull himself together. He told the journalist he would think about it and let him know tomorrow morning when Cheng Eng would meet them in the café again.

When they arrived back there, Walter was still in full flow and one could be forgiven for thinking that he had not even missed them. After their meal they spent the remainder of the early afternoon wandering round the British Museum right up until it closed. They preferred to use the underground rather than a taxi to return home, because the taxi ride to the museum was like something out of a James Bond film. The driver drove like a madman by going through red lights, passing vehicles on the wrong side of the road etc.

One would think he was taking a pregnant woman to hospital. Whatever was on his mind they did not know, or indeed care. They were put off taxis for that day.

Emerging from the underground they parted after arranging to meet in the morning at ten thirty in the café. He asked his mother what she preferred to do, either wait an hour in the lounge for Cheng Eng or take a walk in the park?

"A walk would be fine," she answered, taking his arm for security as they crossed the busy road at a nearby crossing. It was soon dusk and they had enjoyed themselves so much but now it was time to return. Cheng Eng fully understood and brushed off their attempts to apologise for being so late, when they met up in the lounge.

During the meal they exchanged their days experiences and on the whole had a most pleasant time. Cheng Eng said that she had spent the day with immigration and went on to share some stories that the incomers told them. These stories had them in stitches. They laughed so much that some of the other guests were looking at them rather enviously. Later that night Cheng Eng and his mother had a really good sob during a film that they went to see. He couldn't quite understand the point of their tears and was dumbstruck when they both said that they truly enjoyed the film. it was great they said and both agreed they would go to see it again.

Soon it was back to the routine of dropping Cheng Eng off before they returned to the hotel and bed. He had a restless night and took a while to drop off because his mother tended to talk in her sleep. Next morning he was up and dressed while his mother still slept. Even when he returned after breakfast, she was still asleep. He left her a note explaining that not wanting to wake her, he would meet her at the café later on. He was fortunate enough to be able to have a quiet word with Walter before his mother arrived.

On her arrival she apologised for being late and said she could not understand it, as she was usually an early riser. "That's what champagne does for you mother," he said while winking at Walter. The journalist arrived and John went over and began talking to him. The journalist asked John if he could speak to him urgently and in private "The thing is, we have sent six scientists in to investigate the green snow more thoroughly but we have had problems getting them out again and I was wondering if we could use your route to help?"

"Yes you can but how will you get it to them?" asked John. The journalist said, "Oh, I can fax it through to them."

"I'll have to go to the hotel and write down the exact route. You do realise this may take some time?"

Approaching his mother afterwards he said, "I had hoped to take you to Kew gardens today mother, but how would it be if Walter took you instead?"

"That's fine." She replied, as John continued "I'll order you both a taxi over at the hotel and I also insist that Walter joins us for dinner tonight at our hotel."

10

The Ancient Flying Saucer

The receptionist was extremely helpful so he arranged with her for one of the kitchen staff to bring up a pot of tea and some sandwiches for him later on. He was planning to be in his room all day. He arrived there to find the cleaning staff just leaving and sat down to work out the highly complex route. Making sure he didn't miss out any details whatsoever.

Later in the day, room service arrived with his requested tea and sandwiches, which he was ready for. Soon after that his mother returned and reassured him that they were both back safely and that she had had a wonderful time. Walter was waiting downstairs and they were both going for a walk before their evening meal. As soon as his mother left he continued with his task, in the hope he would have it ready for the journalist when he arrived later for dinner.

Even after double-checking his work he finished in plenty of time. Leaving him with an hour to spare. He walked to the local pub where he spent some time with a couple of half pints of beer. When he arrived back at the hotel the journalist was there waiting for him. He took him up to his room and showed him the completed work.

"Why that's just fine," said the journalist, "I'm most impressed and I will fax this off first thing in the morning before I fly back to the states." As they made their way down to the lounge he again assured John that he would be well paid for this information he had provided. Walter, his mother and Cheng Eng were already seated waiting for them.

After a lovely meal he surprised them all by showing he had purchased tickets for the most popular west end show and they should follow him to reception to await their taxis. Walking through to the reception the journalist took him aside and asked if he had broken the news to Cheng Eng about the radiation situation. He said he had not and agreed that he could not put it off any longer.

During a few quiet moments while they waited on the taxi he took her aside and gently broke the news to her. To his utter amazement she took it very calmly and did not seem in the least upset or worried. She went on to say that if that was the price of the adventure of a lifetime, then so be it. He only wished that he could have her attitude. Although he enjoyed the show even the highlights could not erase the thought of such a dreadful death awaiting him and it was on his mind continuously.

As he kissed her goodnight he had nothing but admiration for her, how strong and brave she was. She was still on his mind when he eventually dropped off to sleep that night. Even his sleepless night did not stop him rising early. One thing he must do today was to get his mother new spectacles. Having spent so much time with his mother over the last few days he realised just how poor her eyesight was and come to think of it, he had never ever seen her without her glasses. The big question was however, how would he manage to get her to agree, he had heard her refuse to have her eyes tested before.

Making his way to the reception he was pleased to see that the pleasant and obliging receptionist was still on duty. It only took her a few minutes to look up yellow pages and supply him with an Opticians address. While he was at it he also booked a taxi. Later when his mother had joined him for breakfast she could have been excused for thinking he was rather quieter than usual. He was quiet because he had thought out a plan to get his mother's agreement to have her eyes tested.

He discussed with his mother their plans for the day, which included another round London trip in an open decked bus. "Will Walter be coming?" asked his mother. "Why of course, if he wants to," he replied. "First let's take a trip down town in a taxi, there is a shop I want you to see."

As good timing would have it, they had just finished breakfast and made it down to reception when the taxi arrived. Although their destination was only a mile away they would have been far quicker walking it, even at his mother's pace. The taxi was caught up in the mad rush hour traffic and when it was able to move it did so at a snails pace, even so, they arrived before the shop opened. He stood in front of his mother to protect her from the hoards of commuters who were pouring out of a nearby underground station. The last thing he wanted was for her to be knocked to the ground. Any knocking down that had to be done. He would do it as part of his plans.

By this time they were standing in the optician's doorway and were soon joined by a smartly dressed tall lady who opened her handbag and took out a bunch of keys to open the front door. His heart was thumping and he caught his breath, not because of the beauty of the lady opening the door, but because this was the time for his plan to be put into action. As he stepped aside to allow the shop assistant access. He gently stuck his elbow into his mother's ribs, while at the same instantly flicking her glasses off her face and onto the ground. With one side step he managed to stand on the spectacles breaking them. Apologising sincerely to his mother and to the shop assistant. He felt he should have received an Oscar for his acting.

His mother surprised him when she burst into tears and let out a terrible wail as he bent to retrieve the broken spectacles. Yes he had expected her to be upset but not to the extent that she was. The shop assistant was most attentive and did her best to help. She invited them into the shop and then made a cup of tea in an effort to console his mother who was crying out loud "Oh don't let me go blind, I really do need my glasses."

"It's OK mother don't worry about it, I broke your glasses so I will buy you a new pair," he said quietly and then addressing himself to the assistant he asked if she could possibly arrange for her be fixed up right away? He would pay cash and there would be no NHS involvement.

By this time all the staff had arrived and the assistant, who was in fact the receptionist, went off to see her boss about it. She soon returned confirming that an eye test could be carried out within half an hour and most likely new glasses within two hours if they cared to wait. This news fairly cheered his mother up. She then began to relate a very sad experience she had as a young girl.

When she first left school she worked in a dairy and one of her jobs was to stick labels on milk cartons. Because she was always getting into trouble for sticking the labels on upside down, her mother had arranged for her to get glasses but she hated them and would not wear them. Her father who was a very strict disciplinarian put a tight blindfold on her one Friday evening and did not allow it to be removed until Monday morning. He said this was to teach her what it was like to be blind and that's what would happen if she did not wear her glasses.

This had been such a traumatic and frightening experience that she had never been without the glasses since. "How long ago was that?" enquired the receptionist "About forty years," his mother whimpered. "Are you telling me you've had these glasses for forty years mother?"
"Well," said the receptionist "It's a stroke of luck that they were broken today, they are well past their sell by date."

Soon after that the optician took them both through to his clinic, and John sat aside watching as extensive tests were conducted. When he was finished the Optician said,

"Do you know that you have been permanently wearing reading glasses? It's a miracle your eyesight isn't badly damaged distance wise. You only require new glasses for reading. The last time I saw spectacles like these was when I was a young student. They are now museum pieces and should have been replaced years ago."

She was then allowed to choose her own frames; then he slotted in the new lenses and again given a test card to read but this time she passed with flying colours. He instructed her that she should use her glasses only when reading but there was nothing to stop her wearing sunglasses if she needed to wear something at other times. Back in the waiting room he had a good long look at his mother. Seeing her for the first time without those ugly old glasses and what a transformation.

She really was a nice looking woman. The new spectacles took years off her, even the receptionist remarked on how different she looked. Paying the receptionist in full he included a £10.00 tip, telling the receptionist to treat herself to something nice. Stepping outside, his mother exclaimed how clear everything was and now felt quite comfortable to be without the glasses having being advised by the eye doctor, as she called him.

Throughout their underground journey back to the café she continued to be amazed at the different sights. When they entered the café Walter and the journalist both remarked how lovely she looked without her old glasses on.

"What do you think of my new reading glasses?" she said

250

while putting them on. They both agreed they were very nice and were a thousand times better than the old ones. As they conversed over their coffee, they agreed how fortunate it was that her old ones had been broken in the first place. The subject changed when the journalist gave John his business contact card, and explained that he was leaving for the states that afternoon.

The journalist also told him he had received a newsletter, which mentioned another old Cantonese legend about a huge round bird. Apparently some 300 warriors were sent to capture it but not one of them ever returned, nor indeed were they ever heard of again. He had also received a fax confirming that the scientists had received his escape route plans and were using them. They were returning with some of the green snow for analysis. He had also been given authority to make John a payment of $300,000 immediately on the scientists return.

"The money is of little consequence to me," said John "but the saving of their six lives will be satisfaction enough."

Before leaving, the journalist invited them over to the States for a holiday in his holiday home in Florida. They thanked him and John suggested he might well take him up on his offer. After he left, John's mother said that she had invited Walter up to her home in Scotland. Walter said that he had never been as far as her village before and would be delighted to visit, as long as John approved that was. Getting over his surprise quickly, he smiled and said that it was a great idea and gave his full approval.

By this time they had arrived at the pickup point for their round London bus trip. There was a small group of people queuing up before them, including some children who were having the time of their lives, running round, screaming, and trying to climb up the bus-stop pole. Most people were glad when the bus arrived as the children's antics were beginning to get on their nerves. He noticed with delight that his mother was much more confident now that she could see better and was upstairs in a flash. The time fairly whizzed by and before they knew it they were back where they started.

Next on the agenda was a tour to Windsor castle where they had a light meal and a most enjoyable afternoon. With some people no doubt dreaming of what it would be like to live in such luxurious surroundings. Walter had accepted their invitation to join them for the evening meal at the hotel. They were forced to start without Cheng Eng until her arrival twenty minutes later full of apologies for the heavy traffic. "Thank goodness it's Friday," she said "I'm off all the weekend."

"How right you are," he said "and you are off in the literal sense too, because I have a plan for you to come up to my home for the weekend. We're being picked up by taxi tomorrow morning at ten thirty from the coffee house, so make sure you're there in time my dear." She couldn't contain her excitement and threw her arms around his neck, kissing and cuddling him.

"I'm so excited, I can hardly wait to see your beautiful village in the Lake District." Looking at John's mother she remarked on how much better she looked without glasses. "You really do look so much younger!" she said. They had planned for an early bed that night so until bedtime they talked together in the lounge.

Next morning as usual his mother was up, packed and ready to go before he got out of bed with a yawn. After breakfast with all things squared up at reception they made their way over to the coffee house. Here they pulled two tables together and by the time they had made room for their entire luggage, they had commandeered most of the coffee shop. It was quite embarrassing as on one occasion a waitress nearly tripped over one of the bags while carrying a tray full of dishes.

Dismounting from their taxi at Euston station he purchased the tickets, two singles and two returns, and would not allow Walter or Cheng Eng to pay him, as they were his privileged guests. No sooner were they all comfortably seated than Walter began telling them of his travels through India in a steam train. He pointed out that it was common practise for the native passengers to sit on the roof of the coaches and it was anyone's guess as to how many accidents there were.

The journey passed without incident and they arrived bang on schedule at Carlisle. He hired a car for use over the weekend and his first port of call on his way home was to Carlisle castle. They had a full hour before closing time which gave them time to visit the Border regiment museum which was adjacent to the castle. This was right up Walter's street and they had to literally drag him away because they were closing the gates. During their guided tour John noticed that nothing much had changed since his last visit twenty-five years ago as a school child.

11

Home to Langwathby

All too soon it was time to head for Langwathby but as they passed through Penrith they stopped for fish and chips and a stroll round the shops, which by this time were all closed. As they walked along he pointed to a shop across the street and said, "That's Jack's butcher shop, Jack is a nice fellow, very obliging, he's my brother in law. He is married to my wife's sister, we'll call and see them after our fish and chips."

When they arrived at the chip shop there was a queue for carry outs but plenty of seats for those eating in. The waitress who called at their table recognised him and said, "My John you're a big stranger, do you still have your trendy little sports car?"

"Why yes I do," he answered, "but not with me today, it's too small for me and my friends."

When she had left with their order, Cheng Eng asked if she had been one of his girlfriends. He replied with a laugh, that she had lived in the same village and had a crush on big Tom at one time but Tom didn't fancy her.

"She got a run in my car once and that was it," he said

The waitress brought them their fish suppers including bread, butter and all the trimmings along with a large pot of tea and another of boiling water. The smell coming through from the fish bar had made them all very hungry so they wasted no time in clearing the food from the table.

"You know," said John's mother, "I don't want to sound ungrateful, but the meals we were served in these first class hotels and restaurants in London were nothing like this. The plain food and the atmosphere here is unbeatable."

Looking over at Cheng Eng, John said, "it's also a far cry from some of the meals we had while up there in the mountains of Tibet. When we were huddled up in sub zero temperatures eating dried cereal and vegetables and melting snow for water to drink. Looking back now I wonder how we managed to survive."

This was an obvious mistake to start on survival tactics because very soon Walter took up the subject and related at great length a survival trip he had undergone during his army service. He missed out no detail, even mentioning that he and his mates had been so hungry they had eaten worms, raw fish and other small insects to survive.

John's mother who seemed to be enjoying the gory details asked him if he had ever killed anybody. For once Walter went quiet and said. "Unfortunately many times, please forgive me for not wanting to talk about it. I know that it was done in wartime and it was a case of kill or be killed but I still have nightmares about it and would prefer not to discuss the details." It could be clearly seen that to pursue the matter any further would leave Walter very upset. They had all been so engrossed in his story. They were surprised when John suggested they had better leave the shop as they had been there for well over two hours.

Jack opened the door of his flat above the shop. He was delighted to see them and immediately invited them all in, while commenting on how different John's mother looked without glasses on. Upstairs in the sitting room, Ruth, as normal was stretched out on a couch doing her fingernails with brilliant red nail varnish. Lying scattered around her was a conglomeration of fashion magazines. John made the introductions while Jack got everyone a seat, and then went into the kitchen to prepare coffee.

Ruth asked how the expedition had gone. He explained as briefly as possible that it had been a great success and that is where he had met Cheng Eng. Ruth, well known for being blunt and lacking in diplomacy said, "Just as well you found someone, because according to reliable information, I have been told that queer sister of mine has got herself a lesbian lover." Obviously embarrassed by her crudeness, John changed the subject and asked her if she had heard of the whereabouts of big Tom?

"Last time I heard from him he was somewhere in Argentina, that card there on the mantelpiece arrived some six months ago, I've heard nothing from him since," she answered, while pointing out the card to him. Jack reappeared carrying a tray of hot drinks and biscuits. They all helped themselves to a drink while politely refusing the biscuits and cakes.

From there on the conversation centred mainly on his mother who told them how much she had enjoyed her holiday in London, but at the same time was glad to be back home. When they were ready to leave, Jack offered to run them home in his van. They thanked him and John explained about the hired car, which they had up in the car park. Walking towards the car he thought to himself how pleasant Jack was, a very obliging person who couldn't do enough to help, what a contrast from Ruth who hadn't moved from the couch nor interrupted her nail- painting throughout their visit. He had no time for her, he remembered only too well how insulting she had been to big Tom, her brother.

His mother who had spotted a late open grocery shop interrupted his thoughts. "We will need some messages before the morning, so we might as well get some now," she said. On entering the almost deserted store, he wondered how they could make a profit staying open until this time of night; nevertheless it was a Godsend that they did. Even after reminding his mother to buy only breakfast food. Since they would be mainly eating out, she still purchased a full trolley load from the supermarket.

She also purchased some flowers for her late husband's grave. It was just as well that the car had a big boot with enough room for the groceries as well as their luggage. Driving home in the dark there was not much that could be seen, however it was a short journey and very soon they were gathered in his mother's living room along with a pile of luggage beside them. His mother put the groceries in the kitchen, then sorted out the sleeping arrangements and showed each person to their respective bedroom.

John reverted to his usual sleeping on the couch whenever guests were accommodated. He had spent many a night here before getting his own house. He was first up in the morning so he lit the fire and laid the table, setting it up in preparation for their breakfast. When he opened the curtains he was surprised to see that it was a beautiful morning, most unusual for a Sunday, more often than not it, would be dull and wet at the weekends.

Soon after, Cheng Eng and his mother came downstairs and his mother went straight to making their breakfast. He asked her if she was going to Church later that morning and if so would she mind if he accompanied her. "Oh yes I'll be going," she said, "and you are all more than welcome to come with me."

"I will be more than happy to accompany you in a visit to the Lord's house today dear lady" said the old soldier.

Later Walter was sitting by the open fire, which reminded him of the house in which he had been brought up in London. The pensioners flat he now lived in was centrally heated with boring and lifeless radiators. While they made a marvellous job of keeping you warm, they could never compete with the flickering wonder and the sense of comfort given off by a coal fire. He could remember as a child at night time looking into the fire when the lights were out, and imagining all sorts of things. Not just in the flickering colours of the flames but also from the scary shadows thrown around the rest of the room.

Driving to church later that morning almost became a disaster, when they were about halfway there. They had to return home for the flowers for his father's grave. John did not want to be going into the church late, when all eyes would be on them, however he knew that the graveside flowers had not been changed for a week, so back home it was, he had no choice.

He need not have worried because they arrived at the church in plenty of time. Although he found the service a bit boring, it seems most of the others thought it was ok. As usual when the service was over, the minister stood at the doorway where he shook hands and had a word of encouragement with the congregation as they filed out. When his mother started to tell the minister about her holiday experiences he made a discreet departure to the car park.

When the car park was empty he began to wonder what was holding them up. Eventually Cheng Eng showed up and explained that his mother had the minister riveted with her conversation. He just had to rescue that poor minister, so he collected the flowers from the car, and going back up to the church, he handed them to his mother and said. "Please excuse me for interrupting but it looks as if it's going to rain, perhaps we had better replace the flowers now." The minister said very kindly, "Don't let me detain you" and made a hasty retreat.

No sooner had they replaced the flowers and put the dying ones in the nearby compost heap, than it started to rain, perhaps monsoon would be an appropriate word to explain the rain. After a mad dash they sat dripping in the car,

"What weather," he said, "typical for this part of the country, nice and sunny one minute and torrential rain the next. Never mind it's not going to spoil our day, we are going on a car tour, even if we have to use the windscreen wipers all day." This made them laugh and no doubt heightened their spirits.

Driving leisurely through the quiet country lanes they arrived at Calbeck just in time for a Sunday special bar lunch of roast beef, roast potatoes, vegetables, Yorkshire pudding and gravy. After a drink they decided to go for a walk as the rain had stopped. They visited a local graveyard where the famous foxhunter John Peel was buried. They had a leisurely look round the village before continuing their mystery tour in a Northerly direction. Within two hours they arrived at the Tibetan monastery in Eskdale Muir.

He had been here before, for the others however it was awe-inspiring and a time of wonder. They were particularly pleased with the inside of the monastery. Walter and his mother made their way to the cafeteria while he and Cheng Eng had a word with one of the monks and asked him if it would be possible to have a word with the Abbot. About five minutes later he led them along a narrow corridor, and then into a large and very ornately decorated room. On the floor sitting cross-legged was the Abbot who smiled, and politely asked what could he do for them.

After thanking him for seeing them, John explained that he had purchased a book from this monastery some years ago, which mentioned an old legend about an area of green snow in Tibet which had compelled him to journey there and try to find it. He explained in detail how both he and Cheng Eng had visited the area in the hope of solving the riddle.

He told the Abbot they had proved that the legend was true but their life expectancy was considerably shortened due to a heavy dose of radioactivity from the snow. The Abbot had listened intently until he had finished. Then speaking in a quiet soft voice he said,

"My dear friends of the mission, you have been led by the spiritual forces of the ancient ancestors of the bamboo stone tribe. Who frequented the green snow area, it was your destiny. However you have not told me everything that you found. You are withholding something very important. The guardian spirits of the ancients let you escape, is that not true?"

"You both have a secret which you must take to the grave with you." They exchanged glances with each other and were totally flabbergasted and speechless. They both knew that it was the secret cave he was referring to. His next statement caught them unawares. What he said was even more stunning and left them gasping for breath. He clapped his hands saying "Do not worry about the radiation because the ancient spirits have protected you from it."

He then bowed his head and gestured they should leave while at the same time striking a nearby gong. This was an obvious signal to a monk who entered and led them back outside. As soon as they had parted from the monk it took them all their time to contain their excitement and joy at having a death sentence lifted from them. "I just knew it," he whispered.

"All the time we were in that cave I felt we were being watched. The fact the Abbot knew all about it must prove the point."
"Its times like this" she answered, "that makes me so glad we did not open the second trap door. I'm sure if we had we would have signed our death warrant." They finished their day at the monastery with a coffee and some biscuits.

Returning home he took a more scenic route, firstly to Langholm then through Longtown and a variety of small villages, including Brampton, until finally arriving home in the dark. The change of air had really tired them out so after a nightcap they went straight to bed. Lying on the couch trying to sleep was difficult for him, because he could not clear his mind of the wonderful news he had received from the Abbot earlier.

His thoughts turned to the week ahead, and he figured out detailed plans for the next few days. Tomorrow after breakfast they would all call up and see his twins, and then perhaps stay a few nights at the Boothbay's hotel in the Lake District. From there they could go out on day trips and return to the hotel every evening. At the end of the week they would drive down into Lytham St Anne's to see big uncle Reg, and he would repay him the sponsorship money he owed him and hopefully they would see his neighbours Bob and Margaret who had now retired.

The Blackpool illuminations were now on and if they were really lucky they could get bed and breakfast there for one night. They could stay the final night of their holiday in Morecambe and from there drive back up to return the hired car in Carlisle. Walter and Cheng Eng would then get the train from there back down to London.

Next morning his mother, who was making breakfast in the kitchen awakened him with the rattling of cups and saucers. "There's no point lighting the fire today mother, since we will be out all day, I'll clean it out ready to light it though," he said. He was careful not to tell her that they would not be back for the best part of a week, because he wanted to go over his plans with them all at breakfast. He cleaned out the fire and set it up ready for lighting and then went upstairs for a wash and shave.

However he was soon back down again for some hot water. Their water was always heated by the open fire but not being lit there was no hot water. His mother gave him a pot of boiling water from the Aga cooker in the kitchen. Later he joined the others at the breakfast table and explained his plans for the rest of the week to them. He needn't have worried because they were all delighted with the idea of touring around.

He decided to walk to the local shop for some sweets for his children. Walter asked if he could tag along, as he liked nothing better than a walk first thing in the morning.

As they started to walk along the country road a large mobile workshop driven by John's wife came along side

264

and slowed down. "Ah! That's my wife Ruby, I'll introduce you," he said. As she stepped from the vehicle Walter's face was a picture, he doubted he had ever seen such a tall woman before. After the introductions she said. "I was at the house the other day and read your note on the door about you being away".

"Yes I had mother in London for a week, she fair enjoyed it, it's made such a difference to her, she looks so much younger. Why don't you go in and have a word with her, we are away this afternoon for another week."

"I'll do that now," she said, opening the gate. Seeing the hired car she assumed it was Walters.

"I like your car Walter, it's a real beauty." she said.

Later as they walked towards the shop Walter said, "You told me she was big but that was quite an understatement, she appears very strong."

"Oh yes, she is strong all right," he replied. "She's so much like her brother big Tom and not at all like her sister you met the other day. They're as different as chalk and cheese."

With that he put his hand up to cover his mouth. "Blast and double blast," he said,

"Ruby has gone into the house to see my mother, but she will also find Cheng Eng in there. I do hope she doesn't start a fight." Walter consoled him by explaining that they had never met each other so she could not know who the girl was. He took the opportunity to confide in Walter and explain about Ruby's infidelity with another woman. And went on to confess, if he had known what was happening he would never have returned and would have settled in Thailand. He bought the twins their sweets and noticed Walter buy a large box of chocolates along with a newspaper. He had a good idea who would be getting the chocolates.

Stopping beside a beautifully set out garden he pointed it out to Walter. "It's hard to believe but two years ago all that garden was an overgrown wilderness and nothing but weeds could be seen. I'm sure you can tell it's a professional Gardener who has it now. He's semi retired, so we had him do some work for us up at the farm, you'll see later just how good a job he made. My mother was the home help to Mrs Millburn in that house over there, he said pointing to a small cottage. If you ever want to know the history of a place then go to the post office, the post man usually knows who comes and who leaves." Walter chuckled, "Yes it's much the same everywhere." he said.

Arriving back at the house his mother was in the living room packing her suitcase and he asked her if Cheng Eng was ok and what had happened when Ruby met her. "She's upstairs packing her bag, and that's where she was when Ruby called, so they didn't meet. I was quite pleased about that," she added, "trouble was the last thing I wanted before we go off on holiday."

Later while Walter was packing the cases in the car, John lifted the car's bonnet, and checked the oil level and radiator water before driving the short distance up to the farmhouse. When they arrived they could see the children and their nanny playing outside on the lawn. The nanny approached them, no doubt wondering who was in the strange car but as soon as she recognised them she waved and pointed them out to the children, who seeing their grandmother, ran over to greet her while shouting and waving frantically. The others had stopped to admire the flowered covered archway and the rest of the lovely garden.

After the introductions the nanny went indoors to prepare a drink, leaving them to entertain the twins.

"My they are big for their age," said Cheng Eng. "They sure are," said Walter, "you can tell they take after their mother."

They played with the children and made a right fuss of them, until the nanny reappeared on the scene with a large tray of hot drinks for the adults and soft drinks for the children.

They then enjoyed a little picnic, and had to laugh at the facial expressions of the children as they tried to figure out what was different about their granny. Never having seen her without spectacles on before. All too soon it became time to go, it was always difficult to leave the children behind and today was no exception. He gave them the sweeties, instructing them to leave them with their nanny who would dish them out later.

When they reached Penrith he put fuel in the car and carried on driving for a further three hours until they reached Milam where he knew they would get a good meal in the Bridge café just round the corner from the car park. They trooped into the café and were studying the menu when the waitress who had been wiping the tabletops with a cloth, came over to take their order. Recognising John she smiled "No plaster on your arm now then!" she said. "I'm fine now thanks," he said, "You've got a good memory."

"It wasn't that long ago," she said "must have been about two years ago. When your lady friend sorted out the black five gang." He could see the inquisitive looks on their faces so while she went to get their order he explained the story to them.

As they finished their meal he suggested he change his route, and would they agree to go to Blackpool first and return via the lakes. "You're the driver" they all agreed, "We're quite happy to go wherever you take us."

They stopped off at Carnforth on the way down, and had a trip round the local market. They then went down and looked over the old steam locomotives, which brought back many childhood memories to him, he remembered going train spotting with his father.

Next stop was Blackpool and they were lucky enough to find accommodation in the first hotel they tried. Luck was really with them as there was even room in the private car park adjoining the small hotel. Driving in the town during the illuminations would be a nightmare, so during their stay they would be using the tram system for transport.

They got settled in and had an evening meal etc before going for a walk along the promenade. It was getting dark now and they fairly enjoyed the colourful lights. They had a bit of a job trying to get into a tram because every one was full when they arrived at their stop. Eventually when they did get on a tram they didn't have a clue where to get off. However, Walter reckoned they were about two miles from the Tower. They asked the conductor if he knew where their hotel was, while showing him the hotel ticket. "I'm a tram conductor, not a tourist board official," he curtly replied. "You don't expect me to know all the names of all the hotels in Blackpool, do you?" They wished they had shut their mouths and not said anything to him. So they got tickets to where they thought was about right. When Walter got up to leave they all followed him.

By the time the tram stopped they were a mile or so away from where they wanted to get off. They were really lost now and found themselves passing the same place twice so they had obviously gone round in a circle; his mother was beginning to complain about having sore feet. The place was teeming with people; they were in among the amusement arcades and cafes.

They went into a café and spent a leisurely half hour there where they had a drink and made use of the toilet facilities. Coming out they walked along the promenade to the tower in search of a taxi. Arriving at a taxi rank the first three drivers didn't have a clue where the hotel was, one other driver laughed and said,
"No wonder they can't find it, that hotel has changed name, it's now called the Excelcia and they're still using the old tickets." Although it was nearly midnight the roads were still packed and it took them twenty minutes to travel the two miles in the taxi. It was four very tired guests that

arrived back and went straight to bed.

Next morning they met up at the breakfast table and comparing their key rings, noticed they still had the old hotel name on them. Rather than take the tram this morning they decided on a leisurely walk to the Tower. They took their time, having a seat to rest their legs when they felt like it. The tide was out and they enjoyed looking over the wall and watching the antics of the people on the beach. They went into the tower café where they all indulged themselves in an ice cream cone before queuing for their trip to the top.   His mother decided to wait for their return since she was a bit afraid of the height. She changed her mind however and decided to go along when Walter said he would wait with her. She did not want him to miss out on the experience, after all he was on holiday. Meanwhile John noticed that there was a variety show on later that night which he thought looked interesting, so he asked them if they would like to go. They scrutinised the poster and they too thought it would be interesting. So off he went to get tickets and was lucky enough to have them all seated together.

By this time the queue for the lift to the top of the Tower was reasonable and within a short period of time they were aboard and shooting up to the top. Getting out of the lift he could see that this mother was visibly shaken and he had a pang of conscience about bringing her up in the first instance. She stood well back from the edge and there was no way she would cross over the glass inspection area on the floor, even after he read out the details from a nearby plaque indicating that it was some two feet thick and extremely safe. She still would not venture on it. It was not until they were back down on the street before his mother cheered up again.

After a welcome lunch of fish and chips they spent the rest of the day window shopping and visiting some of the very many Arcades and funfairs. They returned to the hotel tired and weary and also very hungry. By the time they had finished their evening meal it had started to rain and a high wind had sprung up. They could see from the hotel the spray from the sea bursting over the sea wall. What a contrast from the previous night.

The taxi which he had ordered at the reception desk, arrived to take them to the evening show at the Winter Gardens. The gale had cleared the streets and only the occasional pedestrian ventured out, even the trams were empty. Therein lay the great mystery, where had all the people gone? Were they all hibernating in their hotels or boarding houses? One poor soul was seen walking a dog and battling against the wind with her head down, and trying for dear life to stop her brolly from turning outside in.

Some of the many lights which made up such lovely and interesting designs were blown down and swinging wildly in the wind and if the storm did not lessen, there would be a lot more down by morning. Sitting in the theatre waiting for the show to start. He noticed that only about half of the seats were taken, no doubt because of the terrible weather. The show was very good, considering the price of the tickets and the new acts backing up some well-known singers and comedians had very original ideas. The final act, making their debut was a musical group called The Jokers, one of them who was called Dopey wore a pair of gigantic spectacles while sitting on a mat and playing a guitar. He sure lived up to his name. Then there was Ropey who was dressed up in an outfit made from rope with all the trimmings including tassels. He was the drummer.

The keyboard player was called Boaty, and again he was dressed for the part in a full sailor's outfit, cap and all. Last and by no means least was the singer, he was a great singer who wore a most spectacular gown and called himself Popeye apart from the fact that they were good, they deserved ten out of ten for originality. As they finished their act they got a tremendous ovation from the audience, including many shouts of "More! More!"

They got back to the hotel without incident, had a nightcap and then off to bed. He found it difficult to get to sleep because of the noise of the wind howling outside and making the room windows rattle. He made tea twice during the night before eventually getting to sleep. It felt as if he had just shut his eyes when he heard a knock on the door and Walter was there telling him that the rest were down at the breakfast table.

He was deadbeat and bleary eyed when he stumbled to the sink to have a shave. After he was dressed and just before going downstairs. He drew the curtains and was pleased to see that although it was still windy, the rain had stopped and the sun was out. Sitting with the others at breakfast, he could see through the bay window, council workers using a hydraulic lift on the back of a lorry to reach up and repair the fallen lights.

"That was some wind last night, it kept me awake till about four this morning," he confessed.

"Same here," agreed Walter. "Also there was a gate or something that screeched and banged with every gust, I felt like getting up and going outside to fix it."

They just couldn't help laughing at the way Walter expressed himself, they could almost picture him roaming around in the dark with an oilcan and looking for a gate with rusty hinges.

"I just hope our stay in Morecambe tonight is a bit more peaceful, perhaps we should look for somewhere clear of the shoreline," he suggested. "It will probably be as noisy there anyway, because It's a popular place at this time of the year as they have their own illuminations, a sort of miniature Blackpool so to speak."

After breakfast they wasted no time in getting packed and were soon enjoying the lovely scenery on the way to Lytham Saint Ann's to see Reg. They arrived just in time, because Reg was loading his golf clubs into the back of his Volvo estate car. John pumped the horn a few times to attract his attention and stop him from getting into his car and setting off. It worked, because Reg turned to look at them with a vague look on his face, no doubt wondering who were these strangers and why were they tooting at him. He approached the car with caution and bent down to speak through the drivers open window.

His face broke out in a wide grin when he recognised John and his mother.

"Hi there," he exclaimed with obvious pleasure. "Great to see you, you've just caught me, I was off to the golf course, why not come with me? We can have a natter in the clubhouse." When they were all settled in the clubhouse with a hot drink and the introductions were over, he explained about the successful mission he and Cheng Eng had completed.

He handed Reg a cheque for £11,000. as a full refund of the money he had been given, it included £1,000.00 interest. Reg didn't really need the money because he was loaded. However he accepted it with thanks, saying he liked the high rate of interest. When Reg was aware that they were on holiday he invited them to stay at his place and when they refused because they were already booked in at Mrs Boothby's hotel He insisted that they spend a couple of hours on the golf course driving range at his expense. Even although none of them were fond of golf, they truly enjoyed their first time experience and were most thankful to Reg when they later continued their journey.

After a while John tired of driving and they stopped to stretch their legs at Grange Over Sands. What a lovely little seaside village this was, it had kept its Victorian frontage and retained the charm of that age. They went for a walk round a beautiful park which had so many lovely trees, which were particularly beautiful at this time of the year, in their autumn splendour of auburn gold foliage, just like an old oil masterpiece painting.

It was now a lovely day and there was hardly a breeze to be felt. They all enjoyed an ice cream before going into a cafe for a hot drink. It was only while seated and having a coffee that he remembered that he should have called to see Bob and Margaret, not only that. He had missed out his trip to Morecambe. Playing the round of golf had put him off completely; unfortunately they did not have time to retrace their steps. No one seemed to mind for they had all enjoyed their day.

After a two-hour journey on narrow twisting lanes, which would have tested anyone troubled by travel sickness, they arrived at Mrs Boothby's hotel. The night had turned really cold, not surprising since it would be November in a couple of days and by the time they got their luggage gathered and into the hotel, they were shivering with the cold. Cheng Eng joked,
"I wish I had kept the Eskimo suit, it would have come in very handy now."

When they entered the hotel the landlord was not at the reception area but they finally caught up with him at the bar, he greeted them all with a smile and a cheerful wave. "Good to see you again John," he said, handing him a double Brandy on the house. After the introductions they booked in for four nights, and got their luggage settled in their rooms before hastily making their way to the dining room before it closed. After their meal they chatted with the landlord in the lounge until the wee small hours of the morning, and surprise, it was only when Walter started on his war exploits that they realised how very tired they were and made a very hasty retreat to bed.

On opening the room curtains in the morning he saw that it had been a very frosty night, everything including his car was white with a hoar frost. Having plenty of time before breakfast he decided to go for a walk, not just for the exercise but because it usually increased his appetite. Stepping from the heated hotel, he caught his breath in the frosty mists of the air, each breath could be clearly seen, and it was almost as if he were smoking a cigarette. He looked left and right trying to make up his mind in which direction to go. I'll go left, he thought, and made up his mind to visit the hostel he used to stay in while working in this area. It should be nice to see it and old friends again after a six-month absence. What changes would there be, if any? A lot of water had flowed under the bridge in the last six months, but perhaps not so much here.

As he stood outside the hostel he felt quite home sick, this place held so many memories and was an intrinsic part of his life. Perhaps he may even come back here should he decide to return to work. He felt an urge to go inside, although he knew that his old workmates, who worked shifts, would be either at work or fast asleep. Who would be on security duty at the door? It could make things difficult for him if it were a stranger.

He need not have worried because the man who was in charge of the electronic opening and shutting of the door recognised him instantly. "Good grief John!" He exclaimed, "you're a big stranger. I never expected to see you again after you packed in the job up here. Do you still have that grand little sports car?"

"I sure do." He answered, not bothering to tell him that he had given it to his wife. He did explain to the fellow about his six months leave of absence and about the adventure he had just completed and how he was just passing and couldn't resist coming in to say hello.

After they had chatted a while and he caught up with all the news, he made his way back for breakfast. He was feeling on top of the world after his brisk walk, and he ate his massive breakfast heartily. The extra large breakfast was one of the many benefits of coming into these hotels in the off-season. He could never understand how they managed to survive financially with so few guests. Next he had the unenviable job of leaving his lovely warm surroundings and going outside and scraping the ice from the car windows. He searched the cars boot and glove compartment in vain looking for an ice scraper.

He tried using his fingernails, but the ice was far too thick for that. What was he to do? Then he had a brainwave, quick as a flash he was down and had a word with the chef who kindly lent him a fish slice. It worked a treat and he left the engine running to warm up the rest of the car, while he returned the fish slice.

They were soon sitting comfortably in the warmed up car waiting on his mother, who no doubt was putting on her coat and hat as usual, be it hail, rain, wind or shine. A thought crossed his mind as he and his father were forever getting colds or influenza over the years. While his mother seemed to escape it all every year. He couldn't remember his mother ever having a cold, so there must be something to be said for wearing a coat at all times.

Very soon they were away on their sightseeing trip. The route he had planned would take them in a circle, with the first stop being Muncaster castle, then on to see the remains of a Roman bath house at Ravenglass where amazingly, the top protective surface glazed tiling was still adhering to the walls after 2,000 years.

He had been looking forward to showing them a local attraction, a miniature railway, but was disappointed when he found that, like Muncaster castle, it was closed for the season. After a quick look around they went into a local public house for a snack. It was one of these very nice winter days with the sun shining and a bright blue sky, when one walked on the sunny side of the street it was nice and warm, however, when you were out of the sun. It was freezing and the frost was still on the ground where the sun had not reached it.

By the time they walked into their hotel, they had seen many beautiful sights including the lovely Connieston water.

Next morning it was plain to see that it had been another frosty night but there would be no repeat performance of yesterday when defrosting the car. He had bought a very inexpensive scraper while getting petrol the day before. Today's route took them to Calder Bridge, Ennersdale water, Loweswater and all around that area. He made a short detour to point out where he had done his rock climbing; from there it was just a short drive to Keswick where they had a browse around before lunch.

He even showed them the shop where he had purchased all the mountaineering equipment for his expedition. They had a stop in Cockermouth and finished up in Egremont before arriving home in the dark.

Next day it was a coastal trip that took them to, among other places. Sellafield Atomic energy reprocessing plant. The visitor's centre was open so they took a tour round. It was obvious that there were many areas, which were out of bounds to the general public, mainly for their own protection. However what they were shown was a real eye opener, it was fascinating. The very size and scale of things were breathtaking. They learnt for example, that it was called a `Thermal Oxide Reprocessing Plant, THORP for short. The guides were exceptionally pleasant to speak to, so he had no qualms in making enquiries about a particular piece of machinery, which was standing against a wall.

They explained to him that it was a machine for testing radioactivity in their personnel. As they were about to leave the high-risk area. He asked, with tongue in cheek, if he and Cheng Eng could give it a try. For if he were honest, he still had doubts about what the Abbot had told them just a few days before.

They were given permission and the guide even showed them how to operate it. Cheng Eng placed her hands in the appropriate place and then the guide pressed a button. Next there was a loud humming noise followed by a variety of coloured lights lighting up. Most importantly however, the all-important telltale needle flicked up onto the red, but then, thankfully, came to rest on the green area. "Well my dear," said the operator with a large grin on his face, "I can't quite tell when you last had fish and chips, but you are free of radiation."

Now it was his turn and he was nervous and sweating. He could see his mother and Walter staring at him and no doubt wondering why all the fuss. Like the guide they thought it was just a bit of fun. Little did they know of the life and death decision he was about to get! Following Cheng Eng's example he placed his hands in the machine. The operator pressed the button. His eyes were closed tightly, as he considered, were the noises the same as before? Were the same lights showing as with Cheng Eng? He was almost terrified to look. Cheng Eng shook his arm, "Look my darling, another miracle, you are clear just like me."

She had said many beautiful things to him in the past but these last few words he would remember forever as he thought to himself. 'What a wonderful way to finish off their extended holiday.'